Xeno Glitz

The
Blood Purge

Matador
9 De Montfort Mews
Leicester LE1 7FW, UK
Tel: (+44) 116 255 9311 / 9312
Email: books@troubador.co.uk
Web: www.troubador.co.uk/matador

ISBN 978-1906221-072

Typeset in 11pt Bembo by Troubador Publishing Ltd, Leicester, UK

Matador is an imprint of Troubador Publishing Ltd

To Tracey 'Red' Wood, Imelda Lambe, Alison 'Ali Bongo' Cartwright, and Steve Leese, for all their long -suffering support and encouragement.

And to everyone who saw the diamonds in the dirt.

PROLOGUE

Paladin, South West Laurasia.
Primoday, Lutetian 25th, AD 4004

They came out of the blizzard.

The tallest woman was snugly shrouded head to toe in black seal fur; her face masked against the scything wind and the glass sharp particles of driving snow. Her companion was equally swaddled in the pelt of a snow wolf and had her hat pulled down over her brow. Both were mounted on lowly shaggy-haired, long-horned oxen, the traditional and most practical form of transport in this inhospitable part of the world.

Their guide was a native man, bravely tramping the icy wastes as if he were out on a pleasant afternoon stroll, his knapsack casually dangling on his shoulder and his climactically adapted wide, flat-soled boots kicking up plumes of white in his wake. In comparison to them he wore very little attire, preferring relatively simple woollen wrappings since he was more hardened to the inclement conditions. And he was travelling so swiftly they had to very often goad their rides in order that they didn't lose him in the swirling storm which was filling his tracks with fresh snowfall extremely quickly, virtually erasing the traces of his pioneering trek as soon as he'd made any.

Had it been anything else, the two intrepid explorers would've stayed safe and warm in the cabin. But the antiquarians had sent urgent word about finding something, and they couldn't wait to see it.

Excitement and curiosity motivating them, they forsook the refuge of the village, politely ignoring the advice of the wise locals, and set out into the harsh elements. The resident Shaman insisted they partake of the sacrament and receive the blessing of the Ankh before they embarked on their expedition; to which they obligingly concurred, despite wanting to make good headway while the weather was still reasonably negotiable. If they hadn't gone through that ritual they would've been at their destination prior to the storm developing into what they were now embroiled in. So, ironically, the Shaman's desire to protect them from the evil spirits of the encroaching blizzard had delayed them long enough to get them caught up in it.

The guide suddenly turned to his followers, pointing into the whiteout visibility ahead and exuberantly crying in his native tongue, "TAU! TAU A MEI!"

Catching the wind tattered vestiges of his vociferation, the two women brought their oxen to a stop and peered through the raging maelstrom. They saw nothing at first, but after a few moments they just managed to vaguely recognize the jagged outline of a mountain range another few kilometres distant.

"This is it!" the taller one said to herself, impatiently gadding her beast into animation. "The truth at last!"

They plodded on, the savage tempest tugging and flapping their clothing. The oxen were tough, resilient creatures perfectly suited to the environment, but they certainly lacked in the speed department when it came to long hauls. Subsequently, progress was infuriatingly slow and protracted their exposure.

Eventually, they ambled up to the foot of the highest mountain in the range.

Spotting the pitch under a rocky overhang where the

diggers had camped, the guide led them on to the yawning mouth of the cave, accessing the interior of the massif. Once there, they dismounted and took the oxen into the entrance, sheltering them with the other pack animals resourcefully stabled within that retreat.

"Ladies!" a voice resonantly heralded, bouncing around the granite vault.

A figure emerged from the incumbent gloom carrying a guttering torch that threw crazy, elongated shadows on the rough walls.

"Professor Howk!" the tallest woman responded as the short, plump archaeologist shambled to them, her eyes bright circles amidst the smudged griminess of her face. "You have found something, I hear."

"Not just something, my Lady, but him!" Howk enthused in the richer, lighter tones of the southern continent, easily distinguishable from the phlegmatic inflections of northern argot.

"Are you sure, Professor?" the other visitor pressed.

"Come! Come!" Howk excitedly invited, beckoning them to follow her back the way she had just used. "See for yourselves and tell me it isn't so!"

"Pracena," the tall woman's companion said to the guide, offering him an exclusive preview.

He shook his head, saying, "Nao, prith, Contine. Tef deo somnife, af naos ascen." He looked about the cavern, eyes wide with anxious edginess. "Taus nego espiri …"

"What did he say?" the tall woman asked.

"He won't disturb the god while he sleeps, for fear of the curse."

"Indigenous folklore," Howk idly dismissed.

Bearing no superstitious qualms themselves, the three women eagerly went into the passage that had been painstakingly cleared of rubble and debris to reveal a set of steps tooled into the strata, quite obviously artificial and falling away into the dank dimness of the mountain's bowels. The way was lit by flickering cressets mounted at regular intervals on the once plastered walls of this forgotten stairwell, and a knotted rope strung along the route provided a tactile reference.

None of this was new to the two visitors.

For the past year they had stringently overseen the excavation of this intriguing site, avidly analysing each report and every discovery as and when they came. They already knew that thousands of years ago in Palatial history, this entire mountain had been completely hollowed out for some as yet undetermined purpose. The vast array of chambers in the plan and the artefacts retrieved seemed to suggest a temple of sorts, but no definitive evidence had arisen to confirm or disprove this theory.

Until now.

"What have you found precisely, Professor?" the tall woman quizzed Howk as they reached the end of the stone steps and walked into a huge room forested with support pillars. Their footsteps echoed eerily against the strangely painted walls while they passed across the gritty, pitted floor.

"A sarcophagus," the Professor answered.

"Have you broken its seals?"

"No, my Lady. There is no need."

"It's already unsealed?" the tall woman's friend queried, somewhat alarmed.

"No, Contine. It has a transparent lid."

"So you have seen the contents?" the Contine persisted.

"Yeah, my Lady."

"And the preservation?"

Howk looked over her shoulder at the pair, eyes bubbling with glee. "Excellent, my Lady!"

The trio moved on through this the lowest level of the site, briskly touring reclaimed room after reclaimed room in their haste to study the latest revelation.

At last, they came to an antechamber off one of the most recently excavated areas, where picks and shovels and hods of spoil were still lying outside. Within the confines, a group of local labourers enlisted to do the majority of the hard digging and rubble removal were all contemplatively huddled around a shape occupying the lion's share of available floor space.

"Doctor Fossor!" Howk said upon entering. "Here are our sponsors."

A man snuggled inside the coddling warmth of layered woollens and furs stepped from the congregation. "Ladies. It is an honour," he welcomed in a guttural Cadmian accent.

He slapped high fives with them, and when this pleasantry was dispensed with he ushered them to the centre of attention, parting the throng of peons so that the visitors may clearly observe the astounding discovery.

It was indeed a sarcophagus, but unlike any they had ever seen before.

"Icarus!" the tall woman's partner gasped in awe, leaning closely over the casket, her eyes engaged on the perfectly pristine visage still visible through the foggy, almost opaque window inset into the surface of the lid.

"Yeah," the tall woman mused. "I think it might be."

Her friend motioned the sign of the Ankh, muttering, "Nazar."

Approximately two metres by one metre in dimension, it was evident that it had once been white in hue and that its current resting place had been specifically structured as a sepulchre. Other than those established facts, the professed experts were at a loss. They claimed what the thing itself was actually made of was a mystery to them, for it conformed to no known stone, metal or wood. They surmised that it needed more detailed study, especially the abraded hieroglyphics on the shell, so they might be properly documented and perhaps deciphered to unlock their wisdom. Ergo, a few of their cronies would be required in on the job.

The tall woman, who had been bankrolling the excavation, took this as a hint for further funds to be sunk into the venture. To which she magnanimously agreed with a dismissive wave of her hand and the opulent sanction: "Whatever."

"This must truly be the parousia," speculated Dr Fossor, gazing wistfully at their find.

"We won't really know until we open it," said the tall woman.

She grabbed a spade from a nearby labourer and held it over the sarcophagus, ready to strike.

The peons all gasped and recoiled in horror at her intention to desecrate the holy relic. As did the archaeologists, except they were aggrieved by the act of wanton vandalism being threatened upon such an important artefact.

Her friend stayed her hand, advising, "I think we'd better get the Shaman here to bless it first. We don't want to upset local feeling or tradition."

The tall woman considered this for a moment.

"Yeah, okay," she reluctantly endorsed, tossing aside the spade.

Stooping down to within kissing distance of the casket, she gazed into the petrified face of the peacefully recumbent icon.

She smirked.

"They're gonna just love you back home, baby …"

I

Death was a distant stranger.

Not the kind of ominous cloud to overcast the vivacious, romantic mind of a not yet fourteen-year old boy such as Peregrine Farouche, who was brimming with spirit and passion. Especially not when he was care freely gambolling through the rolling glades in the bright, warm afternoon picking clutches of beautiful flowers growing wild; the gentle summer breeze tousling his flowing yellow hair and cooling his fresh, angelic face with its delicately fragranced breath.

Even when he strayed into the dappled shade of the woods, the brooding malice of mortality did not disturb him, although the cautionary tales he'd heard at his father's knee did come flooding back into him like a tide of bad dreams not wholly vanquished by waking.

His father had strictly forbidden him to go near the woods, explicitly detailing grisly consequences that may befall the wide-eyed child if he ever dared wander into those menacing environs.

But he'd been so contentedly engaged in both thoughts and deeds he quite forgot about all the childish fears instilled in him until he was already strolling beneath the lazily stirring and whispering boughs.

Then of course, it was too late.

However, this aberration still failed to arouse anxiety in him, for he reckoned the rewards of his disobedience far outweighed the risks of encountering fabled misfortunes. The woods were so beautiful and inviting it seemed a shame not to enjoy the hospitality. And he could not believe that such a harbour of tranquillity would conceal any monsters. After all, birds perched here and sang their sweet arias, which they surely wouldn't do if dangers lurked nearby.

Comforted by these assertions, Pere sauntered on; pensively arranging the posy of natural flora he'd gathered en route while he listened to the happy choruses high above that stemmed any dark imaginings from curdling his resolve.

Surely enough, the only thing he came across was a deer fawn that promptly pranced away into the deep undergrowth at his approach.

Eventually he reached the edge of the woods, where the land gradually fell away into a shallow river valley. Here he paused to shield his eyes against the sunshine and gaze over the breadth of the ravine to the rolling landscape on the opposite side.

An awe-inspiring rural tapestry lay before him: lush green pastures, golden acres of ripened crops and earthy brown fields were cross-stitched with hedgerows and communal tracks that tied together the tiny farmsteads dotted here and there. Domesticated cattle grazed the grassy enclosures, their lowing and tinkling bells faintly audible on the shifting air. Further in the background, a team of stout plough-horses loyally plodded on with their laborious toil under the encouragement of the gadswoman, their decorative harnesses jingling and sparkling.

Pere grinned in rapturous appreciation.

Then he saw her.

A raven-haired figure standing on the shore of the babbling river, idly skimming pebbles across the glistening watercourse as she patiently waited on his arrival.

He didn't immediately alert her to his presence. Instead, he took a moment to drink in her sheer rugged handsomeness while she was unaware, devotedly admiring every motion of her lithe, slender form as she impatiently paced up and down, nonchalantly kicking at the ground with her riding boots.

When he found he couldn't resist her any more, he called, "*Amoret!*"

She spotted him waving at her.

A huge smile graced her features.

And his heart melted.

Pere began descending the riverbank, giggling with unbridled glee as he recklessly thrashed his way through the thicket covering the slope.

Amoret hurriedly tidied her straggling, shoulder-length locks and breathed against the palms of her hands to check her oral odour before scurrying away to meet him.

He emerged from the bushes just as she reached them, and they both stopped short of one another to silently absorb the beauty they saw before them. Each privately praising the favour fortune had shown in bringing them together.

Slowly they closed the gap, slapped high fives, entwined their fingers and then joined their lips in a lingering kiss.

"Oh, Amoret!" Pere sighed, plunging into her embrace to press his cheek against her chest. She responsively tightened her grasp on him, not wanting to ever let go of this blessed treasure she'd been gifted.

They had met but a week ago.

Amoret had gotten mixed up in a drunken brawl one evening at her favourite tavern, The Creaking Meat Tree. This was quite a regular occurrence for both her and that particular hostelry, except she usually managed to vanish before the Watch was called. On this occasion, however, the Watch Warden herself had been in the bar room playing cards and swigging flagons of ale with her Deputies, all of whom swiftly dispensed instant justice at the scene.

She awoke next morning to find herself in the Rampick town gaol-house, sharing a stinking cell with some vagrant old hag who kept cackling and hacking wretchedly. And while she was in the process of nursing her throbbing head (not just the result of her hangover, but also the after effect of the wardens' liberally applied truncheons), breakfast was served.

By an angel.

Her troubles evaporating into obscurity at the sight of him, Amoret couldn't help staring at the pretty young boy who had come bearing the meals, wondering why one so dainty and refined was condemned to perform such a menial task in this dismal prison. She later learnt from Pere that since his father died a year ago, after tumbling into the cesspit whilst slopping out the cells, he'd inherited the cooking and cleaning chores around the gaol-house at the express command of his mother: the Watch Warden, no less.

As Pere began meekly posting the meals into Amoret's cell, not really taking any notice of the attention being paid to him, the old hag shuffled forward and grabbed the nubile boy's wrist with her grubby mitt. The grizzled crone cackled, nominating him 'the purtiest berd I ever did see', and violently prevented Pere from pulling free of her hooked claw.

Leaping to his defence, Amoret knocked the hag aside, allowing the boy to rapidly retreat clear of the bars.

Their eyes met.

And from that day forth they had been secretly meeting, every moment spent together increasing and developing their impassioned attachment. Both were fully aware of the bleak prospects ahead if anybody discovered their affair, yet undeterred by what might befall them. To suppress their feelings would be much worse, they agreed.

The whinny of a horse disrupted their intimacy.

Pere glanced up to see a fallow stallion towering above them.

"Favel!" he merrily greeted, reaching out to stroke the beast's obligingly dipped forehead. As if in answer, Favel whinnied a second time. "How're you, boy?"

"Are you sure you weren't followed, Pere?" Amoret doubtfully enquired, checking the overlooking surroundings.

"Of course," he reassured her. "Don't worry. My mother's too busy expecting the Sceptral Judiciary to turn up at any minute to bother herself with my whereabouts."

Amoret looked at him earnestly. "They're coming here?"

"Yeah. Straight from Thirlborh."

"When, exactly?"

"Day after tomorrow, if they make good time."

"So soon," Amoret said.

"My mother told me they burnt *five hundred* people in Faubourg," Pere hollowly relayed, swallowing dryly.

"Damn Pherenike and her zealots!" Amoret bitterly chided. "Why can't they leave everyone be?"

"You'll be safe, though, my love," Pere optimistically presumed. "You're a tenant on Lady Mandrake's estate, and you know how she and the Queen are so at odds over their ideals. She will never allow those persecutors on to her land."

"Yeah?" Amoret huffed, unconvinced. "My Uncle Semeion and me are scarcely tolerated in town as it is. With this damned blood purge stirring up the residents it'll be *impossible* for us to have any kind of decent life here."

"All the more reason to quit now," Pere hopefully prompted. "Oh, Amoret. How I long to put Rampick far behind me. Can't we go soon, my darling? You've promised me so many times you'll take me away from all this, but we never seem to get any further than dreaming."

"It's too difficult at the moment," she claimed, breaking the embrace and avoiding the adoring gaze of his doleful eyes.

"I thought you came from a nomadic race?" Pere said, not disguising his disappointment in the sharpness of his tone. "I *thought* travelling was in your veins?"

She turned to face him, divulging, "My Uncle Semeion has been touring this globe for the best part of his life. He's been through The Morro, Cadmia, Argestes, Mulciber, Arcadia. Some even say he saw The Myall in his youth."

At the very mention of this impressive list of distant countries, Pere wistfully pictured himself heroically navigating vast, uncharted territories on the back of a faithful steed.

"Now he's weary of wayfaring and wishes to settle somewhere permanent for his final years," Amoret continued. "And as Lady Mandrake's is the only kindness we've been shown, he chooses to stay here."

"That doesn't mean *you* have to," Pere concluded. "Surely your uncle doesn't expect you to stay as well, not when your heart yearns for other horizons."

He tried to see what her eyes were saying, but she wouldn't let him.

"Your heart does yearn for those horizons, doesn't it, Amy?" he asked, beginning to fear for the first time that all the ambitious plans they'd raked over and over during their stolen moments had merely been empty platitudes on her part, expressed only to please him.

"Semeion can't cope without me," she informed him.

"Then perhaps *I* can!" he retaliated, flinging the withering posy at her. It harmlessly exploded in her face and sprinkled around her feet.

He turned his back on her.

Favel, who had taken to cropping some nearby grass for his own amusement, glanced up at the quarrelling lovers. He offered his equine opinion by snorting then returned to his grazing.

"Don't be like that!" Amoret pleaded, coming up behind Pere and placing her hands on his shoulders.

Pere shrugged off her touch.

"What would you have me do? Abandon the only family I have left? He took me under his wing when my parents died of starvation in Cornucopia."

Guilt seared into Pere like a red-hot needle.

"A wayfarer's life is not all exciting adventures and sleeping beneath the stars," Amoret tried to make him understand, meaning to shatter his illusions.

"I know," Pere fibbed, for he didn't truly comprehend the nature of such an existence.

"I lived it for the first seven years of my childhood. It's hard and rough, even when you're born to it."

"But will you *never* take me away from here?" Pere queried. "Will we be forever hiding our love amongst bushes?"

"Of course not," she hopefully projected.

"Wouldn't your uncle be content to settle somewhere else instead of here?"

"I fear there're few places we'll find a ready welcome like Mandrake has shown us," Amoret mourned. "Her generosity is entirely centred around getting one over on those esteemed inhabitants of Excelsior Montis, of course, but we can live with that."

"How do you mean?"

"Favel, for instance," she said, indicating her trusty mount. Favel reared his head again at the sound of his name being bandied about. "Mandrake won him in a wager against the Delphine Princess Eigne. A thoroughbred from the Royal Mews, and she gifted him to *me*, a Giaour, a dyed-in-the-wool heretic in the eyes of the orthodox Zoetic Church. She couldn't really make her anarchic tendencies much plainer, could she?"

Favel agreed, nodding vigorously and swishing his tail, though whether he was actually confirming his mistress's statement or the nobleness of his lineage was something indeterminable.

"No, I suppose not."

"My tribe couldn't find a home, that's why they were nomadic. They were censured and exiled for their convictions; century upon century, country after country."

"Now they've been accepted in Gegenschein. Or at least their doctrine has," Pere said. "Perhaps we could persuade your uncle that Paladin is the home he's searched so long for."

"Don't talk rubbish, Pere!" she scolded. "That's the reason why that warmongering maniac Pherenike is raising this whole crackpot crusade of hers! That's why the Frithgild tax is robbing Montaigne blind! That's why Customs House gaugers guard the coastline! And that's why we can't risk going *anywhere!*"

"You promised to take me away!" he threw back, whirling round to confront her. "And now you tell me you're too *afraid!*"

She grabbed him and shook him severely.

7

"Yeah, I'm scared! For *you!*" Amoret sharply clarified, her dark eyes blazing. "They'll burn me for sure, but you *know* I'd willingly kill and die for you! That's not my fear! What frightens me is what they'll do to *you!*"

He began crying.

Amoret enfolded him in her arms, immediately regretting her castigation. "I'm sorry, my darling! I'm sorry! Please forgive me!" she apologized, feeling the hitching sobs against her torso and mentally reprimanding herself.

Just then, Favel nudged her with his nose.

She ignored him, so he repeated the action.

"What?" she said impatiently.

The horse nodded towards the thicket.

It was moving; and not by the drift of the breeze, for there was none down in the river valley.

"What is it?" Pere quizzed, noticing the diversion of her attention. "Amy?"

"Stay here," Amoret advised him in a hushed tone, stealing away from him towards the dense plantation along the bank-side.

"Amy?"

She pressed a finger to her lips to beg his silence while her other hand drew a short bladed dagger from its sheath on her belt.

Favel snorted.

Amoret stealthily crept into the bushes, her heart dully thudding, her eyes darting here and there in an attempt to catch a glimpse of whoever might be lurking amidst the vegetation. Pausing, she adjusted her hold on the knife's hilt, which was fast becoming slicked with perspiration. She then went in deeper, secure in the knowledge that Pere was safe under the loyal supervision of Favel.

Pere and Favel stood watching Amoret as she disappeared among the leafy branches. The young boy sighed and thought his secret sweetheart very like some brave hunter tracking a wily quarry, whereas the horse just shook his head despairingly.

A rustling noise suddenly alerted them both.

They looked round in time to see a figure draped in a hooded cloak and brandishing a carved staff surreptitiously creeping up on them from the rear. It halted mid-step, its element of surprise ruined.

Pere gasped, stricken with fright.

Favel whinnied and bolted.

Oblivious to this, Amoret persevered with her nerve-wracking sweep of the bank-side bushes, starting at every shape she saw in the stunted, entangled shrubs and tensing at every tiny crackling of twigs.

Suddenly, something behind her loudly crashed through the foliage.

She stopped, apprehension freezing her solid.

Whatever it was, it was very large and forging straight towards her position.

Amoret stifled a whimper.

Her fingers instinctively flexed around the knife's hilt.

It was gaining on her; its heavy footfalls trembling the ground beneath her and its rhythmic, raging breath blasting onto the prickled hairs on the back of her neck.

Mustering all the courage she could, she prepared to make her strike; a swift pirouette, a hard body jab and then a quick exit. Get in first and get out fast. Those were the rules she lived by when brawling.

A familiar snout urgently bunted her in the back.

"*Favel!*" she gasped in relief, almost collapsing as the pent up tension dissolved. Alarm gripped her again when she realized her horse was where he shouldn't be. "You should be with *Pere!*"

The steed grabbed the collar of her leather jerkin with his teeth and insistently dragged her along, fractiously whinnying as he did.

A squeal pierced the air.

Amoret didn't need any further motivation.

At the riverside, Pere was lying on the shingle, having slipped and fallen whilst trying to escape the mysterious cloaked figure, who was now steadily approaching.

"Who're you?" it demanded from the shadowy depths of its cowl.

Pere cried shrilly.

The figure pulled its staff apart, drawing a rapier blade cunningly concealed inside the shaft. "*Who're you?*" it repeated.

Out of nowhere, Amoret flew at the antagonist, grappling it in her muscular arms and violently bustling it into the water. She plunged the figure below the surface for a few seconds then hauled it up, letting it splutter and gag. Ducked it under once more, holding it down longer this time. Hefted it out before it drowned and then pulled her dagger ready to strike a mortal blow.

Aghast, she hastily stayed her hand.

Recognizing the assailant's face, she exclaimed, "*Uncle Semeion!*"

"*Get off me, you blundering oaf!*" yelled the old man. "That temper of yours will be the ruination of you! And *me* at this rate!"

"Whuh … what're you doing frightening folk?" Amoret questioned, sheathing the knife and doing as he'd requested.

"I came to find out where you've been sloping off to these past few days," Semeion admitted, sitting up. "Look at me! I'm soaked to the skin! You'll be lucky if I don't catch my death!"

"I ought to let you, you silly old fool!" his niece unfeelingly admonished, wading ashore and leaving him where he was. She attended to Pere: helping him to his feet, brushing down his russet tunic and checking his limbs for any bruises or abrasions.

"Well, that's gratitude!" Semeion complained. "After all I've done for you! Raised you! Taught you everything you know!"

He began struggling to stand, but couldn't manage it against the river's current and plopped down. He cursed profusely, causing the innocent boy to blush.

"I could've killed you!" Amoret shouted back at her relative. "You've no business here!"

"You said you were going *hunting!*" Semeion reminded her, trying to fight the flow again and failing just the same. He splashed his hands down in frustration.

Favel snorted and dutifully strode into the river. He plucked Semeion up by his hood and unceremoniously dragged him out.

"*Arrrgghhh!*" the aged man shrieked, gurgling and retching in the water. "*Let go of me, you stupid nag!*"

Heedless, Favel carried on till he could deposit his burden on dry land.

"You want to keep that beast reined, my girl!" Semeion grouchily muttered, indignantly righting himself and glowering at his patient, forbearing saviour.

He turned his gaze upon Pere, slit eyes studying the boy.

"And is *this* what you've caught while out *hunting?*" he directed at his niece. "We can't eat him, he's too skinny."

"You keep a civil tongue in your head, Uncle," Amoret warned him through pursed lips as she elevated herself to her full height beside Pere and curled a protective arm around his shoulders.

"What's your name, berd?" Semeion asked, flicking his sopping grey locks aside and slowly scrambling to his feet. Favel helped, bunting and nudging, but the old codger slapped away his interfering gestures.

Pere first looked at Amoret, who nodded her approval, then back at Semeion.

"Peregrine, sir," he said meekly. "Peregrine Farouche."

Semeion stared at him. "*Farouche?*" he parroted. "As in *Watch Warden Farouche?*"

"Yeah, sir. She's my mother."

"Oh, that's *wonderful!*" Semeion laughed, spreading his hands towards the sky. He went to collect his staff from where it lay. "As if we haven't got *enough* problems," he added, glaring at Amoret, "you have to take a fancy to a neck-stretching bigot's son!" Seriously disgruntled, he stormed off.

Pere and Amoret looked at each other.

"Can you believe I want to stay here with that berd?" she joked, smiling gently.

He didn't find the remark in the least bit funny.

"Will you be missed yet?" she asked him.

"Well, I have to prepare and serve the prison meals at three-seventy five. But there's only old Gaby Cailleach in the gaol-house at the moment …"

Amoret fumbled in the hip pocket of her britches and produced a battered, nickel-plated watch from it. She popped open the lid, studied the dial and checked its reading against the position of the sun. Pere glanced at the watch face and saw the hands claimed it was 2.93.

"Plenty of time." She snapped the watch shut and stowed it. "C'mon," she goaded, chucking him under the chin. "I can't bear to see you unhappy, Pere. I know what might cheer you up."

"What?" he probed, being led to Favel.

"Well, you once said you wanted to see where I live," Amoret explained, effortlessly lifting him and placing him side-saddle style onto the horse's bare back. "So I'll show you."

They set off, Amoret walking alongside Favel as they sedately strolled the curvaceous course of the Talweg River. Coming to a wide, shallow stretch, they forded its breadth and continued traversing the valley until the bank flattened out.

Clinging onto his ride's mane, Pere took the opportunity to survey the magnificent, unspoilt countryside from his elevation; his heart touched and delighted by all the sights, sounds and smells filling his senses.

If there were one thing he would gladly stay put for it was this. But he believed his life to be too unsatisfying even for his over-indulged sentimentality to trap him in the confined sphere in which he dwelt. And although he deeply appreciated the majestic natural beauty that he now saw, the irresistible lure of far horizons and mystical lands tugged more greatly at him.

Eventually they reached the summit of a ridge, affording themselves a spectacular view across the fluctuating hills and dales of Brecham County.

Occupying the majority of the foreground was a huge, densely populated forest, which currently being plundered for its removable assets. Gaping holes opened up by the systematic stripping out of trees marred the lush arboreal canopy, and sooty smoke plumes from brush fires and charcoal-burning rose high into the pastel blue sky. Droves of draught-horses strained to manoeuvre felled forest giants from their resting places to a massive clearing, where multitudes of carpenters crafted the rudimentary trunks into stacks of planks and fashioned beams. These finished products were then being loaded onto trailers by simple, rough-hewn derricks and transported off onto purpose-laid tracks leading, presumably, to the main Excelsior Road.

"What're they doing?" Pere asked.

"Building ships for the fool's errand," Amoret acidly answered.

He looked at her, perplexed.

"The crusade," she expanded. "Virtually every artisan in the country is under contract. You can scarcely get a horse shod because the farriers are too busy producing cannon-shot and broadswords. It's worth more than their regular trade. War is big business."

"Who's paying for it all?"

"The ordinary gys and berds, who else? The same ones who'll pay the highest cost in grief when the battlefields run with martyrs' blood," Amoret said. "It's easy to talk tough in the ivory towers of Excelsior Montis, but it isn't Pherenike who's going to put the money where her mouth is and turn words into action. Nor will it be her who picks up the pieces afterwards."

"My mother said they've already got press gangs working the citadels," Pere imparted, contemplating the activity below as they carried on along the ridge. "Do you think they will come here?"

"They'll go anywhere they think they can rally troops, voluntary or otherwise. No gy is safe from induction into this madness unless she's crippled or dead. And if she isn't either of those, she soon will be."

Pere felt that Amoret had justified his case for their escaping abroad while they at least still had a decent chance of success. But he refrained from stressing the point, as he knew it would probably be of little use.

After another kilometre or so they came upon the end of the ridge they'd travelled. It abruptly curtailed into a rocky outcrop overhanging a sheer drop down to a wide, well-maintained road. On top of this outcrop stood a curious rotunda clad in discoloured marble, its two-tiers constructed entirely of elegant arches and colonnades. Roofing it was a copper-plated cupola capped with a small spire, both of which had gone green in the weather.

"There!" Amoret said, delaying Favel and pointing to it. "Selcouth folly. Home sweet home."

"It's lovely!" Pere genuinely enthused, taken by its oddness in appearance and location. "What's it doing here?"

"One of the estate bailiffs told me Mandrake's Great Grandmother Gallimaufry built it," she relayed as they walked on. "She was completely mad, by all accounts. She stationed her bondswomen up here to watch the Excelsior Road." Indicatively, she traced the line of the carriageway at the foot of the cliff with her index finger.

"What for?"

"Trespassers," Amoret replied. "This was back in the days when feudal nobility had autonomy over their estates, and during the transition when that autonomy was brought under municipal jurisdiction, old Gallimo resisted all legal and strong-arm tactics to make her conform. Hence why Mandragora Demesne is such a fortress today. She used this as a lookout post, garrisoning guards from her private army up here to take pot shots at anyone using this road, so effectively cutting off major communication between the capital and most of the northern territories. Even then this was the only direct caravan route to Excelsior, crossing the Pignon Hills and bypassing the Morasses to the east."

"How did it turn out?" Pere urged her on, intrigued.

"Sieges failed, so they starved them out. Severed all supply lines to the Demesne, waited till their resources ran out, then stormed the place. The few Mandrake soldiers still hanging on who hadn't died of disease or famine or deserted the cause were found to have been resorting to cannibalism and were slaughtered on the spot."

"Eurrgh!" exclaimed Pere, shuddering at the inhuman thought. "What happened to Gallimaufry?"

"Executed for treason. The estate was seized as compensatory payment for lost commerce and divided up between neighbouring aristocrats, leaving only the immediate manor under the family's control. The gossips reckon Gallimo's eldest daughter and heir was forcibly ..." Amoret coughed embarrassedly, "'put with child' by the then Sangreal Prince, to ensure her loyalty to the House of Gerent before she was allowed to inherit."

"Is that why there are so many rumours about Lady Mandrake being related to the Queen?" Pere ventured.

Amoret only shrugged her ignorance. "Could be."

"How come the estate is so big if it was broken up?"

"Apparently, the current Lady Mandrake's mother had the seizure of her birthright quashed through some legal loopholes, reclaiming all forfeited tenure and turning minor nobility off the lands. In truth, Lady Mandrake is entitled to bear the mantle of Duchess, but the Crown never granted reinstatement of that particular privilege."

The trio ascended the beaten track winding towards Selcouth, and as they neared their destination Pere saw it was reasonably well facilitated. Situated behind it was a dewpond equipped with a hand-pump, a large vegetable patch and a fertile glade that sloped away to the woods.

Noticing how his eye was engaged, Amoret said, "Lady Mandrake lets me hunt the game in that copse, and a rill runs through it where I fish and Semeion does the washing. We gather nuts, berries, truffles, fire kindling and much else from there too." She helped him dismount. "We're well provided for."

"Quite a haven," Pere appreciated.

"We're thinking of getting some of our own poultry, and perhaps a few pigs, a cow and maybe a goat."

"You'll be completely self-sufficient," he flatly commented, dismayed her plans for the future centred on putting down roots rather than spreading wings. "You won't need the townsfolk."

"Oh, we will," Amoret corrected, guiding him to the folly while Favel wandered off to graze. "That's the only drawback to Selcouth, its remoteness. Rampick's the nearest town to here."

"Nearer than Slackton?"

"Oh, yeah! Slackton's thirty clicks south, whereas Rampick's barely ten north. The only trouble is, we have to cross the Talweg boundary into Brecham."

As they entered Selcouth via one of the arches at the rear, Pere realized the exterior was in a very poor state of repair. It bore the damage of exposure to the elements and what he suspected were the pockmarks of impacted musket shot, perhaps inflicted in the turbulent times it had previously witnessed. On closer observation he also discovered its fancy arches contained ornate stained-glass windows, some of the fragile panes of which had been broken and crudely replaced by transparent impostors or left empty.

When they went inside the smell hit Pere immediately, compelling him to put his hand to his nose. He soon acknowledged the tangy odour's source, seeing a sizeable quarter of the floor was untidily strewn with horse-dung soiled straw. This left him in no doubt that Favel enjoyed shelter here too.

The interior was spacious, though highly vaulted since the second storey was merely a circular balcony accessed by a spiralling iron staircase and not a real upper level. Of course, this made keeping the place tolerably warm very difficult. There was a single pot-bellied stove squatting in the middle of the cracked blue-brick floor, but this possibly did little to combat the draughts; in fact, it most likely did more harm than good as its bent chimney vented directly into the room.

Furnishings were minimal. Two truckle beds lay headfirst against the blind walls between three of the windows, separated by a cupboard sporting jug-and-basin washing amenities. Set next to the stove was a stout table with cooking and dining utensils littering its surface and several oil lamps hanging about its flanks on deliberately hammered-in brad nails. A few empty crates and kegs resourcefully served as chairs.

At the centrepiece table, Semeion was preparing vegetables for a large stewing kettle, muttering and avenging a sour mood on the blameless foodstuffs as he performed his labours. He was swaddled in a grey wrap-blanket now, having thrown off his drenched habit to hang it on an airing rack beside the stove to dry.

"I brought Pere to see Selcouth, Uncle," Amoret explained, attracting his attention.

"Yeah?" said Semeion, suspiciously eyeing the boy. "To see how the pagans live?"

"Uncle!"

"Well!" the old geezer huffed. "How do you expect me to react? We've just settled nicely here. No taxes. No rent. No bother from bigots. Then you start playing lovey-dovey with a tipstaff's lad!"

"Amy and I love each other very much, Mister Ducdame," Pere proudly announced.

"That's *Master*, boy," Semeion churlishly put him right. "I'm not wed."

Pere glanced across at Amoret then blurted, "We plan to elope."

Shocked, Semeion hit his thumb with the cutting knife.

"*AAARRRGGHHH!*" he yelled, holding up his injured hand as accusatory evidence. "*Now look what you've made me do!*"

"Uncle!" Amoret cried, rushing to his aid. "Are you all right? Here, let me see!"

Her elderly charge indignantly refused her interference. "Oh, no! You were ready to slaughter me in the river not more than ten minutes ago! Leave me be!"

"You need a dressing on that!" she insistently diagnosed, taking a clean handkerchief from her britches pocket. She wrestled with her uncle until he begrudgingly consented to her binding the wound.

"Is this true?" Semeion asked. "Do you plan to *elope* with him?"

Her eyes darted between him and Pere, her mind scrabbling for an answer to suit them both. Naturally, such an ambiguous concession didn't exist. "I have considered it."

"But … but he's just a *child*! Barely pubescent, I'll wager!"

"I'm fourteen this Tortonian," Pere disclosed.

"Well, she's *twenty-four* next Aquitanian!" Semeion ruefully accentuated. He glared at his niece. "There's a word for what you're doing, and it's *perverse!* You're a *grown woman,* for Icarus's sake!"

Amoret deliberately tightened the bandage she'd created, making her uncle wince.

"Yeah, I am. So I think I'm about old enough to live my own life, don't you?" She continued, "Besides, with circumstances as they are, Pere and I have decided to postpone such rash actions for the time being. Right, Pere?"

She looked at him very hard, inducing his compliance.

"I should think so!" Semeion mumbled, picking and fiddling with the wrapping once his niece had finished. "You'll be going enough places if the press gangs catch hold of you, my girl." He glared at Pere again. "You're best off here with me where they can't get at you. Not faffing about on the hair-brained whim of some young bit of tunic!"

"Uncle!" Amoret gruffly chastised.

"Well!" Semeion justified, returning to his chore. "My own niece taking up with a *Zoetic!* It was his creed that harried us here in the first place. Now you want to *run away* with one of 'em!"

"Shut up, you nasty old *goat!*" Pere vehemently insulted.

Both Semeion and Amoret gawped at him, astonished at his outburst: Semeion because he had never before been so disrespectfully spoken to by anyone so young, and Amoret because she had never heard Pere be so rude. She knew he had a fiery temper when roused, but impudence was not a trait she'd attributed to his character.

"You complain of being discriminated against, yet *you* are the biggest bigot I have *ever known!*" the youth condemned, approaching the table.

"If I am so, it's what I've been made!" Semeion retorted. "By the likes of *you!*"

"*Me?* You haven't even seen *me* yet!"

"I've seen *that!*" the crusty hermit spat, prodding the knife he held at Pere's upper chest. Amoret tensed, sure her uncle meant the boy no harm but readying herself just the same. Pere looked down at the gold saltire hanging round his neck on a doubled fine-link chain, which the knifepoint savagely singled out. "And that is enough. I've also seen what that has done in the past, and what it will do in the future."

The junior's wide, inquisitive eyes met the senior's. "What do you mean?"

"My uncle is an Oneiromancer," Amoret replied, with almost as much shame as if she were exposing him as a criminal. "He dreams the future."

Pere stared at them.

"That's *Heresy!*" he whispered, as if hushed tones were required.

"Only to the Zoetic Church, which is so blind it sees nothing!" Semeion contemptuously countered. "Its ignorance has brought nothing but death and destruction to this world, and I have seen what new atrocities are looming under the ill-favour of this latest abomination. Fields strewn with the desecrated corpses of men-folk and children; forests of impaled women set aloft as victory trophies ..."

Semeion paused, seeing something in Pere's docile gaze.

He drew a shaky, fearful breath.

"*You* have seen it too!" he gasped.

Skittishly, Pere ran across the floor and hurtled up the spiral staircase.

"Pere!" Amoret called, concerned by his sudden flight and worried for his safety up there.

"He has seen it too!" Semeion impressed upon his niece, waylaying her and pointing with a dithering hand.

"Damn you and your prophecies!" Amoret cursed, jostling him aside and going after Pere.

High above on the circular gangway, Pere found the only window that accessed the external balcony and threw it open. He staggered out, leant on the wrought iron guardrail to support his quaking body and thirstily drank in the fresh air.

"Pere!" Amoret hollered.

She came up behind him and eased him clear of the rail.

"Careful, darling. It's very unstable. It may not take your weight," she warned. "Are you all right?"

"Yeah," he sighed. "I'm fine."

"Pay no heed to my uncle," she advised, stroking his hair. "He had no right frightening you with his nonsense."

He looked at her earnestly, tears welling up in his eyes.

"But it's *not* nonsense, Amy. I *have* seen it."

"Seen what?"

"What your uncle described." Casting his dewy eyes over the variegated landscape so widely observable from the lofty vantage point, he added, "I've seen it in my dreams as well ... and it *scares* me ..."

II

The time came for him to return home.

Amoret and Favel escorted him back along the river to where they had met. There they had to part company for fear of being seen together, and indulged in an affectionate farewell before he set off back through the woods and meadows alone, by no means as care free as when he had come this way earlier on.

Avoiding obvious places where he might encounter anybody else and invite unwelcome attention, Pere managed to slip into Rampick once again, his secret apparently intact. Several of the locals did bid him good day as he slunk along the back streets trying to blend in, but he was quite certain none of them saw from which way he'd come as he'd deliberately taken a winding route.

Emerging from the narrow alley between the smithy and the bakery, he paused at the side of the muddy main street that passed directly through the centre of the thriving rural community. It was teeming with carts, wagons, carriages, and straying herds of livestock being driven to the market square; and along its edges, rows of cramped, leering half-timber buildings trapped all this hustle and bustle and the sounds and smells of it between them.

Furtively glancing each way before moving, Pere began dodging across the traffic flows, his moccasins deftly tip-toeing around the different types of animal dung deposited on the ground. Once safely on the other side, he carried on up towards the gaol-house, disturbing a few chickens aimlessly pecking about outside the livery.

Looking past his intended destination toward the heart of town, he saw the imposing obelisk of the parish church dominantly towering above the rooftops. A sight that compelled him to touch the X-shaped symbol of his faith that hung around his neck and guiltily reflect on his improper behaviour.

Averting his eyes to avoid feeling any more shame, he concentrated on his padding feet. And as a result of this he promptly bumped into a woman who was just exiting Mistress Morkins' butchery shop carrying a plucked turkey and a side of bacon.

He noticed she was wearing a red cassock.

Startled, he jerked clear of her as if he'd been scalded and stared into her face.

It was Charlatan Fugle, the local minister.

"Good afternoon, Peregrine," Fugle greeted, her affable smile instantly dissolving his inbred fear of divine retribution for impure thoughts and deeds.

"Charlatan," he said, offering a nervous grin and a bobbing curtsy. He was very fond of this young, uncommonly pretty woman of the cloth. She talked a lot of sense and made the scriptural classes she provided him and other village children with every Primoday entertaining and a joy to attend. "How are you?"

"Very well, thank you for asking, Peregrine," she replied. She held up her purchases from the butcher's. "I've just blown the last few ducats of my allowance."

"Already? It's only half way through the week."

"Even Charlatans can't live on faith alone," she chuckled. But when she saw him visibly squirm at her jest rather than share the mirth, it induced her to say in a worried tone, "You looked thoughtful a moment ago. Nothing troubling you, I hope."

"Err … no, not at all," he badly fibbed.

Fugle brushed her long, sandy hair out of her eyes and looked at him. "Sure?"

"Yeah. I'll have to go now, Charlatan. My mother will be expecting me home."

"Of course, don't let me delay you," she said apologetically, moving so she was not obstructing his path. "Give my regards to Mistress Farouche."

"I will," Pere promised.

She touched his arm, waylaying him a little longer. "And if there is anything you want to talk about, Peregrine, you know where to find me. Okay?"

He only gave a half-hearted smile before leaving her to watch after him, concern clouding her thoughts.

The gaol-house loomed ahead; quite appropriately situated opposite The Creaking Meat Tree tavern, from where it obtained the majority of its regular patrons. As he neared it, he saw someone sitting outside on a chair cleaning a musket.

Pere reduced his pace to a hesitant stroll so as to buy time and ascertain who the person was.

His worst fear was realized.

It was Attercop, one of his mother's Deputies. She was a vile, uncouth, lecherous, ale-quaffing layabout with lank, greasy black hair and halitosis. He hated her and how she always ogled him. Her sidekick Skaines was equally repulsive, though she didn't harass Pere quite so much when she was not under the bad influence of her obnoxious cohort.

Steeling his nerve, Pere tossed his golden tresses and held his head high, assuming a haughty air.

Attercop anticipated his arrival, her beady eyes relentlessly staying on him as she scrubbed a calloused hand over her bristled chin and licked her yellowed teeth.

"Aft'noon, young Master!" she hailed when he was within reasonable earshot.

He ignored her and went straight towards the door.

She allowed the quadruple-barrelled firearm she was polishing to drop across the entrance, so blocking his way. He glared at her. She regarded him with an expression of smugness plastered all over her mean, ugly features.

"Where's thee been, then, young Master?"

"Let me by!" Pere snootily demanded.

"Out awalking, eh, young Master?"

"Yeah, if it's any of *your* business."

"Oh, it be my bidness, young Master," Attercop told him. "'Cos I makes it mine."

"Like you make *smuggling* your business?" he ripped into her. "I know the Customs House gaugers don't always declare *all* the contraband they confiscate, and I also know you and Skaines often sneak off out of town at night when you're supposed to be on duty and return with a cartload of stolen goods."

Attercop only laughed that hissing, rattlesnake laugh of hers. "Now if I weren't a lady, young Master, I'd take that as a terrible slight. I be an ossifer of law 'n' order, and I got proof of it." She flapped open one lapel of her frock coat, showing him the silver badge bearing the Brecham arms pinned to the stuffed vest she wore beneath. "I be here to protect thee, young Master. After all, we wouldn't want thee coming to any harm now, would we?"

"I can't *afford* your style of protection!" Pere mercilessly jibed. "Unlike most of the merchants!"

"Oh, I think thee can, young Master …"

She touched his buttocks.

Pere gasped, pulled away and slapped her hard around the face. "Keep your filthy paws to yourself!"

This only made Attercop utter her sibilant little laugh again.

Grabbing the hand he used to deal the blow and resisting his attempts to twist it from her grip, she said, "What would happen if thy mother found out that thee don't keep *all* thy attentions for the prospective suitor she be grooming for thee to wed? That thee has another thee meets when thee thinks that nobody be minding thee?"

He broke free, flustered and blushing bright red.

"I knows thee don't just go into yon fields for the good of thy 'ealth, young Master."

"You know nothing of the sort!" he desperately insisted.

"Like thee don't know if yon smugglers should bundle most of their booty overboard into the water afore the gaugers get near 'em, eh? Or like thee don't know if yon merchants don't show appreciation for our sterling work by making us generous gifts, eh?" Attercop said. "It'd be a right shame if yon Warden should take a personal disliking to anyone in partic'lar hereabouts. Especially with the Sceptral Judiciary on their way…"

Incensed by the indignity of being held over a barrel by such a despicable individual, Pere shoved the musket back at her and hurried inside the house, slamming the door behind him.

Slyly sniggering, Attercop resumed polishing the musket.

The front room of the gaol-house was the Warden's office, fitted out with a few unmatched chairs, a large desk, an unlocked firearms cabinet, a cloak stand, a long-case night-watch clock and a stone hearth where a brewing pot hung on an iron pole above the smouldering fire. On the far wall, a gallery of amateurish sketches depicting local vagabonds and ruffians were haphazardly tacked up, but other than those there were no decorations to mask the cracked, flaking plaster, or any rugs to cover the rough-hewn floorboards.

It was through here that Pere had to pass in his flustered rush to get to the kitchen out back where he cooked the prison meals. Unfortunately for him, it also happened to be here his mother was waiting for him, reposing in her leather wing-back chair and puffing on her clay pipe, her hobnail booted feet propped up on the desk.

"Peregrine!" she said sternly, halting her son dead in his tracks. She was a stout woman with grey hair, bushy black eyebrows and mutton-chop whiskers. She was dressed no differently than usual in black britches, waistcoat, ribbon necktie and white linen shirt. "Where have you been till this time?"

"I'm sorry, Mama," he respectfully apologized, casting his eyes downward.

He realized there was someone else present.

"Mistress Alecost has been waiting on you, my lad," Mistress

Farouche told him, positively identifying the other person who was sitting in the chair opposite his mother.

Avoirdupois Alecost, the landlady of The Creaking Meat Tree, looked round at him as her name was mentioned. She was a blowsy woman whose appearance bore all the hallmarks of rich food and alcohol abuse. On the whole, her public conduct was generally perceived as amiable, but Pere had heard from the kitchen boys at her establishment that she was a violent and miserly employer.

He shuddered to think what she would be like as a wife.

Alas, there was the very strong possibility he would very soon find out if his mother had anything to do with it. She had been persistently encouraging Alecost's interest in her son in order to try and secure him a respectable and valuable marriage partner, regardless of the fact that Pere would rather be stung to death by a swarm of hornets than marry the odious bint.

"Good day, Master Farouche," Alecost boomed, rising from her seat. What remainded of her frizzy ginger hair was parted and flattened to either side of her head, and her piggy little eyes bubbled with eagerness in her grinning face. She'd adorned herself in her best suit and arranged a gaudy display of expensive jewellery about her person in a bid to emphasize her wealth and impress the one she aspired to court.

"Good day, Mistress Alecost," Pere courteously replied, performing a half-cock curtsy. "I beg your pardon, ma'am, for any inconvenience I have caused you. If I had known you were calling …" he began excusing, mentally finishing his sentence *'I would've stayed out for a week!'*

"Please, please!" Alecost graciously dismissed. "No need for regrets, my dear. There's no offence taken."

"He's normally very punctual, Av," Mistress Farouche assured the publican, scowling at her offspring through the haze of smoke rising from her clay pipe.

"No matter, no matter," Alecost waived. "I came by to ask you, Master Farouche, if you would do me the great honour of walking out with me this fine day." She fumbled her watch out of her waistcoat pocket. "But as it is nigh on a quarter of three, I fear the hour grows too late for such."

Just as Pere was privately thanking his lucky stars, his mother remarked, "I don't see why, Av. You're not for opening up till three-sixty, are you?"

"True, true," agreed Alecost. "There is time enough for a decent turn, I suppose."

"I have to do the meals, Mama," Pere timidly reminded his parent.

"Speak when spoken to, Peregrine," Mistress Farouche instructed. "There's only one prisoner in the cells, anyhow. Attercop can deal with her."

At that very moment, as if in answer to her name, Attercop entered the room.

"You can feed old Cailleach, can't you, Attercop?" the Warden said to her Deputy, more as a statement than a question. "While Mistress Alecost takes Master Peregrine out walking."

"Aye," Attercop willingly confirmed as she went to put the musket away in the cabinet. "I can handle that and no mistaking, Warden. We don't want the young Master to be deprived of any pleasure, do we now?" She grinned maliciously at Pere. "Old Gaby b'ain't no trouble."

"Ah, old Gaby's in the drunk tank again, eh?" commented Alecost, chuckling.

"Aye. We had that Giaour in there last week," Attercop said, apparently conversational but looking directly at Pere all the time. "The one that lives up at Selcouth folly, hiding behind Mandrake's bluster."

"That Amoret Artemis?" said Alecost. "I remember the incident, and I'd like to thank you ladies for stepping in when you did. That lout could've cost me a fortune in repairs again."

"It's a pity it wasn't this week," chipped in the Warden. "We could've had her in clink ready for Judge Corsned when she gets here."

"Oh, aye," said Attercop, regarding the boy closely. "Corsned'll sling her on the bonfire if she catches hold of her, and no mistaking."

Pere felt chilled to the bone.

"Well, Master Farouche," the innkeeper concluded, moving towards him and offering her arm, "if we dally any longer we won't get our walk. I have to be back at the tavern to ensure everything's ready for this evening's trade. I can't rely on those servants of mine."

"I will have to go and ready myself, ma'am," Pere referred to his simple clothing and the unsuitability of it, fully intending to take far longer than necessary to change it and so spike the plan.

"There's no need for that," his mother overruled, keen to get him off with his escort. "I'm sure Mistress Alecost has no objection to your appearance."

"Indeed not. You are becoming in any apparel, young Master," Alecost extravagantly complimented. She offered her arm once more. "Shall we?"

Reluctantly, Pere forced a smile and clutched onto her podgy limb with both hands.

Attercop opened the front door for them as they exited the room.

"Enjoy thyself now, young Master," she ruthlessly rubbed it in, that same diabolical grin creasing her mug.

The odd couple promenaded along the main street, Alecost proudly sporting the youth like some newly acquired ornament and Pere trying to avoid the gazes of those they passed on their way.

She paused several times to slap high fives with some of her acquaintances and brag how she was soon to be honoured to have the hand of her beautiful companion. Divulging that his mother's consent was virtually in the bag and how his dowry of 500 signats was not an issue in her choice of groom, though it was a fair sum for such a prize.

For his part, Pere could only helplessly stand by and listen to his life being decided away by other people, forever trapping him in the circle he so much desired to shatter and escape from. But what made his pain worse were the congratulatory wishes, which he felt obliged to accept with false smiles and empty thanks.

While they were going through this routine outside the barber's shop, delaying Mistress Jasey on her doorstep (despite her having a customer waiting for a shave to be finished), Pere saw a sight that gladdened his dejected heart. So much so, he had to repress the exhilarated sigh that rose to express his renewed hope.

Astride her faithful steed, Amoret slowly rode into town.

He saw the intense determination on her strong, prominent features and refreshed thoughts instantly blossomed in the callow boy's mind.

She's coming for me! he exuberantly presumed. *She's coming for me!*

Wildly ecstatic, though not betraying it outwardly, he imagined her riding up to him and scooping him up onto Favel's back, fending off any possessive vengeance from Alecost by decisively striking her to the ground with a single blow. Then he pictured her spurring the horse on to gallop them both away to the far-flung horizons where their destiny and eternal happiness lay.

Nothing so wonderful occurred, however.

Amoret intermittently maintained eye contact with him right up until the point where he believed she might launch the dramatic rescue he expected. But instead of coming to claim him as her own, she just casually trotted past with no hint of romantic bravado about her countenance.

Disappointed to say the least, he looked round to watch her departure.

And was distraught when she didn't even glance back upon him.

"My dear," Alecost distracted him, touching his hand.

Pere took the cue to move on, still snatching glimpses towards his true love as he went, only to see she continued to practice ignorance of him.

"You can be in no doubt, Master Farouche," his escort attributed, "as to my particular affection for you. I have spoken at length with your mother while waiting on you, and she readily considers my attentions to be favourable. Therefore, it only remains for me to ask if you will personally grant me your audience tomorrow so I may apply to you directly. Just as a formality, mind you. Then when that's over and done with I can get down to the business of organizing our nuptials."

He said nothing, being engaged in vainly seeking notice from Amoret as he was.

"What do you say, young Master? May I call on you tomorrow?"

His primal instinct was to push this slob away, screaming undeniable refusal and damnation into her fat face, and run as fast as he could into the arms of his beloved Amoret.

But he suppressed this urge.

For it did not seem Amoret cared enough.

All hopes dashed, he resigned himself to the inevitable and nodded his consent. He was effectively goods and chattel now, anyway. Money had been discussed. Promises made. High fives slapped. He'd been bought and sold in his own absence.

That was bad enough in itself.

But being abandoned to it by the one to whom he'd entrusted his heart cut him deeper.

The dream came to him again. Unchanged, but always new.

He was hand in hand with his lover, strolling through a great forest. High above, the tall trees serenaded them with whispered lullabies that a gentle spring breeze played in the leafy tops, while beneath their softly treading feet, sweetly scented flowers lay abundant.

They gazed adoringly into each other's eyes; sharing a sublime, passionate admiration both were wholly convinced not even the most drastic hardship or misfortune could destroy.

Riding ahead of them on a white mare warhorse was a

knight attired in black armour who bore a standard marked with a blood red saltire.

This warrior chaperone turned suddenly, rearing her charger and setting the standard as a lance, then cantered off amongst the trees until she was lost from sight in the dense greenery.

"Faith!" he called after her.

But she was gone, leaving only branches swinging in her wake to testify to her ever having been there.

His lover's grip began to loosen, alarming him further still. Their interlaced fingers were being unwound and prised apart by an unseen, unfelt force bent on separating them. He tried to resist it, but their firm hold on each other was broken.

And then she was gone too, swept away into the undergrowth.

"Hope!" he cried, to no avail.

He stopped dead.

Before him lay an immense vista of dark, twisted trees that he knew he had to pass through. But this was like no avenue he had encountered before. The trees seemed to have no perspective, becoming larger and taller the further away they were from his viewpoint.

At the far end he could just make out a grassy meadow speckled with the brightness of freely growing flora, lit by what he reckoned to be too brilliant and subtle to be mere sunlight. And in that meadow stood a lone figure completely silhouetted against the radiance behind it.

The figure raised a hand and beckoned him on.

Fearful, he took a few nervous steps into the avenue.

The height of the trees was so great no ambient illumination shone on the forest floor, so he could not see where or on what he trod. But he could feel that the ground was moist and spongy and very uneven. The breeze here was not at all pleasant either, changing to an ill wind that incessantly scythed down the arboreal corridor.

At first, he thought it was this wind causing the movements in the trees, which he caught with the corners of his eyes. But it

wasn't until he looked up into the barren, deformed crowns of those brooding sentinels he realized there were things up there.
Bodies.
Impaled on broken branches.
And still writhing in pain.

Pere woke then, slicked with sweat and breathing raggedly.

Reassured he was still safe in his bachelor bed in the attic room of the gaol-house and not really in that ghastly vale so vividly portrayed in his mind, he threw aside the bedcovers and went to the window on legs weary from the fright of the nightmare.

His intention was to open the window and draw on the evening air's restorative properties, but he saw something outside that perturbed his doing this.

The diamond-lattice dormer looked out on the back yard, where the station's horses were quartered in ramshackle stables, and various bulky items (lost, found or unclaimed belongings) too big to store inside were dumped until providence or decrepitude or audacious thieves took them.

By the dim glimmer of the twilight, Pere could see a buck-boarded cart parked inside the yard's walled perimeter with its tailgate down. Attercop and Skaines were loading barrels (probably containing intoxicating beverages of one description or another) onto the back of this vehicle, obviously taking the opportunity to carry out their illicit act while the Warden was on patrol duty.

Unobserved, he carefully monitored them, resolved to spike their little privateering racket and tell on them to his mother when morning broke.

At that moment another person materialized to speed their progress.

It was his mother.

Pere gawped, the scales falling from his eyes.

She *knew* about her Deputies' enterprising.

Was *in* on it.

A fourth person showed up to uncork one of the barrels,

stick a finger in and taste the wares. It was none other than Avoirdupois Alecost, but this revelation surprised him not in the slightest.

The four conspirators muttered an exchange for the next few minutes, laughed at an unheard joke and went on their different paths. Alecost drove the cart from the yard, while Attercop and Skaines vanished into the darkness of the back alleyway and Pere's mother secured the yard gates after them.

III

Wherever he happened to be that day he made certain he was well within sight of a clock, so he could apprehensively track the dwindling minutes right up to the fateful hour when Mistress Alecost was due to call.

Futilely, he wished some reprieve would manifest itself soon.

Thus far, none had.

Alecost had promised to be there at three, bringing the dray so they may go out driving and find some privacy for her to make her intended proposal. Once Pere had informed his mother of this, she heaped on yet more pressure with lectures on the enormous benefits of Mistress Alecost's bestowed attentions. All of which, he noted, completely excluded any consideration of his feelings on the matter.

Even now, while he was occupying himself cleaning the fire grate in the front office, his mother was contemplatively pacing the room, puffing on her clay pipe and twirling the hairs of her mutton-chop whiskers as she tried to decide what he should wear for the occasion.

"You look very becoming in your yellow chintz chemise," she mused. "Too low cut, though. There's a fine line between fetching and flirtatious ..."

Pere peeked at the night-watch clock.

The hands marked off 2:71.

"That blue chiffon shift is very nice, but too flimsy," Mistress Farouche droned on.

At that moment the front door opened, startling them both but mostly firing a spark of terror into Pere, as he thought the person coming bustling in was Alecost, way ahead of her schedule.

It wasn't, it was Skaines.

"Warden!" the short, tubby woman gasped, puffing and blowing like a broken-winded horse. "She be here! She be here!"

"Who?" asked the Warden, frowning at her subordinate. "Who's here?"

"I," another voice authoritatively announced, compelling them all to look towards the open door where a lean, lanky figure dressed entirely in black stood. Skaines respectfully snatched her tricorn hat off her fat head and quickly brushed away the sweaty strands of dark hair stuck to her brow. "Judge Thesmothete Corsned of the Sceptral Judiciary Bar for Brecham County."

Shocked, Pere dropped the can of ash and cinders he'd swept up, spilling it onto the hearth again.

Everyone else regarded him for a moment until he silently curtsied a servile apology and hastily set about sweeping up the mess.

"Judge Corsned," Warden Farouche acknowledged.

"You have been expecting me," Corsned said matter-of-factly, removing her gauntlets by pulling at each finger in turn. "Word was sent via the County Sheriff's Office."

"Err ... yeah, yeah," the Warden floundered, dousing her pipe and putting it on the mantelpiece to cool. While she was there she urged Pere to hurry his chore and be gone with a swift motioning of her hand. "But we were told you would be here tomorrow, madam."

"Your Worship, if you don't mind," the hatchet-faced judicator sourly insisted, entering the room fully.

Behind her, a hugely muscular character lumbered in

carrying an attaché case. Barely discernible as a woman, this creature was clad in black also: from the britches and boots on her blocky legs to the leather jerkin covering her rippling torso. Her face was partially obscured by a leather mask fitting closely to the top half of her skull, through the roughly hacked eyeholes of which stared a pair of disproportionately sized eyes that lent her a maniacal appearance.

"We rode on ahead of the rest of our contingent, bringing only a few soldiers with us as bodyguards," Corsned explained, unhitching her cloak and flourishing it into the hands of Skaines, charging her with its care.

Four burly women tramped into the office then, all armoured in chain-mail under-jackets, stud-encrusted leather bodices and basic steel helmets bearing the griffin and dragon crest of the Royal Household. They were enough to strike fear into the most committed enemy with their ugliness alone.

Corsned instantly waved them out, commanding, "Have our mounts stabled at the livery we passed." She glanced at Farouche. "The necessary arrangements have been undertaken, I trust."

"Yeah," the Warden had chance to utter before the soldiers obediently departed to do as bid.

"Loon-Slatt," Corsned said, tossing her tall-crowned, wide brimmed hat onto the desk and clicking her fingers at her curious attendant. Loon-Slatt shambled to the beckoning and handed her superior the case. "This is Mistress Widdy Loon-Slatt, Warden. She is the appointed Field Bailiff."

"Hurr hurr!" Loon-Slatt grunted, drooling.

"What's that, Your Worship?" enquired Farouche, puzzled.

"*Executioner!*" Loon-Slatt gleefully elucidated.

She cocked a pop-eyed leer at Pere, who dropped the ash can again in fright.

"Peregrine!" his mother barked.

"Forgive me, Mama!" Pere pleaded, falling to his knees to sweep up the ash for a third time.

"Oh, just leave it! Leave it till our business here is done! Be gone with you!"

"Yeah, Mama," he gladly concurred, scurrying into the hallway leading to the living quarters.

There he paused, eavesdropping on the resuming discussion.

"Now," said Corsned, rifling through her case and producing a wad of documents, "Inspector Gombeen from the Brecham Municipal Revenue Office and Adiaphoron Wanhope of the Brecham Diocese are both currently tying up loose ends in Thirlborh with the County Sheriff. The three of them will be with our party as soon as they are able. Until that time, however, we will liaise with your office and ..." She checked her records. "Charlatan Fugle."

"Our parish preacher," Farouche affirmed. She motioned for Skaines to exit, instructing, "Go fetch her, Deputy."

Obligingly, Skaines hung the Judge's cloak on the rack then rushed out the door.

"Between us, at least we will be able to make a start on the proceedings," Corsned said, sitting in the Warden's chair and reclining.

"And what are those, exactly?"

The white-haired beak gauged the hick tipstaff with her cold, grey eyes.

"My remit is to oversee the legal aspects of all accusations, convictions, confessions and executions of sentence occurring within this County. Adiaphoron Wanhope is the Church representative in the contingent and will, when she arrives, be conducting her specific inquiries on each individual case. Inspector Gombeen's role is wholly fiscal, ensuring all Frithgild revenue has been effectively collected within this municipality. She is currently reviewing the accounts of the Duchess of Brecham's tax collectors for this immediate area. The County Sheriff, her ladyship the Viscountess of Faubourg, is acting as liaison between her officers and us. Strictly speaking, she should be here smoothing the ruffled feathers, but certain ... *matters* ... arose at our last port of call, leading to her unavoidable delay. And as we are slightly behind schedule as it is, Mistress Loon-Slatt and I took the liberty of continuing alone for the time being."

"Right."

"You seem somewhat perturbed by our presence, Warden. Do you begrudge us invading your patch in the absence of the Sheriff?"

Loon-Slatt cracked her knuckles and sniggered.

"By no means, Your Worship," Farouche nervously ensured, gulping. The last thing she wanted was any shadow of suspicion falling on her personally. She'd heard the rumours about this lot hanging folk just for looking at them sideways and had developed a healthy fear of them, the same as every other ordinary citizen in the land.

"Good," Corsned complimented. "It is a common and perhaps understandable reaction, but our purpose here is not to hi-jack your authority in your little pond, Warden. We have a Royal Edict to verify the support of the people, in both faith and finance, for the Queen's forthcoming sacred engagement."

"The crusade."

"Precisely. Our concerns are on a far broader scale than the skirmish politics of … " Corsned clicked her fingers for inspiration, then, after not receiving any, checked her records again.

"Rampick," Farouche reminded her.

"Yeah. Rampick."

"Your Worship will appreciate that your very presence here will affect the townsfolk who are under my charge."

"We will not impede your duties, Warden." Ominously, the Judge added, "And provided you co-operate, you will not impede ours."

"Does that mean you will need my gys to help you with …" Farouche trailed off her sentence to cough and run a finger around the rim of her collar.

"With *executions?*" Corsned finished for her, contemptuous mirth glinting in her wicked eyes. "I am a Judge, Warden, not a despot. My primary function is to consider evidence presented. I have come to get on with the groundwork. Rest assured, no convictions will be made prior to the arrival of the Adiaphoron, the Inspector and the Sheriff. However, at a later stage we may need the services of yourself and your assistants for enforcing the rulings. As for lighting the bonfires under the condemned … I'm sure Mistress Loon-Slatt is the more qualified."

"You bet!" Loon-Slatt proudly stated.

"Myself and my Deputies are completely at Your Worship's disposal," Farouche willingly kowtowed, privately feeling extremely uncomfortable with the whole dubious affair but still preferring compliance to ending up swinging on the gallows.

"Good," Corsned said, as if talking to a child she'd just bullied into some secrecy pact. Her thin lips creased a razor-slash curve across her gaunt face, creating what scarcely passed as a smile.

Widdy Loon-Slatt chuckled diabolically.

"Now, perhaps we can get down to business," Corsned suggested, riffling amongst her papers until she found the document she required. She cleared her throat and relaxed into the wing-back chair. "Tell me, Warden. Are there any undesirables hereabouts that have come to your attention?"

"Undesirables?"

"Yeah. Tinkers, itinerants and those sorts of pariahs … we will of course be systematically inspecting the entire township, but we like to get off to a positive start first."

Catching her drift, Farouche thought for a moment.

"We have a couple of Giaours living nearby," she admitted.

Pere, still hiding behind the dividing wall and listening in on their conversation, clapped a hand to his mouth to stifle a squeal.

"*Really?*" said Corsned, cocking an eyebrow in aroused interest. "Adiaphoron Wanhope will be *most* pleased. She has a high success rate at conversions. Where are they living, exactly? In the town?"

"No, Your Worship. Had they been, I would've had them in the cells waiting upon your arrival. No. I'm afraid they live just inside the boundary of Mandrake County."

"*Mandrake!*" the Judge muttered as if the name tasted foul in her mouth. "Trust *her* to give refuge to *pagans!*"

"Isn't Mandrake County to be included in the blood purge, Your Worship?" the Warden asked.

Corsned scowled at her.

"This is *not* a *blood purge!*" she severely corrected, an expression of bitter resentment clouding her sharp, angular features. "The Queen merely aims to guarantee the faith and loyalty of her subjects, and if during that process we can weed out potential dissidents then all the better!"

"I beg Your Worship's pardon," Farouche earnestly apologized, bowing.

"Mandrake County is a special case and will be dealt with by the Sceptral Cabal."

"The Sceptral Cabal?" Farouche parroted, her fear of the Judiciary paling in comparison to her inherent dread of the power behind the throne.

"Pity," Corsned mused. "A pair of genuine pagans would've started things with a real kick. What are their names?"

"Semeion Ducdame and Amoret Artemis," the Warden blabbed, despite the frantic but silent leniency pleas of her concealed son. "They're uncle and niece, I think. The gy often comes into town drinking at The Creaking Meat Tree."

"Indeed?" the other said with renewed interest. "I believe that is precisely the tavern where my assistants and I will be boarded, is it not?"

"Yeah, Your Worship."

"Soon as this Giaour sets foot in your jurisdiction, Warden, I want to know."

"Certainly."

Loon-Slatt giggled in anticipation.

"With her in our grasp we could possibly lure the other one from the bolt-hole and onto your turf as well," Corsned plotted, smirking her whiplash smile again and rubbing her spindly hands together.

Uttering a tiny screech, Pere ran through the kitchen and out into the yard. Here he hesitated, close to tears and biting his fingernails in anguish. Thoughts clamoured into his racing mind all at once, each compounding his confusion rather than alleviating it.

He had to warn Amoret that she and Semeion were in grave danger, that much was absolutely certain, but how he was going to do it without risking discovery was beyond him. Even by trying to contact her he knew he could be endangering her, yet he knew there was no time to lose, for the wolves were already at the door.

On top of all this, Alecost's visit was imminent, and if he mysteriously disappeared now he was quite sure his mother would not leave any stone unturned till he was recovered, Judge Corsned or no Judge Corsned.

Unable to cope, he burst into tears.

From above, a voice suddenly hissed, "*Pere!*"

Looking up, he saw Amoret squatting on top of the high courtyard wall.

"*Amy!*" he cried in equivalent whisper.

She leapt down, landed agile as a cat then sprang up and took him into her embrace. "Are you all right, my love?"

"I am now you're here," he sighed, mopping his streaming eyes on his apron.

"Why are you crying, darling?" she wanted to know. "Has Alecost done something to hurt you? I'll *kill* her if she has! It made my blood boil to see you with the fat daughter of a dog yesterday."

Putting his hands to her lips to silence her, he spared a wary glance towards the house before warning, "Amy, you have to get away from here! The Judiciary are in town!"

"I thought your mother said they'd be coming tomorrow?"

"Judge Corsned and her executioner rode on ahead of the contingent. They're in the Watch Office as we speak! Please! You have to go!"

"Okay," Amoret wisely agreed. "I'll lie low at Selcouth for a while. They won't dare trespass on Mandrake's ground."

"Selcouth may not be safe for much longer," Pere gloomily forecast. "The Sceptral Cabal itself intends to take on Lady Mandrake. I heard Judge Corsned say so. The Cabal will roll right over even her."

"Damn them!" Amoret cursed aloud. "Damn them all to Erebus!"

Pere begged her to hush lest those inside should hear her.

Deep within him, he was able to pick a tiny thread of consolation from this very dangerous turn of events. He surmised that if Mandrake's benefaction towards Amoret and Semeion were to become more of a hazard than a blessing, they would be forced to quit their settlement whether they liked it or not. And this meant they would be able to fulfil his dearest longing and take him away with them. Away from Rampick. Away from the hideous prospect of marrying Alecost. Away from *everything*.

"*Peregrine!*" his mother's voice summoned. "*Peregrine! Where are you, boy?*"

"Quickly, Amy!" Pere urged his consort, pushing her towards the yard gates. "Quickly! You must go! Mistress Alecost must have arrived early!"

"Alecost?" repeated Amoret, venom in her tone. "Are you to be with *her* again today?"

"Yeah, yeah," he admitted. "My mother has bargained me to marry her and she intends to propose."

"*What?*"

"Never mind that now! Just *go!*"

"*Never mind?*" Amoret exclaimed, anger seething within her. "How can I *not* mind it, Pere? I *love* you and you tell me to *never mind* that you've been promised to another woman as a *husband?*"

"*Peregrine!*" Mistress Farouche yelled, growing more impatient with each passing moment. "*Come here at once, boy!*"

"My mother comes, Amy!" Pere impressed upon her, shoving her harder but not being able to move her sturdy stature since he was far weaker and slighter than she. "You must leave *now!*"

"Let her come!" Amoret challenged through gritted teeth. "I'll show her the strength of true love!"

"No! No!" Pere insisted, pulling at her with all his might to prevent the terrible clash he envisioned. He could hear his mother's footfalls in the kitchen, advancing nearer and nearer.

"Go, Amy! You're no good to me dead!"

This made her think, and she reluctantly abandoned her bearding of the lion in its den. Instead, she stole a kiss from Pere then began clambering up onto a pile of crates crazily stacked in the corner of the yard to get on top of the wall again.

She paused to glance back over her shoulder.

"Don't forsake me, Pere. I won't let you be so cruelly bartered."

"*Peregrine!*" the Warden boomed, almost with them now.

"*Go!*" Pere shooed her on.

Amoret regarded him for a fleeting second before continuing her climb.

The latch rattled on the house back door, spurring her on to rapidly reach the summit of the wall. She peered down into the alleyway below to ensure Favel was still in the position where she'd climbed up off his back, then finally jumped.

Pere glimpsed her just disappearing over the wall when his mother came blundering into the courtyard, face like thunder.

"*Peregrine!*" she shouted. "Did you not hear me calling, boy?"

From the other side of the bricks came a loud gadding cry, a spirited whinnying and the rhythmic thudding of hooves.

"Sorry, Mama," Pere emptily reconciled.

"Do I have to follow you around, my lad? You should be preparing yourself for Mistress Alecost. She will be here soon."

"I will ready myself immediately, Mama," he humbly placated, scampering off across the cobbled enclosure.

"Wait, pup!" his parent further imposed on him. "There is time enough yet for you to clear that mess you made in my office. Be about that, and don't disturb the Judge. She has important matters to attend to."

"Yeah, Mama," Pere said, not relishing the idea of being in the company of Corsned and her ghastly henchwoman.

"Then make haste to your boudoir and pretty yourself."

He curtsied then went swiftly into the house.

Timidly, he re-entered the front office, creeping along in his moccasins to avoid causing any disruption and keeping his eye firmly fixed on the tall, thin figure sitting at the desk studiously bent over reams of paper.

Unfortunately, he didn't spot Loon-Slatt, who was standing by the fireplace trying to spark a match on the stonework so she could light her clay pipe, and he almost collided with her.

Pere squealed in fright when he did see her and speedily back pedalled.

"Hurr hurr!" Loon-Slatt chortled.

Corsned looked round at the rude interruption.

"What do you do there, boy?" she growled.

"Buh … buh … begging your pardon, ma'am," Pere stuttered, curtsying as if his very life depended on it.

"That's *Your Worship*, boy! Show respect!" Corsned harshly tutored. "What is the meaning of this intrusion?"

The youth swallowed hard and justified, "I … I came to attend the hearth … Your Worship."

"Then don't shilly-shally, boy! Get on with it! The quicker you are about it the sooner you will be no pestilence to me!"

Galvanized into action, Pere dodged past Loon-Slatt and went onto his knees. He grabbed the pan and brush he'd deserted earlier and started sweeping so furiously he stirred up a grey cloud of ash.

"And mind Mistress Loon-Slatt's boots, whelp!" Corsned harangued. "She eats brats for breakfast, don't you, Mistress Loon-Slatt?"

"You bet!" Widdy embellished.

Pere was inclined to be convinced.

By 2:99 he was perfumed, preened and presentable, cutting so much of a dash in comparison to the bland drabness of his previous incarnation that even Judge Corsned had to do a double-take when he gracefully glided through the front office on his way outside.

His golden hair was braided in silver, his exquisite complexion accentuated by understated jewellery and his sylphlike form flatteringly sculpted in an elegant jade wrap trimmed with modest flounces and fine lace.

Corsned, Loon-Slatt and Attercop and Skaines (who had since returned after running errands for the Judge) all gawped at him as he passed them by. To them the transformation was astonishing. They were barely able to recognize this remarkable beauty as the dowdy domestic he had been but twenty minutes ago.

Pere could feel the intensity of their lecherous observation burning into him like branding irons and was glad to bang the door shut on them. Being ogled was a frequent occurrence for young males of his age; and while most enjoyed the attention and played to their audiences, he hated it.

Huffing and flicking aside a loose strand of hair, Pere moved to the hitching rail outside of the gaol-house to wait for his date.

It was then that a volley of wolf-whistles and catcalls arose from across the street, rudely attracting his notice. He looked over to see a rowdy gang of teenage girls sitting at the bench tables positioned along the front wall of The Creaking Meat Tree, and when they knew they'd caught his eye they all made lewd gestures at him.

He averted his gaze in disgust, to a barrage of dirty laughter.

Not more than a few seconds later Mistress Alecost came bundling along the main street on the dray, a dancing palomino trussed in the yoke, as opposed to the usual broad-framed draught horse that pulled it when it was laden with ale kegs. Once more she was dressed in her best suit, but this time had added the accessories of a jauntily skewed hat, flamboyant cravat and foppishly frilly shirtsleeves to her outfit.

Pere noted the cart she drove was the same one he had seen parked in the gaol-house yard just last night.

"Master Farouche," Alecost greeted, raising her hat as she drew her transport up to the hitching-rail where her companion was standing. Pere courteously smiled. "By Zoe's name! You are a sight to behold, young Master."

"Thank you, Mistress Alecost," Pere graciously accepted the compliment.

The fat, perspiring woman bumbled down off the dray and

offered a podgy mitt as aid for him to climb aboard. He availed himself of her implied kindness, ascending onto the high perch best he could without compromising his modesty to his willing helper, who was lasciviously disrobing him with her eyes as it was.

That achieved, Alecost eagerly went round the other side of the dray and breathily struggled back into the driving seat, not wanting to waste a moment.

"Hold onto my arm, young Master," she advised, poking out an elbow at him as she took up the reins. "This gelding's not too familiar with the harness as yet, so he may caper a little."

Precautious, Pere did as she said.

"Walk on," Alecost chivvied the horse, lightly smacking the straps onto its hindquarters.

The palomino plunged dramatically, startling Pere into clinging more tenaciously to the whip's arm. Alecost haltered back, causing the beast to rear slightly, then it settled and began moving forward in a frisky prance.

"He needs the practice," she idly informed Pere, "hence why I brought him."

And probably to show off as well, Pere suspected, not in the least bit impressed.

As they trotted along the main street, attracting some attention from the many people milling about, Pere saw Amoret loitering around the smithy with Favel at her side. She made a point of staring directly at him, never tearing her gaze from his as the dray rattled past.

Pere turned his head to maintain the eye contact with her right up until they faded from each other's view.

The drive was pleasant enough.

If the company had been more inspiring then it would have been a whole lot pleasanter. As it was, Pere had to politely endure Alecost's insipid drivel about the tavern trade and dreary anecdotes from it, which were perhaps related to him in hopeful pre-emption of him soon to be intimately dependent on the living. Sometimes she did stray onto shooting, equestrianism and politics, but these subjects also failed to stimulate him into spontaneous repartee.

He compensated for this by enjoying the fine weather, admiring the scenery and thinking of she whom he would rather be with. Letting Alecost tirelessly drone on and on as their skittish gelding, having become more accustomed to his bondage, ferried them through Rampick's outlying meadows and groves.

When the dray slowed to a halt, a disconcerting pang of apprehension alerted him.

This was it.

The moment he'd been dreading.

"Well, Master Farouche," Alecost sighed, slackening the reins. "Isn't this nice?"

"Yeah, thank you, Mistress Alecost," Pere replied.

"Away with all this stuffy formality, Master Farouche! You can call me Av," she generously allowed. "May I call you Peregrine?"

He shyly nodded his consent.

"Peregrine … would you care for a short stroll?"

A tad puzzled by this request, he gestured affirmation. He felt sure there was no real need to get off the cart to make this marriage proposal of hers, unless she intended to go down on bended knee to him in the trendy continental manner, of course. Whatever her reason, he wished she would just get on with it so he could disappoint her pig-headed presumptions and get back home.

She dismounted the dray and waddled round to the passenger side to hand him down from his seat. Then they linked arms like a true courting couple and gently sauntered off the road onto the verge, Alecost leading the way towards a shady little copse.

Once amongst the trees therein, the innkeeper clumsily fumbled in her waistcoat pocket and produced a small, velvet-coated box.

"Peregrine," she said, straining to drop onto one knee. "Peregrine. I can no longer contain my most ardent desires. I am but a simple publican who cannot make fancy speeches, but I can assure you of my undying affection for and devotion to you. You are the only berd I have cast an eye upon in many a year, and I would be honoured ... nay, *privileged* ... if you would favour me with your affections ..." She opened the box, revealing a magnificent ring set with a central ruby encircled by diamonds, and presented it to him. "... and be my husband, forever and always."

Gaping at the richness of the trinket, Pere couldn't immediately convey a response. His own meagre jewellery paled into insignificance against this single piece alone, and it was possibly worth more than his entire collection put together.

"I can't offer you the luxury your fairness deserves, Peregrine, but I am of a respectable trade and I swear I will be steady and reverent to you for all eternity," Alecost persevered, still attempting to influence his decision, although she was certain he had received instruction from his mother as to how he should answer. She preferred to win his heart to reinforce Mistress Farouche's guarantee that Peregrine was hers for the taking.

Finding his voice, Pere finally said, "No."

"*No?*" Alecost repeated, flabbergasted. "What do you mean *no?* There's a lot at stake here, young lad! I think you had better reconsider!"

Pere stepped back from her, shaking his head.

"I'm sorry, Mistress Alecost, but I can't marry you."

"Can't you now, by Zoe?" Alecost dismissively grunted, struggling up onto her feet again. She removed the ring from its cushion and tossed the container away. "Well, I think you *can*, sir! I think you *must!*"

With an agility her size belied, she seized his slender wrist and yanked him to her. Pere screeched as the momentum delivered him into her bear-hug embrace. He tried wriggling free, but she held him tightly and brutally rammed the ring onto his engagement finger, causing him to squeal in pain.

Despite its application, it was a perfect fit.

"There now, sir! We are as good as wed!" Alecost declared.

"Now … let us consummate our understanding with a kiss of those sweet lips of yours, Peregrine."

She clutched him to her harder, pressing him towards her wet, puckered, flabby mouth.

Her right hand mauled his thigh until it found the hem of his gown.

Pere was terrified, fearing for both his safety and that which he prized most highly; his chastity. Bruises would heal; but should he lose the flower of his manhood, he'd never be able to hold his head up ever again for shame and degradation.

There was only one woman he wanted to gift that to.

Suddenly, a voice yelled, "*ALECOST!*"

Startled, Alecost looked up.

She had no chance to react before a fist arced square into her chubby mug and knocked her flat on her back.

Two strong, cradling arms broke Pere's subsequent fall from the publican's grasp. He stared up into the face of his guardian angel and was overjoyed to see it was Amoret who had come to defend his honour.

"Amy!" he gasped.

"Run, Pere!" she told him, pushing him away from the scene. "This isn't over yet."

As testimony to this, Alecost grappled Amoret from behind without warning, picking her off her feet and roughly thrusting her against a tree trunk.

"Amy!" Pere squealed, rushing to her.

Alecost reached out and shunted him to the ground.

"Is *this* the reason you reckon you can't marry me, young Master?" she derisively asked. "Above a decent, honest, upstanding woman you'd choose a thieving, conniving, filthy *Giaour?*"

Amoret propelled herself forward, head down, screaming blue murder as she did. She bludgeoned into her opponent's belly, nailing Alecost up the shaft of another tree.

Despite being winded, the big woman grabbed Amoret between the legs and literally turned her top over tail before violently crashing her to the copse floor.

Disorientated, Amoret started crawling up onto her feet for more punishment. Her burly assailant didn't wait for her and unsportingly waded in with the boot, kicking her in the ribs and putting her back on the deck.

Distraught, Pere threw in his lot and attacked Alecost. Pummelling her beefy chest with his little fists and spitting every expletive he knew, which weren't many and about as effective as his pathetic punches.

Alecost simply laughed and swatted him onto his behind.

This disrespectful treatment of her beloved simultaneously bought Amoret time to resurrect herself and motivated her to do just that. She snatched her knife from its sheath and confronted Alecost, her blade glinting in the sun.

"You dirty daughter of a dog!" she cursed. "*I'll kill you!*"

"No, Amy!" Pere protested, scrambling up, only to be pushed down again.

"You'd better be prepared to use that, bitch!" Alecost said. "Because that's the only way you're going to stop me from shoving it straight up your *vent!*"

Amoret went at her, slashing wildly, the four-inch blade whistling through the air with every lunge and swipe. For her part, Alecost was extremely sinuous, bobbing and weaving and foiling the strikes and courageously diving in at open opportunities to make her own assaults.

Holding his breath, Pere watched in horrified suspense as the tussle continued.

The vying women clashed, blocking each other's arms and bringing the match to a grunting, straining stalemate. They twisted and turned this way and that, shuffling and twirling around in circles, both striving to prove themselves the strongest.

It was Amoret who took the initiative to lash out with her foot, punting the toe of her riding boot into Alecost's meaty thigh. Her spar went down and Amoret dropped on top of her to pin her there.

Alecost wrestled her off and they rolled on the ground, exchanging the advantage as they tumbled along.

Bizarrely, Pere caught himself thinking how Mistress Alecost's lovely suit was being spoiled. These misplaced concerns were soon vaporized, though, when he realized his nemesis had successfully conquered his champion and wrenched the dagger from her grasp.

"Now, Giaour!" Alecost victoriously crowed amidst her hard breathing, poising the weapon over the defeated. "Now I will put you into *the sky* with all the other *pagans!*"

"*NO!*" Pere screamed.

The knife fell.

Amoret shielded herself with her free arm, grimly fighting the mighty intent to skewer the blade into her skull. But she was done for. Her reserves were exhausted and she could feel her resolve caving in to Alecost's superior power. Her arm, the only thing left between her and death, jittered uncontrollably, no longer able to fend off the imminent danger.

Alecost laughed in her face, spraying spittle onto her as a final insult.

Pere's hand discovered a fallen branch lying near him.

Without hesitating he grabbed it, scrambled to his feet and charged towards the theatre of battle, swinging the makeshift club over his shoulder.

Dried leaves still clinging to the bough whickered through the air, alerting Alecost.

She looked round just as he struck and the branch smacked hard against her right temple.

Alecost collapsed onto Amoret.

Numbly comprehending his actions, Pere gawped at the huge woman's body as Amoret struggled to push it off her to escape its crushing weight.

"She … she … she was going to kill you, Amy," he worriedly justified.

"Yeah, she was," said Amoret, retrieving her dagger and going to his side. She looked at him, seeing him in a new light. "You did good, Pere. She got what she deserved, molesting you like that."

"Do you …" He gulped. "Is she dead?"

"Let's hope so," Amoret wished, trying to sound indifferent. If the truth was known, her own fear easily equalled Pere's.

"No!" Pere redressed. "No. Let's not hope *that*, even for her."

Unwillingly, Amoret returned to the stricken Alecost, keeping the knife in her hand in case the publican should suddenly spring back into life.

She kicked the spread-eagled woman.

Not a twitch.

Cautiously crouching down and frisking underneath Alecost's collar and cravat, she searched the neck for a pulse. Meanwhile, her opposite hand habitually mugged the victim, locating watch, purse and jewellery like greased lightning. As for the pulse, she had less luck finding that.

"I think she is dead," Amoret diagnosed, hurriedly moving clear of the fresh corpse and sheathing the knife.

"In the name of Zoe!" Pere gasped, too engrossed in the horrible consequences to notice the loot she was hastily stuffing into her pockets. "I killed her, Amy!" He darted his eyes to hers. "*I killed someone!*"

"No you didn't," Amoret consoled, wrapping him in a comforting embrace. She gently confiscated the blunt instrument he limply brandished and tossed it aside. "I did. You were too busy being ravished, remember."

Their eyes met.

"I told you I'd gladly kill and die for you, Pere."

A crackling of twigs leapt guilty terror into their already drumming hearts.

Favel appeared from behind a bush.

"Oh, great!" Amoret sighed, almost laughing with relief. "Here's the cavalry!"

Treating her remark with the contempt he deemed worthy, Favel plodded over to Alecost. He sniffed her from top to toe then gave his opinion by snorting and shaking his head.

"Now you're here, you can get us out of here," Amoret told him.

Alternatively, the horse gazed out over the road, his ears pricking and rotating.

He began insistently nudging the pair of them towards the bushes he had emerged from, whinnying and causing an awful fuss in order to get them into cover.

"Listen!" Pere said.

They did.

Hoof beats distantly sounded on the road.

Favel snorted an equine 'told you so'.

Amoret peered through the foliage and saw two figures on horseback approaching, riding relatively sedately and not yet within range to identify. She could discern that one was a tall, gangly beanpole and the other a squat roly-poly, though, and that was enough in itself for her to confidently guess. "It's Attercop and Skaines!"

"Holy Zoe!" Pere croaked, clapping his hands to his mouth.

A shout went up.

The steady hoof beats broke into galloping.

"Damn! They've spotted Alecost's dray!" Amoret commentated. She turned to Pere and Favel. "C'mon! We've got to go!"

But Favel was already leading the way, encouraging them to follow him out the far side of the copse before the Deputy Wardens got any closer. And once they were on the open ground, they mounted Favel and he cantered them away down the grassy slope.

Leaving Attercop and Skaines to make the grisly discovery and raise the alarm.

IIII

Semeion Ducdame woke with a start.

He had dozed off in the peaceful absence of his niece, but now he was being rudely roused from his slumber by loud noises. Instinctively, he fumbled under his tunic for the 8mm calibre, eight-barrelled revolver pistol he always carried as personal insurance.

His first thought was of robbery, and through bleary eyes he could make out two human forms, blurred beyond recognition at present, and the shape of a horse. One of the people seemed to be ransacking Selcouth for any removable assets while the second tended the animal.

"Hold fast, scoundrels!" he demanded, cocking the pistol's hammer.

His second thought was that these invaders might be agents of the Watch Warden, sent to recover their mistress's son from Amoret's cradle-snatching clutches.

"It's me, Uncle," Amoret said, ignoring the lethal weapon aimed at her and continuing her rampage, frantically stashing provisions into a set of saddlebags.

"What's happening?" Semeion bad temperedly enquired. He sat up on the edge of his bed, rubbed his eyes and squinted at the other two who had come disturbing his snooze.

Favel, patient as ever, chomped on some of his bedding straw and Pere stood quietly at the door.

Semeion groaned at the sight of the lad.

"What are you doing, girl?" he pressed Amoret, although he thought he already knew the answer.

She came to him and snatched the gun from his grip. Fiddling to uncock it, she asked, "Is this thing loaded?"

"Of course!" Semeion indignantly assured. He slapped the business end down towards the floor. "So don't point it at me!"

"Where's the ammunition?"

"In the table drawers."

Snuggling the pistol into the waistband of her britches, she went about searching the table.

"What are you doing?" he reiterated, still not having received an explanation.

"Leaving," Amoret simply replied, finding a small leather pouch containing a handful of highly illegal homemade cartridges, which infringed the tight restrictions on percussion-cap firearms. She shoved it into the bags. "And you're coming with us, Uncle, so get yourself going. We have to quit here soon as it's dark."

Her uncle stared at her for a long moment, then asserted, "I will do no such thing, young woman! What reason do I have to quit here?"

"The Judiciary are in town," Amoret cited as just cause. "They're after blood to purge. Our blood."

"Pah!" the elderly man mocked. "They have no claim on Mandrake's land. They can't touch us."

"Yeah, but the Sceptral Cabal is coming to deal with Mandrake personally," she countered. "Isn't that right, Pere?"

"Yeah," Pere confirmed. He gazed at Amoret. She had coached him not to say a word about the incident with Alecost; and not being an adept deceiver, he was having difficulty maintaining a buttoned lip. "Soon there won't be anywhere left to run."

"So we're getting out while the getting's good."

Semeion grunted his disapproval.

"Well, don't include me in your foolish scheme," he declined.

"You're coming with us," Amoret inflexibly decreed. "No choice."

"There're always choices. And I choose to stay."

"And be *killed?*" his sole surviving relation said, banging the saddlebags onto the table.

"When you've run as far and for as long as I have, my girl, you eventually learn that the lines are circles."

"This isn't the time for home-spun philosophy, Uncle. The threat is here and very real."

"And when you turn the next corner and go over the brow of the distant hill it'll be different, will it? There won't be just as many persecutors there as anywhere else, will there?" He looked at her and huffed. "Still, I suppose it was inevitable. I hoped you would learn better, but you're as stubborn and headstrong as I when I was your age. Strange how nobody can acquire wisdom without making the mistakes that are made generation after generation."

"I can't persuade you to come?" Amoret summarized, dismayed.

He shook his head.

"I could drag you, you know," she intimidated.

"Wild horses couldn't, so I doubt you could. I'd break your neck if you tried. At least that'd save you the trouble of travelling miles on end to find exactly what awaits you here."

"I have to try," she excused, kneeling at his feet and encasing his hands in hers. Not questioning the probability of the frail ancient beating her if she decided to force him to go, for she knew darn well he could. "I can't just sit here and let *them* say if I live or die."

"And I don't expect you to," Semeion informed her, stroking her hair. "Just don't expect me to share your passion for life."

She glanced at Pere.

"And there's him," Semeion acknowledged.

"I love him, Uncle," she unashamedly professed. "So I have to try for both of us."

"Of course you do. Just don't ask me to stop cursing his

name to Erebus for taking you away from me, Amy." The old man blinked a tear from his eye. "But come," he rallied, clapping her hands and sliding himself off the bed. "There are many preparations to attend to if you are to be provided for and on the road by dark."

He looked at Pere.

"I'll wager you're happy now, boy," he couldn't resist jibing. "You have what you wanted."

"At a price," Pere lamented.

"There's a price for everything in this world, boy," Semeion told him. "The question is whether or not you're prepared to pay it."

"Leave it, will you, Uncle," Amoret implored, exchanging uncomfortably guilty glances with Pere. She began clashing the pots and pans about as a practical distraction. "We need some water boiling up."

"First time I saw you, boy, I knew you would bring trouble. There again, I've been expecting you for a long time now," the old sage went on regardless. "Still, I'm glad to see you're respecting my feelings by not wearing that saltire in my home."

Grabbing at his naked throat, Pere gasped.

"My necklace!" he mewled at Amoret, close to hysteria. She quickly dashed over to him in order to try and calm him before he said anything more. But she wasn't quick enough. He let the cat out of the bag just as she got to him. "She must've torn it off me! It'll be with her *body!*"

Favel whinnied.

Semeion looked at the pair, sharing his attention between them.

"*Body?*" he echoed, frowning. "*Whose* body?"

Neither offered to enlighten him.

"Amoret? What's happened? What've you *done?*"

"I think I killed a woman …"

"You *think?*" her uncle clarified, flabbergasted. "*Empyre above!* You either *did* or you *didn't*, you mad, young fool!"

"No, she didn't kill her!" Pere firmly contradicted.

"Pere ..." Amoret attempted to curb his tongue.

"Thank Icarus for that!" Semeion praised.

"*I* did!"

It was gone 3:70 when they brought her back.

Evening was closing in.

Peregrine had been missing for half an hour and his mother was beginning to fear the worst. Like everyone else, she presumed highway robbers had set upon the courting couple, dispatched Alecost in the attack and made away with the boy, or did something else with him that nobody dared think of let alone mention.

Attercop had her own ideas as to what had occurred, though.

While the Warden was occupied with Judge Corsned, she and Skaines had decided to skive off duty and ride out to see a merry widower and his bachelor brother they often frequented who lived on the Thirlborh Road. It was along this way they noticed Mistress Alecost's dray parked up by a small copse with no one aboard it. Stopping to sneak up on the lovers and catch them 'at it', they stumbled across the prostrate body of Avoirdupois Alecost. Skaines had immediately ridden back to Rampick to alert Farouche, leaving her partner at the scene.

Attercop amused herself during the time she was there alone.

Firstly, by seeing if Alecost had anything on her worth stealing. She found the stiff to be already cleaned out of valuables: a fact that later reinforced the robber theory.

Secondly, she performed a preliminary sweep of the area, which produced some very intriguing circumstantial evidence. According to tracks on the ground she ascertained that there was at least one other person and a horse present at the murder, and reckoned the steed was rough shod with either homemade or second-hand shoes. Also, a couple of interesting items turned up; namely Peregrine's saltire necklace and a piece of leather torn from a jerkin.

Her mind started jamming the pieces together straight away.

There was only one person she knew of who *always* wore a

leather jerkin and who couldn't get her horse shod by any of the farriers hereabouts because of the current social tensions and the more likely threat she might renege on paying the bill.

Artemis the Giaour.

Within fifteen minutes, the Warden arrived.

Once briefed on the awful truth, Farouche desperately assembled a band of willing helpers to search for Peregrine. Judge Corsned, present at the time Skaines burst into the Watch Office with the news on her lips, obligingly volunteered her bodyguards and her right-hand woman Widdy Loon-Slatt to be deployed as the Warden saw fit.

Commandeering carts and horses alike, the posse descended on the copse. Mistress Alecost's corpse was duly loaded onto the dray and Attercop and Skaines were detailed to return her to town, where the local alchemist and apothecary Wiccan Mountebank, who often performed such tasks for the Warden, could examine her. So they rode back on their own horses, guiding Alecost's gelding and her improvised bier between them.

Attercop didn't tell anyone about her finds.

And nor did she stay at Mountebank's house once the body had been delivered, as the Warden had expressly said she should.

She had other plans.

"Where're we going, Cait?" Skaines panted, breathless from carrying the dead weight into Mountebank's front parlour, which the old soothsayer had semi-converted into a laboratory.

"Selcouth folly," Attercop replied as they left Mistress Mountebank ponderously hovering around the hundred and fifty kilograms of publican lying on her table.

"We can't go there!" Skaines forbade, trying to keep alongside her cohort as she descended the house's veranda steps and strode to where the horses were tied to the frontage's handrail. "That be on Mandrake's land. She'll have us shot!"

"We be ossifers of the law, Skaines," Attercop reminded her. "And we be on a murder inquiry."

"What makes you think those Giaours know anything of the dastardly affair?"

"We b'ain't going up there to question 'em, woman!" the other said. "We be going to arrest 'em and recover the young Master."

Pausing to wrack her brains a moment, Skaines said, "Why?"

"Why? Why, 'cos the girl did for the poor seity lying cold in yon quack's clinic, that be why! And she kidnapped Master Peregrine to boot."

"How d'you know that, Cait?"

"I got everdince," Attercop proudly bragged as they untethered the animals.

"Evidence? What kind of evidence?"

"The ifferutable ... the irrefrewtruble ... the kind what can't be argued with! Now stop asking daft questions and check thy pistol's loaded."

"Will we be needing our boom tubes?" Skaines worriedly asked, not liking the sound of this.

Demonstratively, Attercop slid her four-barrel, 12mm calibre Thunderbus out of the holster on her belt and made sure it was fully primed. "Just a percaution. We be going after a cold-blooded killer, don't thee forget. And thee won't want thy pistol to be squibbing out on thee if she comes at thee with a roasting spit, will thee?"

Talked into it, Skaines hastily inspected her more modest 10mm bore Sparquebus twin.

"'Sides which," Attercop said, holstering her own weapon and adjusting her belt, "I knows most of Mandrake's estate bailiffs. I spends many a night shift with 'em up in yon woods. They got a still up there."

"So we'll get by 'em all right, you reckon?"

"Oh, aye. All we has to worry about is taking the Giaour legal-like."

Skaines paled and said, "Aye ..."

"Think of the glory, though, Skaines."

She did, imagining herself and Attercop being the toast of the town for bringing in the heartless fiend who murdered Mistress Alecost and having free hospitality at The Creaking Meat Tree for the rest of their lives as reward.

More cheerfully, she said, "Aye!"

"Climb on, then," Attercop invited her, ascending into the saddle herself and tugging at the palomino's reins to bring it round with her own mount. "We'll stable this nag at the tavern first then ride there directly."

"Will we need the shackles to restrain the young Giaour with?" Skaines queried.

"Nah," her partner dismissed. "I b'ain't planning on bringing her in alive."

"Pere was being *attacked*, Uncle," Amoret patiently explained again, sitting on an empty keg, holding her head in her hands while the old man paced the floor. "It was fortunate I was passing …"

"I don't want to hear your *excuses*, girl! Save them for the Judiciary!" Semeion fumed, wagging his finger at his niece. "Your … *darling* here killed someone! And you choose to go to the *gallows* on his *behalf*? By Icarus! I knew you were *foolish*, but I didn't believe you *suicidal* with it!"

"It won't come to that," Pere chipped in. "Not if we can get away."

"And you can keep your opinions to yourself, boy!" Semeion nastily rounded on him. "Haven't you caused enough trouble already?" Favel snorted discontentedly and retreated outside.

"I didn't ask to be *raped!*" Pere impressively fought back.

"And I don't suppose Alecost asked to be *beaten to death!*"

"Pere's right," Amoret intervened. "If we get away nobody will swing. And the longer we dally here easing your conscience the less chance we have."

"Oh, *he's* right, is he? This *murderer* here?"

"Uncle!"

"Well, that's what you are when you *kill* someone!"

"*Would you rather it was ME dead!*" Amoret yelled, leaping to her feet and sending the keg barrelling across the floor. She pointed in the direction of Rampick. "I know *they* would!"

"Of course not!" her uncle gruffly rectified. "I can live with you leaving, but I couldn't live with you throwing your life away on … on *him!*"

61

"He *saved* my life."

"We'll be throwing away both our lives if we stay here," Pere commented.

"You don't get it, do you? Either of you? I ought to bang your heads together!" Semeion chided. "There is *nowhere* to run! This country is battened down tight as a drum! By running away, you'll make yourselves look even more guilty than you already are!"

"What do you suggest, Uncle? We stay here and surrender ourselves to the tipstaffs?" Amoret sarcastically asked.

"It's worth a try," Semeion recommended.

"With the *blood purge* in town?" she jogged his memory.

"This is no concern of the blood purge! The case'll go before the Sceptral Judiciary, yeah, but not as Treason or Heresy," he surmised. "You have the boy as a witness. He's the Warden's own son. That has to count for something. They won't hang him, I'm sure."

"I never thought I'd see the day when Semeion Ducdame knuckled under."

"This is sound reason, girl, not capitulation! If everything bears out to have happened the way you say it did then they'll show leniency, considering the circumstances. I mean it's not as if you committed any other crime, is it?"

Amoret cast her eyes to the floor.

"Is it?" Semeion almost pleaded.

Digging into her pockets, she shamefully declared the trinkets she had looted off the dead woman, disgorging them onto the table.

"Oh, Icarus!" Semeion moaned.

"Amy!" Pere gasped, moving over to rake through the pile of stolen property.

It was then he realized he was still wearing the ring.

"Oh, my Zoe!" he exclaimed embarrassedly, displaying it to the others. "It's her engagement ring! I forgot I had it on!"

"That settles it," Amoret concluded, scraping the goods into the saddlebags. "We have to leave."

"There may be another way," Semeion hopefully clutched at straws.

"What? Ask Judge Corsned for a pardon?"

"Our host."

"Icarus?" Amoret misunderstood.

"No, no! Mandrake!"

"What do you reckon she can do?"

"She's a Magistrate," the old timer carefully enunciated.

"Yeah. In the wrong County," observed Pere, earning himself a withering glare from Semeion.

"She's also a Mandilion Thane, a wealthy merchant and a very influential courtier."

"She's also forty clicks away and probably not at home," Amoret burst his bubble.

"She could help," her uncle persevered. "She has many contacts abroad through her businesses. The least she could do is get you safe passage out of the country if she can't help you here."

"And what makes you think she would even want to bother?" Amoret trashed the idea, throwing the saddlebags onto the table. "Icarus knows, we're nothing to her! We're just pawns in her stupid, trivial games with the Queen! We're kept here as her pet curiosities!"

"Pah! You're too stubborn to see good sense when it's wafted under your very nose, girl! If you will not swallow your pride and go to her for help then I shall!"

With that, he grabbed his staff from beside his bed and stalked off towards the door, muttering under his breath as he went.

"It's forty kilometres and the time must nearly be four now," Amoret estimated.

"Rot and nonsense! It's less than thirty five cross country!" the elder grumbled, roughly shoving past her. "I'll be back before the hour!"

"It'll be almost midnight by then," Pere said.

Semeion made a point of ignoring him.

"You're wasting your time!" Amoret ensured him. "And ours!"

"When I return with Mandrake's blessing, you'll thank me!" Semeion said as he left.

Favel accosted him outside to offer his services as transport, but Semeion shooed him away in preference of travelling under his own steam and navigation.

"Cantankerous old fool!" Amoret cursed her uncle.

"Do you think his efforts will do any good?" Pere asked her.

"Of course not," she stalwartly denied. "Mandrake's been abroad for the past year, and her bailiffs have been poaching fish and game off the estate and hawking it in the taverns." She shuffled her feet. "They've given us a few trout and hind to keep us sweet."

"Isn't that biting the hand that feeds you?" he self-righteously maintained.

"We're the hands that feed ourselves," she put him straight in no uncertain terms. "Mandrake just grants us free roam to satisfy her ulterior motives."

He forlornly gazed out the doorway after Semeion, who had already vanished from view.

"C'mon," Amoret distracted him. "Let's get some water boiled for our journey."

They'd gone at a brisk gallop, covering the distance within five minutes.

They crossed the Talweg River (which served as the County line, separating Brecham and Mandrake) on the Mandragora Road Bridge, then left the beaten track to follow the meandering watercourse and approach Selcouth from the shielded side of the ridge. Effectively they were trespassing; but this minor infringement did not bother them as none of the bailiffs had spotted them, as far as they were aware. They considered that if ever there was a time when a little professional courtesy was needed it was now.

About a kilometre from the folly's location they purposefully dismounted and stealthily advanced on foot, leading the horses behind them. They skulked in and out of every grove, dell and slightest bit of scrub to avoid detection, using the lengthening shadows of the sun's fading glory to their advantage.

When the rotund structure came within sight, Attercop dropped onto her belly and flapped her arm in a frenzied gesture for her mate to do the same, hissing at Skaines, "Get down!"

"What is it?" Skaines wanted to know, doing as she was told and craning her neck to see.

"It be the other Giaour!"

"The old berd? Is he coming this way?"

"Yeah, damn it!" Attercop swore. "We'll hafta take him 'n' all."

Skaines pulled her pistol and aimed it. "I think I can pick him off from here …"

"No! You idiot!" her partner reprimanded, spoiling her targeting. "You'll ruin the element of surprise!"

"How're we gonna do it, then?"

Attercop briefly surveyed the lie of the land. "That clump of trees there," she said, indicating some birches clustered around a semi-dry pond just down a bank from their position and directly in their quarry's path.

Their plan formulated, they left the horses to graze and scuttled to the ambush venue, keeping low and out of sight. Once there, they drew their truncheons from inside their coats and crouched amongst the foliage until the striding hiker got closer.

"Are we gonna do for him, Cait?" Skaines whispered.

"Nah," Attercop replied, slapping the baton into the palm of her hand while she waited. "The Judge will want one of 'em for burning. Now shut thy craw and go on my signal."

"What signal?"

"Thee'll know it when I gives it."

"How, if I don't know what it be?"

Attercop clouted her round the head with her hand, skewing the tricorn over her eyes.

"Just shuddup and follow my lead!"

They bided their time in silence, until Attercop suddenly bounded from the camouflage as quietly as possible. A bit slow on the uptake, Skaines realized this was her cue and bumbled out after her companion.

Semeion heard the bigger woman's less inconspicuous break

from cover and looked round just as Attercop was almost upon him, truncheon raised to deal a blow. Instinctively, the old man back-stepped to gain reaction room and snatched the rapier blade out of his staff's shaft.

Attercop had to put the brakes on fast to prevent impaling herself.

"Ha! Scoundrel!" Ducdame countered, swishing the foil at his opponent and making her recoil. When Skaines tardily joined the fray he did the same to her, driving her off too. "Hold! Hold! Else I'll slit you both from groin to gullet!"

"Thee be threatening two ossifers of the law, Giaour!" Attercop nervously cautioned, mindful of the sharp-tipped sword being proficiently wielded between her and Skaines. "We'll see thee *burn* for this!"

"Pah!" Semeion derided, mock thrusting and warding Attercop back a few skipping paces.

The gangly custodian stumbled and fell onto her rear.

Semeion dimpled her doublet with the rapier point. "I know you have come for my niece, but I will *not allow it! Do you hear? I will run you both through first!*"

Skaines seized the lapse in his concentration on her.

She skinned her Sparquebus, cocked one hammer and fired.

So quickly Ducdame didn't know he'd been hit until he was lying on the ground pumping blood onto the grass through the fresh hole punched into his chest.

Attercop hurried to her feet and stood next to her second to watch with macabre fascination as the old geezer gurgled, reached out a clenching and unclenching hand then lay very still.

"I suppose that's muffed up our surprise element," Skaines presumed, re-priming the expended charge from her morsing-horn.

"Not necessarily. They might think it were just poachers in the woods," Attercop said, rubbing her chin. She prodded Semeion with the toe of her boot and said, "C'mon. Let's get rid of him. We don't want any of the bailiffs finding him and jumping to conclusions, does we?"

"Where we gonna dump him?" Skaines asked, packing her piece.

"In yon pit hole," Attercop designated, jabbing a thumb at the watery grave to be. "Thee grab hold of him and I'll get his gear."

Unerringly, Skaines dragged the demised hermit to the stagnant pool and flung his rag-doll body in. Attercop did the same with the discarded staff and rapier after collecting them.

That done, they resumed their mission.

Amoret was filling glass jeroboams and wooden pails from the dewpond when she heard the shot resound over the open countryside, setting up crows and inducing the alarm calls of peacocks and pheasants alike.

Startled, she looked out across the observable landscape, her eyes scouring the darkening hills and shadowy woods and her ears intently straining to detect anything else amidst the dying cries of the frightened fauna.

But she neither saw nor heard any additional disturbances.

Her instincts were on full alert, telling her there was something wrong.

Sidetracking them with the assumption that it was the estate bailiffs having captured an inept poacher or bagged themselves a free dinner, she carried on, though she did keep a cautious eye and ear trained on the surroundings in case things were not as she thought, as the niggling doubt troubling her seemed to imply.

While she worked her mind turned to Semeion and his odyssey to Mandragora Demesne, wondering how he was getting along. She harboured no doubt about his being quite safe on his own, for there were few who had tangled with him in the past that were willing to take him on again. Perhaps he did look old and feeble, but he was very capable and a shrewd operator. Semeion hadn't survived the last seventy-seven years out in the world by being a pushover. He was a Giaour. And if that didn't condition you to hardship, nothing would.

Her thoughts were still dwelling on her uncle when a shape suddenly shifted in the dewpond's reflective surface.

She whirled round fast as a cat, hand clasping the pistol at her waist.

But Attercop's Thunderbus was already pointing at her and two of its four hammers were cocked in readiness.

"Don't thee move, Giaour," the Deputy Warden commanded, grinning. "Or I'll put thy brains in the dirt!"

Pere was busy boiling water at the stove. Humming a merry tune and mopping his sweat-slicked brow, he stood over the steaming cauldrons set on the scalding hot plate, watching them froth and bubble.

It wasn't until Favel, who was relaxing on his straw while he wasn't required, whinnied loudly to attract his attention that he turned round and caught Skaines creeping up behind him.

Gasping, Pere went to scream a warning to Amoret.

The Deputy lunged forward, though, and clamped his mouth shut with a fat paw before he could utter a syllable.

"It be all right, Master Peregrine!" Skaines reassured him in a subdued tone. "But we have to stay quiet while Deputy Attercop nabs the Giaour!"

Favel deserted his bed to clip-clop across the blue-brick floor and gnash his teeth onto the collar of Skaines' coat, much to the protest of the woman herself. He shook her vigorously, trying to unfix her hold on Pere.

"Sod off, you stupid nag!" Skaines cursed, slapping at Favel's nose.

The horse persisted, shaking her more roughly, so she grabbed her truncheon and fetched him a swift crack on the edge of his eye socket.

Favel staggered backwards, dazed.

"Didn't like that, eh, Dobbin?" she taunted, taking another swing and hitting him dead centre of the forehead.

Pere clawed at Skaines.

"Don't you worry none, Master Peregrine. I'll get rid of the brute!"

She fetched Favel a third bruiser.

Deciding enough was enough he cut his losses and ran.

Consumed with anger, Pere jammed Skaines' tricorn down over her eyes and stamped on the toes of her buckled shoes extremely hard. Needless to say, Skaines gave up her grip on both him and the truncheon so she could dance around the floor alternately nursing each foot, cursing explicitly as she did.

Pere ran for the door yelling "*AMY!*" at the top of his voice.

Pere's shouting distracted Attercop for a split second, which was all Amoret needed.

She was on her feet and throwing the contents of a pail into the face of her assailant so fast, the gunwoman had no chance to react. The water blinded Attercop momentarily, giving Amoret time to leap on her and knock her to the ground.

Grabbing the Deputy's lapels and hauling her up, Amoret smashed a fist onto her opponent's jaw. Then, briefly reminding herself of all that Pere had told her of this female chauvinist sow's lewd conduct towards him, she did it again and again and again as payback on his behalf.

Letting Attercop flop drunkenly onto the deck at last, Amoret rushed towards the folly to find Pere and met him in a mutual collision; him running out, her dashing in.

"Pere! Are you all right?" she anxiously enquired, embracing him tightly.

"Yeah!" he answered, relieved at it being she he'd bumped into. "Are you?"

"I'm okay," she said, starting into Selcouth. "C'mon. We've gotta grab our things and move!"

"Skaines is in there!" Pere warned.

As he said this, the very woman herself sallied forth, baton brandished.

Amoret snatched the revolver from her belt and pointed it into the Deputy's piggy face, instantly halting her rampage and compelling her to drop the truncheon.

"Take her gun, Pere," Amoret instructed.

Hesitantly he complied, wary of going near Skaines, lest she should grab him. She didn't attempt this, however, since she was too mindful of the deadly threat she was under from Amoret, so he was able to slide the Sparquebus out of its holster and quickly retreat.

"Get rid of it," Amoret said.

He lobbed the hefty shooter into some bracken.

"*YOU'RE A DEAD GUY, GIAOUR!*" Attercop bellowed as she lurched round the curve of the folly wall, Thunderbus presented.

No messing, she fired the two cocked barrels.

There came an impotent fizzle and the ball shots lazily trundled out of the tubes.

Bemused, Attercop gawped stupidly at the soaked gun.

Wanting to settle this, Amoret turned the pistol onto Attercop and squeezed off a round above her head, clipping the building and dusting her with a fine spray of marble.

"*Fico!*" Attercop squawked, diving for cover.

Skaines attacked Amoret, tackling her extended arm and wrestling her for possession of the lethal tool. They lost their balance and went tumbling down together, the pistol slipping from Amoret's grasp and opening the field for all comers. Like spoilt brats fighting for a toy, they tussled and rolled, both desperately baulking the other from obtaining the prize.

Squealing what his naivety believed to be obscenities, Pere bounded onto Skaines' back, trying to scratch her eyes out or rip her nose off. But his spirited effort didn't deter Skaines in the least and she flicked him aside as if he were no more than a bothersome insect.

Amoret gained a few scant seconds of recovery as a result, though, and she smacked her knuckles slap bang between Skaines' eyes, sending her sprawling backwards.

Seeing her chance, Attercop scrambled for the gun and successfully claimed it.

Before she could actually discharge it in anyone's direction, Amoret lashed out with one foot and caught her square in the gob with a boot heel, putting her on the ground as well for the time being.

Amoret bounced up, shouting "*Favel!*" and scouring the area for her trusty steed as she hurried over to where Pere was still recuperating from his fall. She scooped him up in her arms and began racing down the path, calling again for her horse. "*FAVEL!*"

The equine familiar broke from the undergrowth approximately half way along the track, neighing wildly and galloping to intercept them.

"You coward!" Amoret verbally laid into him soon as he got to them. She hoisted Pere onto Favel's shoulders. "A time when we could've done …"

She realized the stallion was bleeding.

"Oh, boy!" she sympathetically exclaimed, tentatively touching the wounds. "Did those sluts do this?"

Favel snorted, bravely shrugging off her mollycoddling.

"I'll kill the bitches!" Amoret vowed.

"Amy!" Pere encouraged, watchful for the re-appearance of the Deputies. "Let's go!"

Ratifying the advice, Favel bunted his mistress.

Taking the hint, Amoret expertly mounted behind Pere, wrapped her arms around him then snagged handfuls of mane and cried, "*YA!*"

At her behest Favel launched into a flying break for freedom, churning up the path beneath his pounding hooves. Once at the bottom of the slope, he took a short cut onto rough terrain, pelting over the open glade.

Cursing their prey, Attercop and Skaines hurtled along the path to the leafy spot where they had hidden their horses, Skaines trailing as she plucked bits of bracken out of her newly retrieved pistol.

Attercop stopped dead, goggling at the empty space previously occupied by the two sleek mustangs they'd tethered to a tree.

"They be *gone!*" she stated the obvious, exasperated at being thwarted at this crucial stage in the chase. She thrashed back the branches, disclosing nothing. "Where be they?"

Skaines found the ends of the reins still knotted to the slender tree trunk.

"They've been nibbled!" she said, wiping slobber off her hand onto her coat. "That stupid nag musta done it!"

"There they be!" Attercop barked, pointing at the grazing plain beyond where the pair of mustangs could be seen happily cropping the lush fodder.

The Deputies went after them; and following a lot of frantic chasing around, a bevy of swearing and Skaines being dragged along on the trailing straps of her skittish mare at one point, they regained their rides.

V

Favel was a fine figure of a horse.

Strong and powerful.

But these attributes were weighing mightily against him, for he was not bred for speed like the much more agile mustangs sprinting hard on his heels and gaining at an astonishing rate from so far back in the field. He'd been groomed at the Royal Mews as one of the elite Mandilion war-horses, specifically selected for the Field Marshal of the Thanes herself; the Delphine Princess Eigne.

Sturdy in frame, stout in heart, steely of nerve and swift enough to devour short lengths at full tilt, but not so lightweight he couldn't take a stumble without it crippling him. Bold enough to loyally go wherever his rider steered him, no qualms fogging his fortitude. Resilient enough to weather the brunt of the assaults aimed at his dominator in the midst of battle. Intelligent enough to exercise discretion as the better part of valour when the going got too rough, saving himself and his beaten burden so they both may live to fight another day.

As a getaway driver he was less well trained.

His determination and dauntless fidelity were doing a good job at present, however, which was greatly admirable considering he was feeling groggy from the blows Skaines had dealt him. Thus far he'd managed to keep a decent lead, but the exertion was beginning to take its toll.

What he needed was some cover, so he made towards the woods where he could easily lose his pursuers.

Stampeding through the rampant greenery with all the finesse of a careering boulder, he curved and swerved amongst the closely packed trees, leaping the innumerable deadfall obstacles littering the floor. But the mustangs followed unflinchingly despite this tactical ploy, still bearing down on him. Although the adverse terrain slowed their pace somewhat, they enjoyed the advantage of being able to travel in his wake.

The first shot buzzed through the bush, missing Amoret's head so narrowly she felt its passage before she heard the report.

"*They're shooting at us!*" Pere squealed, clinging onto her for dear life as Favel carried on crashing the vegetation asunder, goaded by the detrimental sound of the gunfire.

A second shot rang out.

"*YA!*" Amoret harried the already flagging steed, digging her knees into his ribs for extra emphasis. "*YA! YA!*"

A third bullet skimmed a nearby tree, gouging the bark.

Amoret glanced over her shoulder to see exactly where Attercop and Skaines were and was shocked to witness how close they had advanced. Both of them were well within range and neither sparing the horses.

Attercop levelled the eight-barrel revolver for another pop.

"*YA!*" Amoret yelled, pressing Favel harder even though she truly knew he was about at his limit.

Her brave companion responded magnificently, selflessly straining his core strength and sapping all his energy reserves trying to outrun the dogged hunters.

But against firearms he might just as well have stood still.

A shot whistled past him, biting the dirt instead.

Ahead he saw a sharp drop in the geography where a dry, disused meander of the Talweg cut through the woodlot, and he thought (much as a horse might) that if he could clear the majority of it in a single bound they might just be in with a chance of escaping. It was risky, he was smart enough to appreciate that, but he also knew he couldn't go on much longer at this rate of knots without keeling over in mid-flight. And if that happened, they were all dead for sure.

Putting on a final spurt, Favel romped faster towards the point at which he'd estimated he must propel himself from and then he took the dramatic leap.

Pere and Amoret screamed in unison, unpleasantly surprised by the sudden aerial jaunt they were forced into. Terrified, they clung to each other and Favel so tightly their knuckles went as white as their faces.

It was a breath-taking spectacle that probably would've worked if Skaines hadn't discharged her Sparquebus at the same moment as the horse went airborne, ripping his flank open with a shot that might've missed him had he remained on the ground.

Favel whinnied in agony, throwing his head up and baring his teeth before he came hurtling earthwards, crash landing amongst the thick fern growth smothering the basin of the dry river course.

Amoret curled her arms firmly around Pere then physically ejected herself off Favel's back prior to impact, wrenching her love along with her. Attempting to minimize their injuries by abandoning the wounded beast, lest they should be crushed beneath him.

Their fall was broken thanks to the ferns, whereas Favel hit terra firma awkwardly.

"Bull's-eye!" Skaines celebrated as she and Attercop pulled up on the crest of the slope to survey their handiwork.

"Hoss's fud, more like!" Attercop quipped.

They cackled and slapped high fives.

"We got 'em now, Skaines, mate! They can't get far on foot. C'mon."

Spurring the mustangs, they began their descent.

"Pere?" Amoret said, slowly releasing her hug on the boy. "Are you okay?"

"Yeah," he replied weakly, his eyes bright with fear. "You?"

"Few bruises," she groaned, stiffly rising from the vibrant undergrowth that had cushioned them. "Nothing serious."

"Favel?" Pere conscientiously queried. "Where's Favel?"

"Over there," she sated his curiosity, pointing at a large mass just visible through the foliage.

Together they scrambled up and beat aside the ferns to get to their noble friend, taking care to keep hidden under the shielding canopy.

The stallion was lying on his right side breathing harshly and bleeding badly.

"Oh … Favel!" Amoret mewled, almost gagging on the grief at seeing the proud thoroughbred so dreadfully laid out. She rushed to kneel beside him and comfortingly stroke his muscular neck, lamenting, "Oh, boy! I'm so sorry! I'm *so* sorry!"

Favel only snorted and shook off her wet-nursing.

Then he struggled to haul himself upright.

Failed.

Had another go.

All Pere and Amoret could do was helplessly watch him fight to re-attain some of his former dignity with little more than sheer grit and bloody-mindedness as incentives. Painful sorrow and loving respect simultaneously tugging at their heartstrings as the pitiful display overwhelmed their emotions.

"C'mon, boy! You can do it!" Amoret egged him on. "That's it!"

After a few abortive endeavours he rolled himself onto his belly then paused, exhausted.

He pricked his ears.

Attercop and Skaines' voices, bullying along their horses, came floating on the air accompanied by the rhythmic swish and clink of a sword chopping.

Amoret poked her head just above the sea of feathery leaves and saw the Deputies wading towards them, Skaines slicing the hindering flora with a cutlass.

"They're coming!" she informed her fellow fugitives, ducking back down. "C'mon, Fav."

Favel grunted at her as if to question her sanity and shook his head.

"We can't leave you here!" Amoret pleaded rather than stated.

He nodded to urge their departure.

The rabid dogs could be heard getting ever closer.

Scrawling onto the knees of his forelegs, Favel began dragging himself in the direction of the oncoming hunters. He looked over his shoulder and nodded his mistress away once more, whinnying to impress upon her the importance of her obeying.

"There's nothing we can do for him, Amy," Pere interpreted. "Let's go."

"*NO!*" she cried, thumping the ground, tears stinging her eyes. "I can't!"

"Over here!" they heard Attercop shout, Amoret's outburst having betrayed their position.

Favel whinnied again, flicking his head at them.

"Amy!" Pere induced, gripping her arm and pulling her. "We have to *go!*"

Amoret didn't budge. Sobbing, she looked on as her most faithful ally crawled into the ferns to die.

"*C'mon!*" Pere demanded.

Finally she went with him, pausing to spare one last backward glance.

Attercop and Skaines saw the movement in the ferns and rode their animals in galumphing lopes to the spot, certain their chase was at an imminent and desirable conclusion.

"Gotchya now, Giaour!" Attercop trumpeted, pointing the revolver at the waving ferns. "Show thyself!"

Favel came unexpectedly lunging out from beneath the rippling emerald surface like some bizarre jack-in-the-box, his nostrils flaring and craziness fiercely burning in his wide, bulging eyes.

Spooked, the mustangs reared upright onto their hind legs, spilling their equally alarmed riders from the saddles, then promptly bolted.

Swearing terrible oaths, the unseated Deputies quickly got to their feet just in time to glimpse their mounts disappearing far down the old ravine at an incredible lick.

Favel, semi-recumbent in the ferns, whinnied at the fallen duo.

"*Damn thee!*" Attercop scorned him, cocking her pistol.

The stallion wrinkled his upper lip as if he were grinning.

Pere and Amoret halted when the shot echoed through the woods and were both pierced in the heart by the strangled neigh that superseded it.

"*FAVEL!*" Amoret shrieked back.

But only the frightened calls of disturbed birds answered her.

"*YOU SOWS!*" she screamed at the culprits. "*I'LL KILL YOU BOTH! D'YOU HEAR? I'LL KILL YOU BOTH WITH MY BARE HANDS!*"

"Amy," Pere tearfully called, not really knowing whether he was more hurt by Favel's receipt of that bullet or at seeing his beloved in so much pain.

She lingered a minute more to glower in the general direction of Attercop and Skaines, perhaps hoping to slay them with her malice of forethought alone.

"C'mon!" she said at last, biting down on her anger and distress. "Let's make sure he didn't die for nothing."

Meanwhile, Attercop and Skaines clambered to the top of the bank on the other side of the ravine.

"What're we gonna do now, Cait?" Skaines asked as they surveyed the woods for any sign of their quarry.

"Well, we b'ain't gonna give up," Attercop told her, striding off.

"Why not? We b'ain't gonna catch 'em like this!"

"'Course we will. They should be pretty easy to track," Attercop contested, briefly studying a snapped twig and scuffmarks left in the windfall leaves on the ground.

"It'll take a damn long time," Skaines complained, using the lull in proceedings to reload her Sparquebus. She looked at the darkening sky. "And it be nigh on dusk."

"Stop whining, wench!" her cohort admonished. "Summat will turn up."

The neigh of a horse caught their attention.

Looking over to their right they saw a well-dressed gentleman sitting sidesaddle on a prim little pony; obviously out for a leisurely trot along the deer trails on his favourite colt.

Attercop smirked.

Today he'd be getting more than he bargained for.

Motioning for Skaines to copy her, she began slowly sloping among the trees, covertly approaching the wayfarer who was as yet unaware of their presence. They reached the edge of the deer trail, and squatting low behind an oak they waited until the foppish jockey and his aloof horse drew closer.

At the most opportune moment Attercop jumped out, executing the same stunt as Favel had done across them minutes earlier. Scared witless at her sudden appearance in its path, the colt reared and sent its screeching rider tumbling in a flurry of layered silks and fine linens. Attercop hastily snagged the pony's harness before it could vamoose and yanked it into subordination, then Skaines came to help calm its fractious prancing so as they could comfortably mount it.

"My Zoe!" the gentleman squeaked, sitting up, apparently unscathed other than having had his feathered hat knocked crooked. He fluttered his mascara-laden eyelashes at his attackers. "Are you *ruffians?*"

"If thee likes," Attercop said.

"Oh ..." he breathily gasped, putting a kid-gloved hand to one rouged cheek. "I ... I do hope you are not going to ... *ravish me!*"

"Thanking thee for the offer, sir, but I b'ain't got the time," Attercop cheekily declined.

"Are you *quite* sure?"

"Aye."

"What about you?" he said, looking at Skaines. "I do hope you are not going to force your *powerful femininity* upon my soft, fair flesh ..."

Skaines glanced at her colleague, uncertain what she should say.

"She b'ain't got the time neither," Attercop replied on her

behalf, treading in the stirrup and swinging herself onto the pony's back. She leaned down to assist Skaines' ascent onto the animal's haunches.

"Do you *know* who *I am?*" the gentleman huffed, planting his fists on his hips. "I could have you hung, drawn and, I dare say, quartered!"

"And I could have thee shot," Attercop countered, cuing Skaines, who drew her pistol and pointed it at the miffed hussy. "So pray I don't find out who thee be, sir."

She smacked the reins on the horse, gadding it, and they cantered into the woods.

Leaving the gentleman for the real ruffians.

Amoret and Pere were flagging.

They had been running for what seemed an eternity, scarcely granting themselves any rest since they were convinced Attercop and Skaines still had horse power and would be on their tails. So, expecting company every second, they had slogged onward to put as many precious centimetres as they could between them and their stalkers.

But as they had neither seen nor heard anyone anywhere thus far, Amoret decided they should take five, for if they didn't now they may not get the chance again. Besides which, her legs felt like they were lagged with lead and she was virtually carrying the totally pooped Pere anyway.

They sank to the roots of an ash tree, propping their backs against its trunk.

"Amy? Where are we going?" he asked her.

"The Slackton Road can't be much further," she estimated. "If we get onto that we can rejoin the Excelsior Road a couple of kilometres down and see if we can hitch a ride."

"To Excelsior?"

"I was thinking we could make for Havenstrand or Salter Bay."

"Then?"

"Stowaway to Monte Creston."

Pere looked at her. "We're going *abroad?*"

"Yeah. We've no choice now. The odds on us succeeding are narrow if not non-existent, but I'd rather die trying." She choked back a sob. "Like Favel did."

He had to contain his overwhelming joy (which wasn't easy) in respectful memory of Favel's selfless sacrifice so that they may get this far in their bid for freedom. Inside, though, he was deliriously happy. At last he was breaking out of the microcosm he'd been imprisoned in since birth, actually casting off the manacles of subservience to explore the world beyond his limited scope.

His dreams were coming true.

"What's that?" Amoret said, starting to her feet.

"What?"

"Shh ... listen ..."

He did, but nothing came to his ears except the soft rustling of the trees and the twittering of the birds perching high above in them. Then he began picking up a steady thrumming, and a voice geeing a horse echoing from the near distance.

About twenty metres away on their left he glimpsed a pale shape darting in and out of the trees.

"Holy Icarus!" Amoret swore. "It's them!"

Pere didn't need to ask whom she meant.

"C'mon!" she cried, grabbing him and dragging him into a stumbling run.

"There they be!" Attercop hollered, violently turning the pony about to bring it to bear on the two scampering figures she'd spotted.

Skaines leaned over her buddy's shoulder and fired the Sparquebus. The shot went wide, decapitating a sapling instead of the targets.

Sneering at the bad markswomanship, Attercop had a go with the revolver. Yet she fared as poorly, ricocheting the round off a gnarled hawthorn and endangering them more than those she aimed at.

Amoret and Pere staggered up the incline of an embankment, slithering uncontrollably on mulched leaves and tripping on scattered twig debris that seemed to deliberately entwine around their pumping limbs. Their momentum slowed to a stodgy, shambling hike as the gradient increased and they resorted to practically crawling on all fours to the summit.

Once there, they found the woodland floor abruptly fell away into an almost sheer drop that sharply plummeted to a pot-holed cart track at the bottom.

They stood on the brink, gawping down the escarpment with sinking spirits.

"Oh no!" Pere gasped. "How're we going to get down there?"

"I think I know," Amoret said, attracting his attention to a vehicle coming along the rough road. It was a buck-boarded farm trailer motored by a lazily sauntering mule and driven by a half-asleep bumpkin with her hat tipped forward to shade her eyes from the dying rays of the setting sun.

"Wait for it to come under us," Amoret tutored Pere, hooking her arm about his waist and drawing him backwards for a longer run at the edge. "Then we can jump into the cart."

"*Jump?*" Pere debated, gawking at her and then at the drop again. "I can't jump *that!*"

A bullet sizzled past them.

"*Oh!*" he cried. "*Yes I can!*"

Together they charged toward the precipice at full tilt.

And leapt.

They made it, striking the cart dead centre, their impact completely absorbed by the cargo: the moist, brown, smelly cargo. The mule awoke from its drowsy plodding upon their landing. Widening its eyes and issuing a startled bray, it jerked in its harness and very nearly broke into a trot.

"What in the blue blazes!" the bumpkin muttered fuzzily, fumbling with the reins. "*Whoa, Lurdane! Whoa there, boy!*"

Lurdane did as bid, bringing the wagon to a stand.

"*Euurggh!*" Pere squealed, disgustedly inspecting precisely what he and Amoret had flung themselves into. "It's *manure!*"

"Who be thee be?" the rustic wanted to know, shoving her hat back on her head and regarding the uninvited passengers. "What be thee doing in my trailer?"

"We're on the run," Amoret explained. "Can you keep driving, please?"

"Who be thee be on the run from, then?" the farmer asked, chewing on a stalk of barley while she considered their plea.

Without warning a shot plucked the hat off her head, exposing a scabby scalp thinly coated by ginger hair.

"Aurora Borealis!" she exclaimed, clutching at where the hat had been a moment ago.

"*Them!*" Amoret replied, indicating Attercop and Skaines, who had just reached the brow of the embankment.

"Gerron with thee, Lurdane!" the bumpkin chivvied her mule. "*Gerron!*"

Obediently, Lurdane walked on. A few more slaps persuaded him a gear relatively unknown to him was required and he accelerated to a brisk dawdle.

"I be Joskin, by the way."

"I'm Amoret, and this is Pere."

"Pleased to meet thee, I'm sure," Joskin greeted, offering a spare mitt for the slapping of fives low, which the grateful pair duly accepted in turn.

"Could we go a bit faster, Joskin?" Pere requested, glancing back at the progress of Attercop and Skaines.

They were descending the deceptively perilous cliff face, and although this was hindering them, they were still making fairly fast work of it.

"Oo-ar," Joskin complied, geeing Lurdane. "Who be them what's chasing thee, anyhow?"

"Deputy Wardens," Amoret said.

"Not them from Rampick?"

"Yeah. You know 'em?"

"Oo-ar. Them shot one of my best milkers last year when I took her to market there. Them said she didn't have a bell on whilst on the Queen's highway."

"How far are you going, Joskin?" Amoret asked.

"Slackton."

"You can get us onto the Excelsior Road, then."

"Oo-ar. No trouble."

"Not at this speed!" Pere whinged. "Drive faster! They're coming!"

Sure enough, Attercop and Skaines had survived their treacherous trek and were currently goading the colt into a galloping frenzy, anxious to reclaim the forfeited distance.

"Gerron, Lurdane!"

"*Faster!*"

"*Gerron, Lurdane! Gerron, old son!*" Joskin futilely chanted, for Lurdane was quite set in his ways and had a definite aversion to exerting himself.

"They're going to catch us!" Pere gloomily predicted, worriedly staring as the two custodians grew larger and larger in his sight the more ground they gained. "*Drive faster!*"

"Old Lurdane be doing his best!" Joskin protested. "Any more of this and he'll have a blasted *blue fit!*"

Amoret climbed onto the bench Joskin was sitting on then sprang onto Lurdane's back. Not taking too kindly to this treatment, the dozy animal brayed and tried shaking her off, but she resisted all his efforts and brought him into her mastery, soon showing him who was boss.

"*YA! YA!*" she yelled, slapping him and thumping her knees into his flanks.

The ploy worked, for Lurdane started moving faster than perhaps he had ever moved in his entire life, goosing their rate of knots to a more competitive level.

Panicking at the Deputies' blistering pace, Pere began snatching handfuls of manure and lobbing them at their horse, attempting to dissuade it.

Relieved from her post as helmswoman, Joskin got into the wagon with Pere.

"I got a better idea, young Master," she said, staying his hand.

She waded towards the rear of the cart, sinking to the tops of her boots, and unhitched the latches holding the tailboard shut. She let it flap open and spill the load onto the road, spreading a filthy swath right down the middle.

Attercop and Skaines' requisitioned ride cantered straight into the mess, slipping on it at first but managing to retain its balance. Then it skidded again; slid, skittered, slipped and fell, pitching the pair into the muck.

Joskin and Pere guffawed, triumphantly smacking high fives.

They were still laughing when the bullet ripped Joskin's ruddy face apart, spattering Pere with her blood.

Her body back-somersaulted out of the trailer, and the last he saw of her were her gaiters and boots vanishing over the side.

He screamed.

"*Pere!*" Amoret shouted to him. "*Pere!*"

But he couldn't answer.

Only scream.

Lurdane was really belting along at full stretch now, and not only because he was going downhill. His output was so improved Amoret was having difficulty curtailing him for the junction with the main Excelsior carriageway, which she could clearly see looming ahead. She vigorously snatched at the straps, employing the conventional method of applying the brakes, but her labours failed to sway his frantic romp.

The beast was possessed.

Desperate to reinstate her influence on the monster she'd created, she shinned along onto the length of his neck, hooked her hands into the bridle and physically grappled with him to raise his head. His strength prevailed, shaking her loose and almost throwing her, so she just clung to him and hoped for the best.

It was too late, anyhow; they were at the junction.

Damage limitation was all that mattered now.

Recklessly swooping onto the Excelsior Road, they encountered an entourage of armoured cavaliers escorting three ornate coaches, which until that point had been obscured from view by a grove of trees dividing the main thoroughfare from the tributary lane.

Terrified at the impromptu appearance of the horses, Lurdane uttered a shrill bray and diverted his course at an acute angle, twisting the wagon's limbers and capsizing it into the entourage's immediate path, equally upsetting his equine cousins.

Pere was bundled from the cart shrieking and deposited onto the hard gravel, while Amoret dived clear as Lurdane succumbed to the restraints binding him to the vehicle and tipped onto his side with a fretful cry.

"*AMBUSH!*" one of the metal-clad cortège bellowed; her voice lent a tinny resonance by the closed visor of her helmet. Professionally bringing her dancing steed to its senses, she reiterated, "*THE ATHELING IS AMBUSHED!*"

Sinuously dismounting and drawing multiple barrelled pistols from belt holsters, the four forward escorts rushed to the crash site.

Two of them obstructed Amoret, who was just on her way to her lover's rescue, threatening her with their guns and ordering her to "Hold!"

With little option, she concurred, forced to stand idle while the other two knights tyrannically accosted Pere, pulling him up by his hair and slapping him to quell his hysteria.

"On the ground!" commanded one of the knights detaining her.

"Wait! I can explain!" Amoret said.

"I don't give a fig, slut! If you don't kiss the dirt, we'll put you down *permanent!*"

She soon bit the dust when a shot whistled past her nose, millimetres shy, and the knights hastily followed suit since neither of them had spent the round.

"What the Malison!" one of the other knights yelped, forgetting about hurting Pere.

"*Assassins!*" her colleague jumped to conclusions.

They scurried to the mouth of the junction, as did their two associates once they'd scrambled up and brushed off the dirt soiling their gold-leafed silver armour. Attercop and Skaines, remounted and diligently resuming their quest, came into their view plainly sporting pistols.

The knights brought their weapons to bear on the Deputies.

Hauling the pony to a halt, Attercop and Skaines gaped at the fearsome welcoming party.

"Fico!" Skaines gasped. "Them's *Douzepers!*"

"Ladies! *Fire at will!*" one of the four escorts instructed.

"Which one's Will?" another wittily remarked.

"Let's get outta here!" suggested Attercop, turning the pony and hastily galloping it back the way they'd just come. Their retreat was chased by an awesome volley of firepower as the Douzepers discharged round after round in rapid succession, shaving them at frighteningly close quarters. It was only due to sheer good fortune they didn't get wounded or killed.

Whilst the knights were occupied, Amoret scampered to Pere to check he hadn't been seriously injured in the accident or from the disrespectful conduct shown him, concerned that the blood she saw on his face was his own.

"No," Pere told her, still sobbing as she tore a strip from her shirt and wiped him clean. "It's Joskin's."

"Thank Icarus," she said with relief.

"Thank Joskin," Pere contradicted. "No god had anything to do with this."

A bevy of regular soldiers less finely attired in chain mail and studded leather emerged from the wagon train and rudely estranged Pere and Amoret again. More uncouth than the regal bodyguards, they brutishly searched them, confiscated Amoret's dagger and held them prisoner until the Douzepers returned.

"And next time I give you an order, Fougade," the apparent authoritarian amongst the knights said, banging her fist against the breast-plate of another, "you carry it out! Not make stupid jokes!"

Fougade slid open her visor, revealing a young, handsome face.

"Sorry, Sarge," she apologized, affable smirk on her lips. "Just wanted to be sure who you wanted us to shoot."

"Bah!" her Sergeant doubted, breaking her pistol and extracting the used cartridges. She stowed them in a pouch on her garrison belt for recycling, then refilled the pistol's chambers with fresh loads stored on a bandolier also wrapped about her waist.

"Sergeant-at-Arms!" an unseen member of the entourage called from within the foremost carriage, to the sound of which the Sergeant hastily attended.

"My liege," she saluted, snapping open her helmet's frontispiece.

"What on Gaea is happening? What was all that shooting?"

"Our party was ambushed, Your Highness, by Federaries."

"Federaries?" questioned a man's voice. "Are you sure, Sergeant?"

"We can only speculate, Governor."

"And did you kill them?" the eminent personage coldly enquired.

"Begging your pardon, Your Highness, no. Two escaped, but we have captured their accomplices."

Walking toward Amoret and Pere, Fougade holstered her pistol and prised the boy's chin up off his chest, drawing his eyes to hers. "You don't look like a dissident, boy," she commented. "What's your involvement here?"

"We – " Amoret began for him.

The knight clouted her in the mouth with her metal plated chain mail gauntlet, saying, "Was I talking to you, bitch?"

Fougade's familiars guffawed.

"Again, boy. What is your true involvement?"

Pere looked at Amoret who was tending a bleeding lip.

"Don't look at her! Look at me!" Fougade brusquely asserted, tweaking his ear and causing him to squeal, much to the mirth of her pals. She stood away then, pinching her nose. "*Pheeew!* You *stink*, boy! I know peasants aren't too particular about personal hygiene, but there is a *limit!*" More cackling laughter. "It's those rags you're wearing. We ought to get you out of them. What d'you say?"

"*No!*" Amoret cried, struggling against her captors but failing to break their strict arrest on her.

The soldiers holding Pere chuckled and tightened their grasp on him as Fougade stepped closer, removing her gloves and breathing on her hands to warm them.

"Be a good lad now and I can probably stop you from being lynched," she promised, grinning lecherously.

She went straight for the family jewels, roughly shoving her hand up his frock and squeezing his groin.

Pere screamed.

Before she could go any further the Sergeant-at-Arms appeared from the opposite side of the first coach, issuing the command: "Atten'hun!"

Douzepers and regulars alike snapped into rigid discipline.

"Her Royal Highness Atheling Princess Anheires!" the Sergeant announced.

A dark-haired young woman robed in a gaudily braided military uniform self-importantly swaggered around the corner of the carriage, one hand casually resting on the hilt of a sabre sheathed in an ornately decorated scabbard that dangled at her side from a regimental baldric.

Closely shadowing her was a baby-faced man in a black cloak and wide-brimmed hat.

"My liege," the Sergeant-at-Arms heralded, quickly genuflecting along with the other guardians.

Pere and Amoret had their knees crudely bumped out from beneath them, effectively ensuring they met the same kneeling criteria as the soldiers keeping them.

"Yeah, yeah," the Princess said sniffily, flapping a limp-wristed wave at the venerating throng.

"These are the captives, Your Highness," the Sergeant fawned, guiding her towards Pere and Amoret.

Anheires strolled back and forth before the pair; but as their eyes were being forcibly cast downward they saw no more of their royal audience than her exquisitely polished boots and the gilt, heraldic designs borne thereon.

"And they are Federaries, are they?" the Princess asked.

"We assume, Your Highness."

"Do these look like Federaries to you, Governor Cauchemar?" the Princess sought a second opinion.

"Indeed not, Atheling Princess," the baby-faced young man readily backed her doubt.

"Come, berd. What is your name?"

89

Pere glanced up at her.

"Show Her Royal Highness respect!" the soldier behind him angrily growled, pushing his line of vision down again.

"Come. Speak."

"Peregrine, my liege," he timidly replied. "Peregrine Farouche."

"And how did you come to be here, Peregrine?"

"We were being chased, Your Highness."

"Really? How *thrilling!* By whom?"

"The assassins," Amoret butted in.

"Bite your tongue, bitch!" one of the regulars raged, pressing the cold steel of a knife to her throat.

"No, no. Let her speak," the Princess permitted.

"We learnt of a plot to ambush you, Your Highness," Amoret lied, "and we came to prevent it." Recalling Favel and Joskin's tragic sacrifices, she added, "Friends of ours died so we might preserve Your Highness."

Pere spared her a side glance, ashamed at her brazen dishonesty and pondering on just how many lies she had told him since she was obviously so capable of spinning yarns.

"Very commendable," the Princess congratulated. "Though implausible, for no one but a select few knew of my engagement here."

"Somebody must have leaked it, my liege, else they would not have plotted to ambush you here and we would not have learnt it and rushed to save you from the assassins, would we?"

The Atheling considered this for a moment.

"Perhaps," she said, unable to untangle the deception. She turned to the Sergeant-at-Arms for counsel.

"What are your thoughts, Cacafogo?"

Twirling one end of her handlebar moustache, the Sergeant said, "Did they have any weapons about their persons, Ronyon?"

"Fougade was just frisking them when Her Royal Highness came to inspect the prisoners, ma'am," Ronyon falsely testified.

"Yeah," affirmed Fougade. "They had nothing."

"'Cept this, my Lady," said a soldier who had frisked them for real, presenting Amoret's dagger to Cacafogo.

"Personal defence, Your Highness," Amoret conveyed.

"Well, if your story is true we owe you a debt of gratitude," the Princess ascribed. "Is that not so, Governor?"

"As you say, my liege," Cauchemar toadied, rubbing his gloved hands together.

"Come. You must ride with us to Mandragora Demesne. I trust Lady Mandrake will not mind extending her hospitality to accommodate these dauntless champions. A wash, a change of clothes and a hearty meal will go some of the way at least to rewarding your brave deed."

"Thank you, Your Highness," Amoret bowed to her generosity.

"Very well, very well. Unhand them."

The soldiers let them get onto their feet, allowing Pere to curtsy his appreciation.

"You can travel in front on your mule. And if any more bandits set upon us on our journey, we will look to you for salvation," the Princess jocularly designated. She laughed to indicate she had cracked a funny, stimulating everyone else into counterfeit mirth.

"My liege," Cacafogo said, concerned. "Are you certain you desire this?"

"Yeah. Why not? Is there a problem, Sergeant?"

"No, Your Highness." She regarded the dagger. "But I'll keep this all the same."

That settled, Lurdane was released from the shattered remains of the cart and put into the charge of Pere and Amoret, while the rest of the entourage prepared the procession.

"It seems as if we'll be imposing on Lady Mandrake after all," Pere said as Amoret helped him mount Lurdane. "Maybe your uncle will be there by now."

"Yeah, maybe," she humoured him, gazing into the growing gloom of eventide.

She thought of loneliness and shuddered.

VI

It was getting dark when they came across the Mandrake estate's official entrance. It lay on the side of the Excelsior Road, marked by a pair of grandiose pillars at least five metres high. Supported between these was a carved stone arch inscribed with the legend *Mandragora Demesne*, which in turn was capped by a sculpture of the Mandrake family crest, depicting a phoenix spread-eagled over an escutcheon bearing a rampant dragon.

Pere gazed in awe at the towering structure as he and Amoret rode under it on Lurdane, bringing up the rear of the entourage and not spearheading it as the Atheling Princess had flippantly decreed. To have so magnificent a gateway led him to believe Mandrake was even wealthier and more important than he'd originally supposed, and he could only marvel at how wondrous the house itself must be if this edifice were merely garden furniture.

A long, winding driveway ushered the visitors through the vast parkland immediately purveyed by the Lady of the Manor, showing them it from all the best angles and impressing upon them her status. In reality, Mandrake was the landowner of the entire County and therefore the nation's largest stakeholder in economic development. What her guests were now viewing was but a fraction of the fiscal influence she wielded.

Eventually, the caravan reached the house.

Well, they reached a wall. A soaring, formidable stone limit akin to a castle curtain, bristling with turrets and battlements. It had probably once served as the encircling curtilage of the Demesne, until it was drastically remodelled into a reinforced wall so lofty it was difficult to tell whether there was in fact a building concealed behind it. The only clues to there being one were the barely visible chimneystacks poking above the secrecy of the parapet.

"See, Pere," Amoret said, "I told you it was like a fortress."

He blinked disbelievingly.

As if the insurance were needed, a wide moat surrounded the entire enclosure. This obliged the party to grind to a halt so they may be observed from the barbican of the wall's gatehouse by some of Mandrake's bondswomen who were stationed there, rifles trained on their rivals. The portcullis of the gate was down and there seemed to be no conventional drawbridge or turn-bridge facility available.

"*Phew!*" Pere exclaimed, cupping a hand over his nose. "That *smell!*"

"It's the moat," Amoret told him. "The sewers empty into it, I guess."

Pere looked into the deep, black waters below, and he thought he glimpsed a fleeting shadow shift beneath the surface.

"*WHO GOES THERE? FRIEND OR FOE?*" one of the sentries in the barbican shouted to the Douzeper advance guard. Trick question in this case, for the relationship between the House of Gerent and the Mandragora line was indeed ambiguous.

"*HER ROYAL HIGHNESS THE ATHELING PRINCESS ANHEIRES! LET US BY!*" the Sergeant-at-Arms yelled back at the guards.

There was some delay as discussions and other formalities took place.

Finally, the sound of large machinery clanking into gear emanated from either side of the gatehouse. Slowly but surely, a crossing platform projected out from under the gatehouse foundations and locked into a flange on the far bank of the moat.

Cacafogo motioned for the entourage to move forward.

It did so; though, it had to impatiently linger on the bridge whilst small defensive cannons were hauled from their positions at the portcullis and more engines were employed to steadily raise the obstructing armoured grid. Whenever the Lady of the Manor or any of her internal staff wanted to leave or re-enter the premises, these security measures were usually stood down in unison. In the case of invited callers, however, the disengagements were deliberately done in stages as standard practice.

Pere watched the dark moat with a cautious eye as Lurdane plodded along the platform, wary of whatever might be lurking down there. He had heard wild tales of Mandrake keeping a sea serpent somewhere on her estate and was now nervously wondering if that is what he'd seen.

Once past the hostility of the outer defences, the whole contingent was amazed to see further earthworks and battlements situated ahead of them, protecting this country mansion as if it were sovereignty in itself.

Mandragora Demesne stood on the most prominent grade within the enclosure. It was a sprawling range of inter-communal buildings, constructed of locally quarried stone, all gathered into the encompassing girdle of an inner bailey aggressively rife with cannons peering out from the narrow gaps in a palisade of wickerwork gabions. Before that, there were another two bailey walls to negotiate; their purposefully misaligned gates both turn-bridging anti-cavalry pits that hid sharpened stakes within their three metre deep traps.

None of the party, except for Pere and Amoret, were unaccustomed to these kinds of precautions since the Royal Palace Excelsior Montis was a complex approximately ten times the scale of this and implemented ten times as many devices to counter infiltration. So their surprise was not at the magnitude, but at the conceited arrogance and audacity of Mandrake's family for utilizing such martial defences on a minor manor house.

They considered the attitude to be very distasteful, especially as they were victims of it. Mandrake was well aware of the delegation's impending arrival, yet she had not ordered the removal or disablement of the defences so the emissaries may pass through unhindered, choosing instead to treat Members of the Sceptral Court no better than commoners rapping at her door begging for alms.

That really niggled.

Consequently, daylight had virtually evaporated when they wearily trudged through the wrought iron gates of the house itself and sidled down the gravelled approach, the blazing beacons set along the road's length lighting the way to hospitality. Either side of them, beautifully tended formal gardens delightfully spread out, where fragrant shrubs and perennials permeated the night air with sweet, rich aromas that eliminated the stench of the stagnant moat.

The house loomed ahead. Its primary range was a hulking silhouette against the twilight; a plethora of flying buttresses incorporated into its design thrust many sculpted pinnacles toward the sky, competing with the succession of apex roofs ridging the uppermost storey. Its square-glazed windows were brightly illuminated from within, cosily promising the travellers congenial respite.

A horde of willing footwomen and servants poured forth from the vestibule of Mandragora Demesne to meet the entourage and fulfil every requirement necessary for debarkation, swarming around the first two coaches like flies round cow cakes, crudely vying to pay the prestigious inhabitants the best courtesies possible.

In the case of seeking to pay Anheires homage they were rudely thwarted. Trusting nobody else, Cacafogo and her knights swatted away the aides in favour of handing the Princess and Cauchemar out of the carriage themselves.

Amidst the rest of the confused bustling, Pere saw two figures alight from the second coach. A shrewish woman dressed in the finery of a middle class dignitary and a woman wearing the flowing orange and yellow garments of a priestess; though, of what clerical rank she was he couldn't ascertain as he wasn't familiar with the specific garbs she had on.

Dismounting Lurdane and putting him in the care of a bamboozled stable-lass – whom they left wondering why she should be expected to give attention to a couple of peasants who smelt worse than she did – Pere and Amoret squeezed towards the front of the mob.

Fougade collared them, asking, "Where do you think *you're* going?"

"The Princess invited us into the hospitality of Lady Mandrake," Amoret reminded her, squaring up for a confrontation.

"No, no," Fougade challenged. "You feed at the kitchens on the scraps the dogs don't want and sleep in the stables where the mounts won't lie."

"Let us pass!" Amoret fumed, trying to shove her aside.

Grabbing a handful of her jerkin, Fougade spat, "D'you wanna make a scene, *fumet breath?*"

Pere gasped at the expletive.

"Yeah, *fudhead!*" Amoret retorted, making him gasp again.

"What goes on down there, Fougade?" Cacafogo wanted to know.

"These *peasants* claim places at high table, Sarge."

"They dine with us!" Princess Anheires ardently ruled from her position at the top of the flight of steps leading into the portico. "I promised them so for their deed, and as I am as good as my word then it shall be so. Let them by!"

"My liege," Fougade conceded, bowing to her wishes.

Amoret took Pere's hand and proudly led him on.

They passed through the cold, bleak austerity of the vaulted vestibule's unadorned stonework then entered into the capacious foyer, which was a total contrast in décor terms. Here, no expense had been spared: mirror-polished oak panelling lined the chamber; rich tapestries and embroidered draperies festooned the white plasterwork not crafted with extravagant friezes; and sparkling crystal chandeliers hung from the high ceiling like dripping jewels, warmly casting their flickering glow.

The master staircase was the predominant feature; centrifugal and elegantly gliding to the upper echelons, its ascension embellished by framed daubs of Mandragora ancestors. Beneath it, doors accessing the lower rooms frequently punctuated the walls, but all were firmly shut against prying curiosity.

A butler awaited them at the foot of the stairs.

"Your Highness," she greeted the Princess, obsequiously stooping, "My Lord Governor; My Lady Chancellor; Your Sacred Grace," she included, extending her bows to Cauchemar, the shrew and the priestess respectively. "My Mistress the Lady Mandrake is regrettably detained elsewhere at present. Please allow me to conduct Your Highness, Your Highness's Ladies and Your Highness's Lord to the principal drawing room."

"This is outrageously intolerable!" the Chancellor protested at the shoddy manner of their treatment so far.

"Indeed," agreed the Atheling. "Fetch your mistress at once and tell her I *insist* on her receiving us *in person*."

"In that case, you won't be disappointed," said a voice from above.

Everybody's eyes turned to watch the tall woman coming down the stairs.

Pere's breath caught in his throat.

She was *beautiful*. The first *really* beautiful woman he had ever seen, bar none.

Her hair was as jet black as her whole outfit and mingled into the flowing lines of the satin frock coat draping her shoulders. Her gracefully contoured figure was achingly accentuated by the haut couture silk and lace bodice tightly hugging her every curve, and calfskin leather trousers snugly moulded her exquisitely long legs.

Enraptured, he stared as she minced towards them, her shapely hips rhythmically sashaying.

And he felt a stirring in his fledgling manhood.

Greatly disturbed by this base reaction, he averted his gaze and tried thinking about the Primordial Precepts to curb his arousal. Until now, Amoret was the only female who had ever stimulated him in any way; but the awakening she had instigated in him had been of the romantic passions in his heart and not the realization of hormonal precedence. This was the first time in his life full-blown carnal lechery had imbued his loins.

"Mandrake," Anheires said flatly, enmity already souring her tone.

"Call me Maugre," Mandragora informally granted.

"And you may call me Your Highness," the Princess snootily demanded.

"Nah," declined Mandragora. "I'll call you Annie."

All present drew sharp breaths, expecting Anheires to blow her stack at this insult.

True to form, she did.

"*How dare you?*" the Atheling exploded, her hand falling to the hilt of the dress sabre sheathed at her side. She was by no means a great swordswoman, but with four Douzeper Knights of the Realm and thirty soldiers at her command, she didn't need to be.

"Oooh! Now that's not very diplomatic, dear!" Mandragora mocked.

"Your Highness!" Cauchemar intervened before things got ugly. "Does not Your Highness think we are at liberty to waive certain small points of order as a gesture of good will in the spirit of our ambassadorial role?"

"Yeah. I mean you don't want to queer the pitch … " Mandragora mercilessly jeered, smirking in self-satisfaction, " … or else what will Mummy say?"

"Your Highness?" Cauchemar solicited.

Ungraciously, the Princess gave way.

"Aren't you going to introduce me to your friends, Annie?"

"Allow me, m' Lady," the butler tactfully volunteered, bringing Cauchemar to her mistress's attention to begin with. "This is the Lord Governor of the Sceptral Cabal, ma'am, Mister Guignol Cauchemar."

"That's *Mzter*, actually," he rectified, accepting Mandragora's extended hand and brushing it with his cherubic lips. "Charmed, my Lady."

"Pleased to make your acquaintance, *Master* Cauchemar," she said, mispronouncing on purpose the title he had stressed just to see the look on his face. She needn't have bothered, for little of what occurred in Cauchemar's mind was ever betrayed on his cold countenance. He offered a vapid, emotionless smirk in response and nothing else. Determined to get some sort of rise out of him, though, Mandragora went on with her jibing. "How are the other jackals in the Cabal these days, hmm? Still wearing cloaks and daggers?"

Cauchemar bowed, saying only "My Lady" in an irritatingly glib manner.

"The Lady Chancellor of the Sceptral Treasury, Lady Baselard Snollygoster, the Marquess of Herdwick," the lackey distracted her mistress to the shrewish woman.

"Ah, the Chancer of the Sceptical Usury," Mandragora impertinently affronted.

"Mandrake," Snollygoster curtly addressed, prepared to ignore the remark and give high fives.

"I would, dear, but I'm afraid my fingers might become as sticky as yours."

Snollygoster bit her tongue for the sake of the delegation's remit.

"Her Sacred Grace Primitial Chamade, the Holy City of Goshen's Ecumenical Equerry to Montaigne," the butler continued.

"My Child," the priestess said, crossing her torso with the shape of the saltire and stretching the same hand out for the hostess to humbly kiss.

"I suppose you've come to convert me, Your Sacred Grace," Mandragora openly broached, rejecting the obligatory custom.

"If I am able to lead you towards enlightenment, My Child, then it will be all the better."

"For who?"

"You, My Child, without a doubt."

"And the Church's pocket, without a doubt. What's the price tag on a consecrated burial these days, hmm? Do I get to lay in the blessed bosom of the Earth Mother Gaea for less than a thousand signats?"

"That is entirely upon your own conscience, My Child," Chamade deferred. "You are well aware of the alternative, I trust?"

"Ignominious cremation and the forfeiture of all possessions to the Church. Yeah, I got your number, Primitial. You gys are shrewd operators, you know that? Acolyte or Agnostic. Boxed or burnt. You win!"

"The Church only asks you to look into your heart to decide your own salvation."

"But Zoe's open to the odd bribe, though, eh?"

Bored with this theological sparring, the Lady of the house moved on and Pere, crowded out of the limelight by the Douzepers, caught her eye. She stopped dead, staring directly at him.

"And this is?" she asked, looking to her butler. "Abigail?"

"Pray, forgive me, m' Lady," Abigail politely begged. She ran a sly eye up and down Pere and Amoret, "I am not aware of the names of these ... *individuals*."

"They are two brave champions," Anheires relayed. "They spoiled an assassination attempt on myself on the way here. A noble act of loyalty some less reverent than they could learn from."

"Ouch!" Mandragora sardonically quipped.

"I gave my word that you would graciously extend your hospitality to include them for the service they rendered me. Is that agreeable to you, Mandrake?"

"Of course, Annie!" She held Pere's gaze. "I'd be honoured. What are their names?"

"Peregrine Farouche and Amoret Artemis," Amoret informed her, pushing forward and pulling Pere along too. She bowed and he curtsied, "At your service, m' Lady."

"I know you, don't I?" Mandragora said, pointing at Amoret.

"Yeah, ma'am. I'm a tenant on your estate."

"At Selcouth folly."

Anheires scowled and said, "Isn't she the gy you gifted my sister's Mandilion thoroughbred to, Mandrake? The *Giaour?*"

At the very mention of that word everyone gasped.

Chamade crossed herself again and moved away from Amoret as if she were diseased.

"Yeah," Mandragora shamelessly confirmed. "Yeah. How is he … err …"

"Favel, m' Lady," Amoret jogged her memory. "He's dead."

"Oh, shame," Mandragora genuinely consoled, "damn fine steed."

"Ate him, did you?" the Princess acidly presumed.

"Actually, *Your Highness,*" Amoret retaliated, "he was killed by the very assassins who attacked *you.*"

Glancing at her, Pere fought the urge to come clean. It was difficult but he managed it. She'd fibbed them in too deep now anyway, and to confess the deception at this late stage would be tantamount to suicide for them both. He would have to brass it out all the way now whether he liked it or not.

"Oh, Zoe!" somebody suddenly cried. "A thousand, thousand apologies!"

A gentleman in a ruffled silk gown came pattering across the foyer, the dark ringlets of his hair bouncing as he ran to where they were all gathered.

"Hildie!" Mandragora saluted. She turned to the visiting party and introduced the new arrival. "Ladies and gentlemen, this is my husband, Hilding Fainéant Lord Mandrake."

"Oh, Zoe alive! Am I awfully late?" Hilding breathily enquired. He instantly curtsied to the Atheling. "My liege, I beg Your Highness's pardon for not being here to receive you."

Flicking her wrist, Anheires granted her dismissal.

"I do so apologize, everyone!" he went on, flapping open a fan and wafting himself. "I was out riding in the woods …"

"You weren't ravished by any ruffians were you, my dear?" Mandragora quizzed her spouse, a wry smile on her face.

"No, indeed."

"Not from a want of trying, I'll wager."

"Actually, Mo-Mo," Hilding said, "I *was* set upon by two ruffians, but they only took my Lysart."

"Your favourite pony? The pride of your veritable fleet?"

"Yeah. Scoundrels!"

"Well, I suppose there's no accounting for perversion," Mandragora mused. "Deviants!"

"No, no! When I say *took*, I mean they *stole* him!"

"Oh, right."

"Anyway," he resumed his tale, "I had to walk home. As luck would have it, I came across one of our bailiffs and she gave me a ride."

"And after that she brought you back here," his wife finished.

Hilding blushed and fanned the fluster.

"Excuse me, m' Lord, but what did these ruffians look like?" Amoret interjected.

He looked at her and he giggled. "Why, one was tall and thin and one was short and fat," he coyly answered, flirting like crazy. He was an attractive man, and despite the fading of the beauty he'd enjoyed in his youth, he could still turn heads once he'd healed over the blemishes with sufficient cosmetics. "Neither of them so … *strong* and *handsome* as you, my dear."

It was Amoret's turn to go red.

"Those were the very likenesses of the assassins, Your Highness!" Cacafogo declared.

Fougade, Ronyon and their fourth colleague, whom Pere had heard referred to as Scarmoge, all swore the same as their Sergeant.

"Did you not give chase to these *assassins*, Sergeant, if that is what they truly were?" Mandragora asked.

"No, m' Lady. Our duty is to protect the Atheling, not pursue Federaries all about the countryside."

"Federaries?" She sniggered. "But you have footsoldiers. Couldn't you have deployed them in such a fashion?"

"Their duty is to protect the remainder of the delegation, m' Lady. After all, it may have been a rouse to divide our numbers."

"Hmm, yeah, well …" Mandragora deflated the conversation. "Come come! Why do we all stand here in the lobby when a roaring fire and the finest wine await us in the first drawing room? Abigail, show the ladies and gentlemen the way."

Duly, Abigail started ushering the esteemed guests in the appropriate direction.

Mandragora and Hilding lingered with Pere and Amoret.

"What a lovely ring!" Hilding exclaimed, taking Pere's hand and admiring Alecost's betrothal trinket. "Are you two an item?"

"We're engaged, m' Lord," Amoret lied, if only to deter this insatiable woman-eater.

"Dinner will be at four-ten," Mandragora threw in. "So if you are to dine with us, Peregrine and Amoret, we had best get you cleaned up a little first."

"We are indebted to your generosity, m' Lady, but we don't wish to intrude on your entertaining. It will be sufficient for us to feed in the kitchens," Amoret humbly suggested.

"Nonsense," the hostess denounced, "I won't hear of it."

"Of course you must dine with us! And I will *personally* see to the young Master here," Hilding gushed, bagging Pere. "I've already got a gown in mind for you, my dear."

"I was thinking more of Dandiprat, Hildie," his wife said.

"Whom?"

"The under-chamberboy. He's more his size."

"Don't be ridiculous, Mo-Mo! What has *he* to wear that is suitable for high table, for goodness sake?"

With that Hilding whisked Pere off up the staircase.

"Berds!" Mandragora sighed, watching after them until they vanished from sight. "C'mon, Amoret. I've got some spare duds that'll fit you, I'm sure." She led her towards the stairs then shouted: "*FARAND!*" She glanced at Amoret, explaining, "My valet. She'll sort you out while I tend to my guests."

"You're too kind, m' Lady," Amoret thanked. She hesitated

before asking, "M' Lady … could you tell me if my uncle, Master Ducdame, called on you this afternoon?"

"Your uncle?" she said, cogitating. "No, not that I'm aware of. I'll ask Abigail, but I'm sure no one has called all day. I returned from abroad late last night and have been recovering in bed the best part of the day."

Before long a rather wild-haired character dressed in a high collared jacket and knee-britches appeared on the first landing of the staircase.

"Ah, Farand. Can you prepare a bath for Mistress Artemis here and find a few of my clothes that will fit her," Mandragora detailed, "she is to dine with us this evening."

"I'm sure we'll be able to conjure up something, my Lady," Farand positively replied, her fingers literally itching to get a hold of the sartorial nightmare being put into her charge.

"Good, good," said Mandragora, satisfied. "See you at dinner, Amoret."

Attercop slammed against the wall.

"What d'you mean *lost them?*" Mistress Farouche growled into the face of her Deputy, the latter's coat lapels tightly bunched into the former's clenched fists.

"We tried firing warning shots, Warden," Attercop pathetically excused, wheezing.

"*WHAT?*" She slammed her up the wall again. "You *fired shots* at *my son?* You bungling buffoons! I ought to have *you* shot at!"

She sniffed at some foul odour she could smell, wrinkling her nose in disgust.

Realized it was Attercop and let go of her.

"We feared for the boy's life, Warden," Skaines chipped in, nervously running the rim of her tricorn through her flexing and unflexing hands as she stood in one corner of the Watch Office like a naughty girl.

"So you *shot* at him?" Farouche said, failing to see the logic. "What were you hoping to do, in the name of Zoe? Kill him before anybody else got a chance?"

"We was protecting him, ma'am."

The Warden shook her head in disbelief. "Remind me never to ask *you gys* to mind my back if that's your idea of protection!" she huffed. "I've spent most of the afternoon on a fruitless search, and when I come back you tell me you've been chasing my son and his abductor half way across Mandrake County! Zoe Almighty! If Mandrake finds out about you two idiots trespassing on her land shooting the place up, the fumet will really hit the whirligig!"

"At least we found the young Master," Attercop compensated, adjusting her coat.

"Oh, yeah? And *exactly* how did you do that, pray tell?"

Smugly smirking, the gangly woman dug into an interior pocket of her frock coat, from which she produced the necklace and torn leather she had discovered at the copse where they had found Alecost. She dangled them in front of her superior as if she were coaxing a dog to heel.

"Be that your proof what can't be argued with, Cait?" ventured Skaines.

Farouche snatched at the pendant and examined it. "That's Peregrine's!"

"Found by Alecost's still warm corpse, ma'am." Attercop put forward the leather swatch. "With this."

"What's that?" the Warden asked, taking it and turning it all ways but still ending up none the wiser as to its identity.

"It be a piece of a jerkin, Warden," Attercop clarified for her. "I dunno about thee, but I only knows one body what wears a leather jerkin all of the time."

"Larrikin the lumberjill," Skaines guessed.

"No. It b'ain't hers!" Attercop denied, motioning for her associate to keep quiet.

"She wears a jerkin most of the time."

"It b'ain't hers!"

"Gambo the farmer, she got one 'n' all."

"Shuddup, Skaines!"

"And Martel the farrier, she do 'n' all."

"Artemis! The Giaour!" Attercop told the Warden. "I also

105

found hoss shoe marks on the ground what were in real bad shape. I knows for a fact Artemis can't get a farrier this side of Faubourg to shoe her hoss."

"You call this *proof*, Attercop?" Farouche took the Deputy to task over the evidence she'd submitted. "You ought to go and work for the Judiciary!"

"Are you implying the Judiciary does not make competent judgements, Warden?" a stern voice enquired from behind them.

They looked round to see Judge Corsned and Loon-Slatt, both of whom had softly entered the office via the rear access.

"No, no, Your Worship!" Farouche hastily redressed her loose tongue's aberration.

"That's what it sounded like to me," Corsned sourly asserted. "Was it not so, Loon-Slatt?"

"Aye," her henchwoman gratified.

"It was just a joke, Your Worship."

Glaring icily at Farouche, the Judge removed her cape and handed it to Widdy. "Have you found your murderer and missing son, Warden? The Adiaphoron and Mistress Gombeen are due at any time, so I could do with you and your women available."

"My Deputies seem to have discovered them both, yeah."

"And have you said murderer behind bars and said son safely incumbent at home?"

"No, Your Worship."

"What is your delay?"

"We b'ain't kind of sure where they went, Y'r Warship," Attercop admitted.

"Have you raised a search party?" Corsned relentlessly interrogated. "I can let you have my soldiers again for a while if you need them."

"We were just discussing it, Your Worship," said the Warden.

"Well, the longer you discuss it the further away they are getting. Who is your suspect, anyway?"

"Amoret Artemis," Farouche nominated, "one of the Giaours I told you of."

"I see …" Corsned said, mind calculating. "And she has taken your boy hostage?"

"We assume."

"Why don't we ask the Douzepers?" Skaines said.

They all looked at her, perplexed. Except Attercop, who clapped the palm of one hand against her forehead and rolled her eyes.

"What are you blithering about, woman?" Corsned witheringly interviewed.

"Well, while we was chasing 'em, they sort of collided with a group of Douzeper Knights … and they seemed to win favour with 'em, 'cos they turned on us …" Skaines conveyed, getting the feeling she was digging herself into a deep hole. "Maybe we could ask 'em to give 'em back."

"Douzeper Knights? Where was this?" the Judge troubled her for more information.

"On the Excelsior Road in … in Mandrake County …"

Attercop mimed a slashing gesture across her throat and pointed at Skaines.

"A little out of your jurisdiction, wouldn't you say, Deputy?"

"Heat of the moment, Y'r Warship," Attercop justified. "We gets carried away with our work when we gets into it."

"Did you not declare yourselves as Watch Deputies and claim the suspect as a prisoner?"

"That was a bit difficult, Y'r Warship."

"Aye," agreed Skaines, "with ten mil shot parting our hair!"

"They fired on you?"

"I think they had us down as a threat to 'em, Y'r Warship," Attercop astutely determined.

"Yeah, well the Douzepers do tend to be a trigger-happy bunch," Corsned remarked. "So you believe your suspect may be imposing herself on the good will of these knights under some contrived artifice?"

"Aye, to get 'em to fire on ossifers of the law," said Attercop, rubbing her chin. "I'll wager they're in Zoe knows where by now."

"Zoe may know, and I think I can take a shrewd stab too," the Judge contributed. "I believe what your suspect ran into was a delegation of the Sceptral Cabal sent from Excelsior Montis."

Silence fell at the very mention.

Corsned continued, "Destination, Mandragora Demesne."

"How does that help us, Your Worship?" asked Farouche.

"Aye. If Artemis has wheedled her way in with them lot, we b'ain't got a hope in the sky!"

"You forget," Corsned said, "I am a Sceptral Judiciary Judge."

"And?" prompted Farouche. "I don't mean to be disrespectful, Your Worship, but this is politics we're getting mixed up in here, not legislation."

"The Sceptral Cabal is not a law unto itself, Warden, contrary to popular belief. Even it must submit to the sworn oaths of the land."

"I wouldn't bank on it," muttered Skaines.

"So, your Deputy's suggestion to simply ask them for your son and your suspect back is not quite as absurd as it seems. With the support of my authority, I am certain concurrence will not be a problem once the delegation are made fully aware of all the facts and learn of the conniving trickery implemented upon them."

"What do you get out of it, ma'am?" the Warden wanted to know. "I appreciate your willingness to assist us, but I wouldn't want to distract you from your business here."

"There is a slight catch," Corsned confessed.

"Which is?"

"I don't want you to hang the Giaour as a murderer."

"Why not?"

"Because I want to burn her as a heretic …"

VII

It was 4:07.

The rest of the congregation were assembled in the first drawing room, casually socializing, sipping red wine and swapping chitchat while they waited for the serving of dinner to be announced.

Pere and Amoret met on the third floor landing of the staircase on their way down to join the party, both feeling like mutton dressed as lamb in the bourgeois attire they'd been allotted and each eyeing the other with similar certainty about how they'd turned out.

"You look … err … *lovely*, Pere," Amoret carefully professed, her gaze tracing up and down the hideous makeover she saw before her. He had been draped in a scarlet silk gown puffed up at the shoulders and narrowed at the hips and layered in flounces. His throat and wrists were decorated with gaudy, lavish jewellery, far exceeding the understatement of his own preference. The natural beauty of his complexion had been almost obliterated by the liberal daubing on of death pallor foundation, heavy rouge, thickly applied black mascara, deep burgundy eye shadow and several coats of the kind of lip-gloss Amoret had only ever seen bordello catamites wear. As for the cloying perfume that had been lashed on him, it fair took her breath away with its overuse rather than in any appreciation of its fragrance.

"I look like a *tart!*" he self-depreciated.

"Well, you were dressed by one."

He gave her outfit the once over, which was definitely in the style of Mandrake, being entirely black leather and satin orientated and concentrating on squeezing Amoret's curves into the positions they should be. Had it all fitted as tightly as Mandrake's he might've been turned on again; but the owner's tall, slender stature didn't correspond well with Amoret's shorter, stockier build, so the clothes hung loose in some places and cut in too much at others.

"We could pass for their children," Pere concluded.

"Yeah. Even your mother wouldn't recognize us," Amoret quipped. She offered her crooked arm to him, saying, "Shall we?"

They trotted down the stairs arm in arm.

A footwoman waiting in the foyer directed them to where the others had retreated. She threw the door open on a large, high-ceilinged room lit by ornate candelabra fixed on the pilasters. Elaborate scatter rugs patchily camouflaged the lacquered wood floor; expensive, richly crafted furniture provided elegance and functionality alike, and sophisticated works of art in frames probably worth more than the paintings themselves sporadically broke the continuity of the flock wall covering.

Cautiously, Pere and Amoret went in.

Conversation instantly desisted and all interest centred on them.

"Well!" sighed Hilding, admiring them both but particularly absorbing Amoret's metamorphosis from something beautiful to something scrumptious. "What do you think, Mo-Mo?"

"A definite improvement," Mandragora hailed, "though, I think you've put too much powder on Peregrine, Hildie. He has a natural radiance."

"Oh, pooh!" her husband contested, pouting. "You just don't know chic when you see it!"

"Come," Mandragora said, beckoning the two reluctant mannequins into the social circle gathered round the marble mantelpiece, "have some wine."

Dubious, they went over. Amoret very gingerly indeed, since

the shape-manipulating corset she wore was so rigidly laced she had trouble breathing and walking properly. Farand had planted her foot against Amoret's butt and yanked on the straps with what seemed like a team of untamed buckaroos just to get the sturdily boned body vice shut.

Mandragora filled a pair of goblets from a crystal decanter containing a red liquid, which came out rather viscously when she poured it, glugging loudly. She handed them the glasses and bid them to "Drink."

Amoret looked at the beverage, frowning.

Sniffed the bouquet.

And glanced at the smirking noblewoman.

"There is someone I'd like you to meet," Mandragora said then, placing an arm over the shoulders of each and escorting them across the room to where a solitary figure stood.

The woman was average height, blonde and had a fair, wispy goatee beard. Her choice of clothing possessed an air of quality but no sense of current fashion: the collarless camise, suede waist jacket, culottes and buskins were all frightfully démodé in Montaigne and on The Pangaea generally.

Her head bowed and eyes closed, she whispered some sort of enchantment over her brimming glass and tapped the rim with a curious loop-topped cross before reverently sipping the wine. She smacked her lips and uttered something that sounded to Pere like "Nazar."

"Fran," Mandragora called to her once she'd performed her strange ritual.

Looking round, she started at the appearance of Pere.

"In the Holy name of Icarus!" she invoked.

"I want you to meet a couple of my friends," Mandragora went on, satisfied by her reaction. "Amoret … Peregrine … this is Contine Franion Ahithophel."

"I am honoured to make your acquaintance, madam," Ahithophel said, graciously bowing to Amoret, who returned the courtesy. She tentatively took Pere's hand and delicately kissed it, engaging his eyes with hers as she did. "Delighted, sir."

The other members of the party regarded the display with a degree of disdain, muttering some things derogatory about foreigners and collaboration.

"Contine? You're a Caroline Countess, then, my Lady?" Amoret guessed.

"You're from *The Holy Land?*" Pere gasped, impressed.

"Paladin, actually," replied Ahithophel, checking her answer with Mandragora via a glance. "Gegenschein, to be precise."

"*Really? Are you safe here?*" Amoret wondered. "I take it you know what's being planned at Excelsior Montis."

"Quite safe," Lady Mandrake assured her. "Fran is an ambassador for the new regime in Paladin, and if Pherenike hopes to win any favours abroad she won't try any funny stuff against a peaceful envoy. Right, Fran?"

"Let us pray she is not that stupid," the Countess toasted, tipping her goblet at Princess Anheires, who was looking in the direction of the clique. The Atheling responded, imitating the attaché's gesture. "It does show a glimmer of hope in her understanding in that she has sent her own daughter as a negotiator for a peaceful settlement to the differences between the Montaigne crown and the Antichthon Confederacy."

"I wouldn't hold much in store by that," Mandragora commented. "Fact of the matter is, Pherenike just can't find Annie anything else useful to do that she's any *good* at. Sending her along with this crowd is pure tokenism. She couldn't negotiate a turn."

"Your Queen means to make war, no doubt," Ahithophel bluntly recognized. "But if the Confederacy makes every effort to be amicable then they will have nothing to reproach themselves for. And any ensuing hostilities will be entirely at the instigation of Pherenike, her allies and the Holy City of Goshen. Paladin wasn't taken by force; it just became converted. The fact the Matronit doesn't like having 'infidels' on her doorstep is hardly grounds for a massacre. How will they be able to ease their conscience after condoning slaughter as a means to curtail free will?"

"Witchcraft," said Amoret. "They'll brand you all as witches and spend the next thousand years convincing the world they did it a favour by rooting you out."

"You sound as though you speak from experience," Ahithophel remarked.

"Amoret is a Giaour," Mandragora explained.

"Ah, I see. Where was your homeland?"

"Giaours have never truly had a homeland, but I spent the largest part of my childhood in Cadmia. Until the Arimaspi Diaspora, of course."

Ahithophel placed a comforting hand on Amoret's shoulder. "You will have a home in Paladin now."

"But for how long?"

"Pherenike intends to make this ridiculous crusade a symbolic pilgrimage, paying homage at every Zoetic shrine between here and The Morro, from where the crusaders will launch their assault on Paladin," Mandragora told them in a low murmur so no one else eavesdropped on the information.

"A pilgrim crusade?" Amoret reflected. "How ironic."

"How do you know that, m' Lady?" asked Pere, his eyes wide with fascination.

"Ah," said Mandragora, tapping the side of her nose. She continued, "The point is, Pherenike is not well received on the continent and may not find a ready welcome in every country she hopes to pass through, despite having the blessing of Goshen. Consequently, she has to hedge her bets and rally support both here and abroad, hence the infamous blood purge. Above *sixty per cent* of the Frithgild surtax revenue is being ploughed into blatant wooing of potential allies on The Pangaea."

"That's a lot of signats," Amoret estimated, raising her eyebrows in surprise.

"We're talking *millions.*"

"People in your country are being bled dry and inducted into martial service while their neighbours' aristocracy, politicians and clergy get fat and rich on their money," the Countess plainly outlined. "Any sovereignty on The Pangaea with a gram of democracy will see this for the brazen imperialistic usurpation it is."

"You wish," Amoret huffed.

"We do, most fervently. Though, I fear it may be in vain."

Abigail entered then, announcing dinner as served.

Everyone eagerly abandoned their drinks in favour of following the butler out into the foyer and towards the dining room, which was only on the opposite side of the reception area. The door stood ajar ready for their influx, delicious aromas wafting out like invisible fingers come to beckon them forth to the feast within.

The banqueting hall had the proportions of a gallery and accommodated a long, wide, brightly burnished table. Sideboards lined all four walls, literally groaning with tureens, covered dishes and carafes of every shape and size. Footwomen methodically worked along these sideboards filling fine porcelain plates as the guests filtered in to take their positions. The table itself was set with a plethora of condiments, dressings of many descriptions, complimentary snacks and floral decorations. Each place was neatly denoted with intricate lace mats and laid with more cutlery and flatware than Pere reckoned he had in the kitchen at home.

"Fish soup for starters," Mandragora mentioned to Pere and Amoret. "Venison, beef or partridge for main, and chocolate mousse or meringue for dessert. Hope you don't mind eating catch as catch can. The culinary staff had begun the meal when you arrived, so there wasn't chance to take into account your preferences. Hope you'll enjoy it."

"Yeah, m' Lady," Pere anticipatorily reassured, overwhelmed by her cordial attentions. She had accepted them in her house and at her dining table at a moment's notice, and here she was concerned with pleasing their tastes. He felt a very warm respect for her.

"Thank you, m' Lady," Amoret said.

Mandragora left them to seat herself at the head of the company while Lord Hilding was installed at the furthest end. Ahithophel joined Pere and Amoret on their side, happily putting herself at Pere's elbow. Across the table Cauchemar sat nearest to

Mandragora, then the arrangements went: Anheires, Primitial Chamade and finally Snollygoster.

The Douzeper Knights remained; Ronyon and Scarmoge posted as sentries on the doorways at either end of the room, and Cacafogo and Fougade keeping close guard on the Princess and other dignitaries they'd been sent to chaperone.

When the food was dished up, Cacafogo stopped each of the footwomen as they came to the Atheling and, demanding a fork or spoon as appropriate, she tested every course for any traces of poison prior to allowing the plate to be set before the regal heir. Similarly, she sampled the wine from each carafe used to recharge Her Royal Highness's glass.

Besides that insulting charade, the meal was a success. Light conversation did intersperse the awkward atmosphere, but the subjects were mainly mutterings about the weather, the price of horse oats, the latest continental trends and so on. No meaty discussions or gristly debates, other than idle boasts about the number of kills on hunts or shoots and the pedigree of the game Mandrake had put in the pot for the main course.

Towards the end, however, things got more heated.

"I hear from Paladin that the Icarusians have found a relic, which they claim is the tomb of Icarus himself," Mandragora pitched in, using it as a verbal grenade and delighting in the reactive detonation.

"Damn fatuous, idolatrous balderdash!" Anheires denounced.

"Quite so," Primitial Chamade bolstered. "Mythical propaganda, I'll be bound."

"On the contrary," Mandragora disagreed, "I understand some distinguished Cadmian antiquarians have verified it."

"What else can you expect from the Cadmians?" Cauchemar contributed. "They should rename their country Middle Ground, because they're forever on it."

"They are a peaceful nation, sir, not a warring one," Ahithophel said.

"Are you making a veiled comparison, madam Countess?" Anheires haughtily suspected.

"Not at all, Your Highness. I was merely pointing out the reason for their neutrality. It doesn't mean the Cadmians lack the resolve or resources to sustain armed struggle if needs be. They effectively repelled the Arimaspi back in Ninety Six."

"The fact remains," Chamade cut in, "that their so called Holy Grail is but a fatuous myth, no matter how many grave robbers have looked at it. It is a wraith. A fantasy. A fallacy, I dare to venture."

"In more ways than one," Mandragora vulgarly punned, though nobody got the gist.

"That is the basis of their idolatrous creed; the veneration of invented relics," the Primitial shared. "That is how they recruit their disciples, by making empty promises of their false god's *second coming*, which will occur at some unspecified date and have a universally curative effect! Whereas the Zoetic Church advocates the tangible constancy of the Almighty Mother's bountiful blessings, rather than perpetuating wild conjecture about putting the world to rights at the wave of a magic wand when the magician turns up to wield it." Her associates guffawed. "The Zoetic Church deals with the here and now, not the there and then."

"I can understand your feelings, Primitial," Ahithophel rose to the bait. "Hope is something you are not familiar with. You prefer things to remain the same as it guarantees you retention of the only influence you have and will ever have, namely *fear!*"

"Disciplined guidance is a terror to none other than the uninitiated heathens!" Chamade ranted in riposte. "They wouldn't know commitment if it bit them!"

"And your kind *does* bite! It bites those with free thought and spirit. Those not so dull witted they need to trail after your glorified bandwagon, paying to pray in the dirt and then paying again to lay in it! *You* are the heathens!"

"Ladies! Ladies!" Mandragora intervened, although amused by the passionate slanging match. "You are meant to be peace envoys."

Both Ahithophel and Chamade grunted but said nothing more on their differences of opinion. The confederate resumed eating her pudding and the priestess motioned for a servant to refill her wine goblet. They glowered at one another across the dining table, though.

"Well, at least they're talking," Hilding remarked.

Unsettled civility held sway again, but not for long.

"How do you like your wine, Primitial?" Mandragora politely conversed. "You fancy yourself as a connoisseur of the grape, don't you?"

"Mmm, yeah. It is very fine, My Child," Chamade responded, inspecting the colour and nose of the specimen Mandragora had liberally supplied them with all evening. She sipped it and savoured the flavour. "What is it, precisely? It is certainly no vintage I have had before."

Ahithophel and Amoret almost choked themselves on their desserts.

They looked at each other then at Mandragora.

The Lady of the house smirked and answered, "Ichor."

The priestess spat a mouthful out onto the table.

Pere squealed, for it splattered his way and reminded him of Joskin's blood.

"*Holy Zoe! Forgive my sin!*" Chamade distressfully cried; spilling the rest of the goblet and getting to her feet so quickly she knocked over her chair. Spluttering and gagging, she desperately wiped her mouth on a serviette and simulated the sign of the saltire on her torso, shrilly babbling: "*The foul blood of pagan idolatry! Oh, my sweet Zoe! Forgive me!*"

"*What is the meaning of this, Mandrake?*" Anheires chided, her guardian knights rushing to the Primitial's aid and trying to calm her.

The Princess picked up her own half consumed wine and threw it into the hostess's face.

"*Aaargh! BITCH!*" Mandragora cursed, clumsily rising to wipe her eyes out and brush herself down. "*Do you know how much these clothes COST?*"

Ronyon and Scarmoge hastily moved in.

"How *dare* you serve us this *filth!*" the Atheling roared. "We come to you as *peace envoys*, and all you can do is play *childish pranks!*"

"Get real, honey!" Mandragora disrespectfully advised. "Pherenike's a despotic warmonger!"

"You insult my mother the Queen, cur!" Anheires seethed, standing and laying her hand upon the hilt of the dress sabre for the second time that evening. "And you a *Mandilion Thane!* You are not fit to hold the title, Mandrake! A Thane dons her sword and straddles her horse when the Queen rallies her to a cause, not sits back to collaborate with her enemy and slag off her name!"

Ahithophel's hand secretly touched a pistol tucked inside her jacket.

"I insult the Queen, but not your mother … because she *isn't* your MOTHER!"

"I think I smell bridges burning, Your Highness," Cauchemar glibly quipped.

"Yeah? Maybe it should be *her!* Along with all the other *pagans!*" the Princess raged, looking daggers at Ahithophel as she articulated the last word.

The equerry's grip flexed around the butt of the pistol.

Spotting the characteristic twitch of somebody pulling artillery, Scarmoge drew her pistol in a split second and pressed it against Ahithophel's temple, grittily issuing the challenge: "Do it and die!"

Declining, Ahithophel showed a pair of empty hands.

Scarmoge frisked her and tossed the offending six-barrel 9mm onto the table.

"Federarie scum!" Cacafogo berated. "Arrest her!"

Accordingly, Scarmoge and Ronyon grabbed their prisoner.

"*Hey, tin-heads!*" Mandragora waylaid. "She's a guest in *my* house! What *I* say goes! And that's YOU!" She pointed straight at Anheires.

"Gladly!" the Princess declared, storming out of the room with her chaperones trailing after her like devoted hounds, the Chancellor and distraught Primitial in tow. "I won't stay a minute longer in this *blasphemous house!*"

"Don't let the door hit you in the fud on the way out!"

"You've clearly distinguished where *your* loyalties lie!" Anheires delivered as a parting shot, turning to jab a loaded finger at Mandragora. "Be ready to reap the consequences of your treachery!"

With that she went, retinue at her heels.

Cauchemar paused to say, "As of now the crusade is in motion."

"It was anyway," Mandragora countered.

The Governor smirked then left.

"Well," said Hilding from the other end of the table. "That went better than expected."

"I guess you can kiss goodbye to an amicable resolution, Fran," Mandragora sighed.

"There's a surprise," Ahithophel grunted, re-pocketing her pistol.

"If you'll excuse me, I will go and change," the hostess pardoned herself. "Then perhaps we can retire to the study for brandy and cigars, ladies, while the gentlemen amuse themselves as they please."

Mandragora exited, removing her damp frock coat and tossing it at Abigail, requesting it to be immediately dealt with by the washermen.

"What's Ichor?" Pere naively asked, suspiciously examining his goblet of wine.

"The blood of Icarus," Amoret replied.

"Eeuurgh!" he said, squeamishly recoiling from the glass. "We're drinking *blood?*"

"No. We're drinking wine, my dear," Ahithophel allayed his fears. "It is only symbolic blood."

"It's the custom of the Icarusian faith," Amoret schooled him. "My faith."

"It's ghoulish!" he condemned, superstitiously crossing himself with the saltire as the Primitial had done.

"Not dissimilar to the Zoetic rite of Primordial Renascence," Ahithophel paralleled.

"We don't *drink blood!*" Pere contested.

"No, you *bathe* in it. In your church's teachings the baptismal seas are Gaea's lifeblood. In our ritual the essence of our god is represented by the wine and ingested, mingling it with our own. Do not be afraid to drink it, for it is only wine you have there. It gains no sacramental properties without first being blessed by the orthodox cantillation, and of course, it has no meaning whatsoever to those who have not the faith. I am not afraid to bathe in the sea because of your baptism ritual."

He thought about this a moment.

Then drank the wine.

The hour was 5:00 dead.

Midnight.

Amoret had left Mandragora and Ahithophel in the study smoking richly aromatic cigars and swigging strong brandy, engrossed in good-natured disputes over those countries likely to capitulate to Queen Pherenike's bribery and corruption to pave the way across the continent for her crusaders. They were at the point of striking a bet as to whether The Morro would surrender itself as the much-needed launch pad to Paladin or if there would be a fight for it.

Admittedly it had been a pleasant, relaxed evening devoid of any awkwardness or class distinction, with Amoret joining in the discussions freely and candidly airing her opinions, being treated more as a friend and equal than a lowly peasant, wholly different to the way she had felt under the condescension of the Atheling Princess.

But the conversation began to run beyond her depth, so she claimed she was getting a little fuddled on the brandy and politely bid them good night.

In truth she had reached the limit of her knowledge of global politics and travel. More importantly, for all her social tolerance, Mandrake still retained that flippancy regarding money most of those born to it had bred into them; a trait which Amoret despised.

Pere, who had been in one of the house's parlours playing cards with Lord Hilding, had gone to his bed a long time ago as far as she could tell. When she quietly opened the communicating door between their bedrooms and peeked through she saw him swaddled in his sheets, fast asleep. She had hoped to talk to him about what their next move from here might be, but she supposed it could wait till morning.

She mercifully released her body from the crippling stays that had tortured her for the past hour with long sighs of relief, gratefully tossed them aside and donned the crisp nightshirt that had been laid out for her use.

Then she doused the candles before slipping into the clean, smooth bed linen.

Lying there gazing into the gloom, she reflected on the day.

Two people were dead. A molesting slob that deserved all she'd got, namely Alecost, and a bold and generous woman they had only known but a few scant minutes before she gave her life to help their escape, namely Joskin. And of course a brave, noble horse had also gone the same way.

Favel.

Amoret shed a tear thinking of him.

Added to all this, she had assaulted two Deputy Wardens, cheated death she didn't know how many times and lied to a Princess of the Realm.

She began to wonder what tomorrow had in store.

Her mind turned to Semeion, cogitating on the possibilities that may have befallen him on his unfinished mission to Mandragora Demesne. If he hadn't made it this far what had happened to him? Had robbers attacked him? Had some wild animal set upon him? Or had he just exhausted himself and dropped asleep under a tree somewhere along the way, and since woken and given up and returned to Selcouth?

These thoughts soon wearied her and she gradually drifted off into slumber.

It wasn't long before she snapped awake again, though, alerted by a noise. She held her breath and listened, but only heard owls screeching and wheeling outside and a distant fox barking at the night.

Her eyes darted here and there like caged creatures testing the boundaries of their cells, straining to see in the dim luminescence thrown by the moon's eerie glow.

The main door of her room slowly creaked open, admitted a small, shadowy figure and then lightly clicked shut again. Whoever had entered stood stationary for a moment, their delicate respiration panting into the gloom.

"Pere?" Amoret hissed. "Is that you?"

Bare feet softly padded towards the bed.

"If you want me to be," whispered Hilding Mandrake, leaning over her with only a black lace trimmed scarlet negligee to scantily shield his modesty.

"My Lord!" she gasped, sitting up. "What're you doing in here?"

"Oh, come, come," he cooed. "You're a woman of the world. Isn't it obvious?"

"Nuh ... no, m' Lord," she fibbed.

"I want *you*, silly!" He reached out, trembling, and caressed the exposed upper area of her chest. "I want every big, muscular centimetre of you!"

"My Lord!" Amoret complained, trying to stop his wandering hands. But no matter how much she dissuaded him he persisted. "This isn't proper!"

"Oh, pooh to properness!" Hilding giggled playfully, clambering onto the bed.

"The man I love is in the next room!"

"Oh, don't worry about *him*, darling! I got him a teensy bit tipsy on gin. He'll sleep like a log for the rest of the night." Hilding licked his glossed lips at the prospect. "That gives us *plenty* of time to get to know each other a whole lot better."

He lunged at her, but she dodged him and he fell flat on the mattress.

"You don't understand, m' Lord! I *love* him! I can't hurt him! I *won't!*"

Hilding propped himself up on an elbow and looked at her, leaning his head to one side and winding a ringlet round his forefinger.

"Do you want me to scream rape?" he asked.

"What?"

"Do you want me to scream … *at the top of my voice …* RAPE!"

Amoret clapped her hands to his mouth. "No! No, I don't!"

He took her wrists and moved her hands down onto his chest.

"Then be a sport, darling …"

Pere stood on a shore of jagged rocks, where billowing waves surged forth from the hostile grey waters before them to crash and break into foaming maelstroms. He stared out at leaden clouds quickly gathering on the horizon, the wrap sheet he had draped about his person doing little to protect him from exposure to the bitterly cold wind that pressed against him.

Patiently, he waited.

He knew something terrible was going to happen.

The storm clouds boiled overhead with grim inevitability and shed their freight, sending bolts of forked lightning crackling all around him and hammering thunder through the sky and ferociously thrashing some sort of precipitation into the turbulent sea.

Unflinching, Pere just stood and watched until the heavy weather cleared as fast as it had come.

Then he waited expectantly.

Finally, something came out of the water. A figure clad in armour, washed ashore like jetsam and now exhaustedly crawling up onto the craggy coast, its progress hindered by the constant battering it suffered from the vicious swell.

It was a woman, that much he could determine; her long, blonde hair obscuring her face from view as she laboured to drag her carcass over the shattered rock debris beneath her, which squealed against her metal skin like screaming babies.

He watched her painfully slow advance towards his position.

"Go back!" *he commanded when she eventually arrived at his feet.* "Go back!"

"I have come so far!" *the dishevelled stray moaned.*
"This is no place for you!"
She started to haul herself up off the ground.
"I claim my right!"
"This is not your right!" *Pere sternly reproached.*
She looked at him.
Yet she had no face.

He awoke with a jolt.
"Holy Zoe!" he invoked, breathing hard.

His head swimming queasily, Pere lay back on the pillows regretting caving in to Lord Hilding's insistence and imbibing those three glasses of gin. He only ever drank alcohol at Lammas; and even then his mother allowed him but the smallest of drams to celebrate the festival, so his system just wasn't accustomed to such excessive quantities.

The cold, remnant imagery of his dream filtered into his mind again and he shivered.

According to the conceptual laws of his belief, prophecy was akin to reincarnation: a blasphemous impossibility. All life was subordinate to natural selection and progression; therefore, predetermination was anathema to the Zoetic Church. This was exactly what he and every other child under the tutelage of their local Charlatan had been taught at religious instruction classes, and this is exactly the reason why the dreams scared him so much. He truly thought he was either going mad or being demonized into a heathen by some arcane mysticism, for another teaching of the Zoetic faith was that the only dangerous monsters in the world dwelt within the minds of humankind.

He stopped himself suddenly.
The wine.
He had drunk Ichor, the blood of a pagan idol!
Mistakenly attributing the vision to this aberration and frightened he might forsake salvation in the soil, he crossed his arms over his chest in the shape of the saltire and frantically

repeated the Purgatory Prayer into the dark. "Holy Zoe, Purveyor of Light, hear my prayer and heed my plight. Purge my seity of Malison's blight, and spare my purity for divine delight. Grant me still my blessed grave, so to make use of my bountiful remains. From the wretched pyre save, all that I am and have, I pray." Earnestly hoping the exorcizing chant would be enough to absolve him and dispel the nightmare from his subconscious.

How could he be so stupid? Letting himself get talked into libation was bad enough, but to abandon all his inherent principles and participate in the practice of paganism was unforgivable. What made it worse was that Amoret had coerced him into it. Did she care for him so little that she would treat with such disdain what he held so dear?

Just then he heard voices.

Well, not voices as such but giggling, and it seemed to be coming from Amoret's room.

Curious, he slipped out of the bed and crept across the floor to the door connecting his room and hers, a silky nightgown his only clothing and the light of the moon streaming through the unshaded windows his solitary source of illumination.

When at the door he bent close to it and listened.

Yes, there was definitely someone else in there besides Amoret. And whomever it was they were having a marvellous time, judging from the amount of shrill laughter. His first thought was that she had brought Ahithophel up to her room and they were continuing some intercourse they had begun in the study.

That was until he heard the slapping of bare flesh.

Pere lightly dropped to his knees and peered through the keyhole; only to discover it was Lord Mandrake in there with her, and that they were indulging in intercourse of a very different kind.

Clapping a hand to his mouth to stifle a squeal, he fell back and pedalled himself in reverse towards the bed, his wide eyes staring at the door that concealed heart-rending infidelity behind it. His whole world demolished and coming crashing down to earth.

How could she? he mentally chastised. *How could she be so wanton?*

All the plans they'd made together and all the promises she had given him, everything he had to cling onto, simply meant nothing any more. They were all worthless now. Lies and deceit expressed for ends he could only guess at since he didn't know why she would desire to keep him dangling on a string of untruths. Unless she was no better than Avoirdupois Alecost, declaring undying devotion in order to butter him up in the hope he would let down the guard on his honour and compromise it to sate her lust.

A few minutes ago he would never have believed that of her, but now it gained a horrible clarity.

"Amy!" he sobbed, tears cascading down his cheeks in black rivulets of mascara. He crammed his fist into his mouth to bite down on so he didn't scream her name aloud. "Oh, *Amy!*"

He had to get away from here.

Run into the night alone.

Acting quickly, chiefly motivated by his pain, he leapt up and grabbed the scarlet gown he'd cast onto a chair. His own clothes were spirited away to the laundry by Lord Hilding's groom when he changed, so the on-loan frock would have to do. He doubted his Lordship would miss it anyway, considering the copious wardrobe he had impressed the boy with; and seeing as he was correspondent to Amoret's romping, Pere reckoned he owed him.

Whilst putting it on very skew-whiff and rumpled, he formulated a plan of escape.

He supposed he ought to steal down to the kitchens to purloin some bread, cheese and a drop of milk as provisions for his journey. The trouble was, he hadn't the faintest idea whereabouts the kitchens were located in the Demesne, and if he were to go sneaking around he might be discovered and be prevented from leaving or, worse still, be shot as a burglar.

Putting that aspect aside, he instead concentrated on the actual feat of slipping out of this fortress unnoticed. But simply turning the hazardous adventure over in his mind was as far as he got with it, for he hadn't the wit to tackle such a mammoth challenge. Amoret had presided as tactician to get them here, not him. The chances of him being mistaken for an invader would undoubtedly increase a thousandfold even if he did succeed in exiting the house itself. And then there were the gates, the walls and the moat.

His brain whirled.

Unperturbed, he decided he'd just play it by ear, and if necessary use his beguiling boyish charms to impinge on the mercy of anyone he might meet. Not a totally sound policy on which to proceed, but it was the only policy he had available that didn't require too much thinking about. The fact still remained that he *had* to get out of here.

When he was ready he left the room.

Creeping onto the landing, he first checked there was no one in sight before he began making for the stairwell. Guttering candles mounted in wall brackets shone him the path as he fleetly padded along in the dainty shoes he'd borrowed from his hated rival, holding up the layered flounces of the frock to avoid tripping on them.

Voices murmured on the stairs.

He almost skidded to a halt, the carpet runner rucking under his feet.

Peeping over the banister, he saw Mandragora and Ahithophel climbing the steps. He retreated before they spotted him, pressed himself back into a shallow alcove (one of many in the corridor containing more portraits of dead Mandrakes) and waited with bated breath, listening.

"What do you think of Peregrine?" Mandragora was asking.

After a pause, Ahithophel said, "I think he is of the bloodline."

Mandragora looked at her. "The resemblance *is* uncanny."

They reached the top of the steps and turned to each other.

"We shall have to have him," Ahithophel said.

"And Amoret?"

"She speaks like a rebel, but I think her heart is settled to complacency."

Pere found that sentence perfectly summed up feelings he'd had growing in him for some time now and silently nodded his agreement.

"No true faith," attested Ahithophel.

"We will have to separate them."

"You don't mean to kill her, do you, Maugre?"

He gasped, shocked.

They were plotting to murder Amy!

"Nothing so drastic," Mandragora dismissed. "We'll just surrender her to the County Sheriff in the morning."

"On what pretext?"

"Well, the way my other half was eyeing her up this evening I wouldn't be surprised if he's got his claws into her by now, so ravishment, I guess."

Fraught with dilemma, Pere glanced towards the chambers he'd come from, in two minds whether to dash back and warn Amoret of the devious conspiracy to have her thrown to the wolves. Despite the hurt she'd caused him, he couldn't stand by and let her blindly walk into their trap.

"She is a Giaour, Maugre," Ahithophel reminded her friend. "They'll put her to the bonfire. Surely you can't want to martyr her to that madness."

"Of course not!" Mandragora said. "*I'm* the County Sheriff, Fran. And Magistrate and Lady of the Manor, all rolled into one. She won't be going anywhere without *my* say-so. She'll just be kept out of the way while we deal with the boy."

His concern sharply transferred from Amoret, who was apparently safe, to himself who was fast becoming unsafe. There was no question about it now. He *had* to escape. Zoe only knew what sort of hideous fate they were cooking up for him.

Mandragora and Ahithophel kissed then.

Not as friends might, but as lovers do.

Pere gagged at the spectacle, a profanity in his pious eyes.

Encircling each other's waist with an arm, they sauntered off down the opposite corridor and disappeared into a room together.

Seizing the opportunity, Pere scurried out of his hidey-hole and swept down the staircase as fast and noiselessly as he could, which wasn't easy with the rustling silks impeding his stride and threatening to pitch him down head over heels.

He'd nearly got to the front door when a heavy banging suddenly fell against its sturdy oak structure, resounding in the foyer like thunder and frightening him.

Again he stopped dead, caught between a rock and a hard place.

The booming racket continued incessantly, certain to rouse the whole house and rumble his surreptitious departure.

"All right! All right! I'm coming!" somebody moaned.

Pere looked every which way, seeking convenient concealment. Then in sheer panic, he darted into a shadowy recess under the stairs.

Abigail the butler hurried into the lobby, the flame of the candle she held fluttering as she went along. When she reached the front door she loudly scraped back the bolts and rattled the locks and opened it.

"Good evening, my Ladies," she greeted some unseen callers.

"Is your Mistress at home?" a horribly familiar voice curtly cut to the chase.

"Yeah, m' Lady. May I enquire as – "

"Judge Thesmothete Corsned, Sceptral Judiciary Bar for Brecham County. I have a warrant for the arrest of one Amoret Artemis, whom I believe the Lady Mandrake to be harbouring here." The imposing figure of Corsned stalked into the foyer, closely followed by her soldiers and an assortment of others Pere couldn't quite identify from his viewing angle.

"At this late hour, m' Lady, I am afraid my mistress has retired for the night," Abigail apologized, reluctant to disturb her employer.

"Then awaken her," the Judge snappily instructed. "And that's *Your Worship*."

"Very good, Your Worship."

"Do you have a boy here as well who may have arrived with Artemis?" Pere's mother piped up, labouring the butler's attention. "Peregrine Farouche?"

His ship had come in. Here was his way out.

"*Mama!*" he hollered, breaking cover and running to his redeemers.

"Peregrine!" the Watch Warden cried with genuine relief in her tone.

"Yours, I believe, Warden," Corsned dourly commented as the repatriated mother and son embraced deeply.

"Are you all right, darling?" Mistress Farouche worriedly fussed, wiping the smeared make-up from his face.

"Yeah, Mama, yeah," he reassured her.

"One down, one to go," Attercop said, impatiently fingering the butt of her pistol, eagerly spoiling for a rematch with Amoret.

"Aye," Skaines confirmed.

"What is the meaning of this intrusion?" Mandragora's voice spoke.

Everyone looked up to see her poised on the stairs glowering down at the uninvited hoi polloi, Countess Ahithophel shadowing her very closely.

"Faubourg," she said, addressing one of the party. "This isn't a social call, I presume."

"Mandrake," acknowledged a burly woman with a dark, bushy goatee beard, stepping forward. "I am here in my official capacity as County Sheriff, yeah."

"Well, you've lost your way, sweetheart. You're the Sheriff of *Brecham* County. This is Mandrake turf."

"I am Judge Thesmothete — " Corsned began introducing herself.

"I know who *you* are," Mandragora rudely interrupted. "I just want to know what you're doing in my house? Who let you through the gates?"

"Your bondswomen were less intent on perverting the course of justice," Faubourg said. "They recognize real authority when they see it, to their credit."

"Treacherous bitches!" Mandragora cursed. "I'll have them all flogged!"

"I have in my possession," Corsned officiously commenced,

flourishing a legal document at the noble as if it were a lucky charm capable of warding off evil spirits, "a warrant for the arrest and detention of one Amoret Artemis, a tenant on your land."

"Artemis … Artemis …" Mandragora repeated to herself, frowning at the ceiling and clicking her fingers for inspiration. "Nope," she concluded her fake cogitation. "I have at least ten thousand tenants on my property, Judge. Have you tried her farmstead?"

"She lives at Selcouth folly."

"There you go. That's where you should be. Not cluttering up my front hall."

"These Deputy Wardens pursued her from there to here, Mandrake," Viscountess Faubourg stated, motioning towards Attercop and Skaines. "We have reason to believe you are harbouring a murderer and a kidnapper, and that is a very serious offence. Don't make things more difficult for yourself, Mandrake. Just tell us where she is."

"I don't have to tell you anything, Faubourg!" Mandragora hotly retorted. "*You* are trespassing, don't forget. And as such you are at the discretion of my tolerance, which happens to be wearing pretty thin!"

"You are ignoring a warrant of the Sceptral Judiciary," Corsned slyly informed her.

"You betchya!" Mandragora said, folding her arms. "Your move, slick."

"Search the house!" Corsned ordered the soldiers.

"Over my dead body!" the owner protested.

Ahithophel presented her pistol over Mandragora's shoulder, supportively declaring, "And mine!"

Eight guns reactively pointed in their direction.

"If you wish," Corsned smugly granted.

"Of course, we could perhaps negotiate the situation," Mandragora redressed, gesturing for her companion to stow her firearm. "I'll swap her for the boy."

"No!" Warden Farouche angrily denied, clutching her son

close to her. "Does it look as if this lad wants to stay here a minute longer?"

Pere gazed at Mandragora and Ahithophel and they at he.

"No deals," Corsned adamantly stated. "Either you give her to us or we arrest you for obstruction of justice and take her anyway."

Mandragora nibbled her lower lip.

"We only want the Giaour," Faubourg told her. "Don't do anything stupid, Mandrake."

Finally she concurred, sighing, "Okay."

Corsned stepped forward in readiness, her soldiers minding her.

"But not *you!*" Mandragora refused the Judge. "Just Faubourg and the Deputies."

"May I come, my Lady?" Pere blurted, acting on a whim.

Everybody regarded him as if he'd asked for the world on a gold salver.

"I want to see her before she's taken away."

"Yeah, of course, my dear," Mandragora realized the strange request.

"Pere?" his mother queried.

"Please, Mama. I must."

Although bemused as to why he should wish to see his abductor, she consented.

"Well," sighed Hilding Mandrake, resting his chin on Amoret's chest and drowsily gazing at her. "I dare say I shan't tire of you easily, darling."

"Don't get used to the idea, my Lord," she muttered, feeling thoroughly ashamed of herself for betraying her beloved Peregrine. "It won't happen again."

"Oh, it will if I desire it," Hilding asserted. "For if it doesn't, I could have you locked up for ravishment."

Amoret pushed him off her and sat up on the edge of the bed.

"Oh, don't sulk, darling!" he affectionately reprimanded. "It's not as if it was *so* dreadful, was it? At least I hope not, because that would mean I'm losing my touch. You enjoyed it as much as I."

The worst of it was she had.

This fact made her feel even more ashamed and dirty. She was besotted with a boy so pure and beautiful any woman with a milligram of sense would be proud to call him hers; yet it took a salacious incubus like Hilding to arouse her like never before. It made her physically sick to the stomach while at the same time it titillated her. And she knew that all her mustered willpower would not be able to stop this adulterous union happening again if she stayed here, no matter how much she rejected its temptation.

Therefore, she and Pere would have to leave at first light if she wanted any chance of saving their relationship. It would mean deserting favourable shelter, but if this was the price it levied then they would be better off gone.

Hilding pressed himself against her back and whispered into her ear. "Come to me, lover."

Just then the bedroom door burst inwards, succumbing to the forced entry of Faubourg, Attercop and Skaines.

Lord Hilding screamed, gathering the sheets about his person to cover his modesty.

"Amoret Artemis!" the Viscountess authoritatively claimed, standing with arms akimbo so her badge was visible. "You are under arrest!"

"Get yer britches on, wench!" Attercop rousted her, Skaines close at her elbow with pistol unholstered in case of any hi-jinks.

"What's the charge?" Amoret demanded to know.

"First degree murder and kidnap."

"And assault of two law ossifers," Attercop appended, the injuries of her beating still very colourfully evident on her face.

"Aye!" Skaines said, equally smarting.

Mandragora and Pere appeared behind the Sheriff.

"Mo-Mo!" Lord Hilding gasped. "This isn't what it looks like!"

"It never is, Hildie," his wife said.

"Pere …" Amoret guiltily crawled. "I … I can explain this …"

He only looked at her with an aloof disregard that killed her inside.

Simultaneously, Amoret and Hilding pointed at one another, each declaring the other seduced them.

"Take her away!" Faubourg urged the Deputy Wardens.

"C'mon, Giaour!" Attercop harried, dragging Amoret off the bed.

"Get your mitts off me, fudbreath!" Amoret spat, slapping her hands aside. Skaines swiftly reminded her the gun was present, jabbing the cold barrels into her ribs. "I still owe you *bitches* in spades for killing my *horse!*"

"Wait a minute!" Hilding interjected. He pointed at the Deputies, who both took a close look at him then glanced at each other with a sense of impending doom. "I remember you! You're the ruffians who stole my pony!"

"Is this true, ladies?" Faubourg asked the Deputies. "Did you steal Lord Mandrake's pony?"

"Requisitioned it, m' Lady," Attercop amended, "in the execution of our duty."

"Aye!" Skaines readily endorsed, nodding her head as if her neck were made of jelly.

"They threatened me with a gun!" Hilding further testified.

"A necessity, Sheriff," Attercop hastily defused the argument. "Due to the nature of the pursuit we was conducting 'n' what not, there weren't no time for ettykit."

"Aye!" Skaines agreed.

"*They raped me!*" he tried again.

"Oh, do shut up, Hildie!" Mandragora entreated. "You told me yourself the ruffians who attacked you in the woods weren't up to the job."

Attercop and Skaines both huffed, affronted by the insinuation.

"*I demand justice!*" he screeched like a spoilt brat.

"Well, all you're getting is your negligée," his wife said, retrieving the garment from where it had been tossed. She handed it to him and held up the bedclothes while he put it on.

"You've made a big enough fool of yourself for one day, dear."

When he was decent she grasped his wrist and yanked him out of the room, mentioning to the Sheriff on the way, "I want that pony returned, Faubourg. It's pedigree bloodstock and worth a small fortune."

"Indeed, Mandrake."

Amoret had crammed on the leather trousers over the nightshirt and was just pulling on the boots when her fidgety escorts decided she was adequately dressed. They roughly jerked her to her feet and shoved her towards the door, unwilling to wait any longer.

"Pere," she importuned, begging the audience of the spectating boy. In the scant seconds she could delay her captors they searched each other's eyes. "Forgive me!" she beseeched.

"Gerron!" Attercop harangued, shoving her into stumbling advance.

A single tear tracked down Pere's cheek.

"Come, young Master," Faubourg ushered.

And they left.

VIII

Two days had elapsed, allowing him plenty of rest and recuperation.

Now the kid gloves were off.

Pere sat in the front office of the gaol-house looking at the assembly of women. His mother was there along with Judge Corsned, the County Sheriff and the local minister Charlatan Fugle. Also present was a newcomer whom he'd not had the privilege of meeting, since he'd been gallivanting around the neighbouring County when she arrived in Rampick.

She was Adiaphoron Wanhope, the incumbent diocesan superior invested with the task of supervising the religious aspects of the blood purge in Brecham. Her robes were sumptuously layered satins of varying orange colours, much grander than the relatively rudimentary red cassock of the humble Charlatan but not so grandiose as those of the Primitial. Slung about her neck was a silver saltire set with an array of precious jewels, again not so dazzling as that larger gold ornament Pere had seen Primitial Chamade wearing. Her hair was long, straight and black, her eyebrows heavy and bushy, and her face seemed permanently pinched into a haughty expression of looking down her nose (an effect exacerbated by her propensity to regard everyone through the bifocals she precariously perched on the very end of her hooked proboscis).

Sat in a chair that had been moved to the centre of the office, Pere meekly watched them all one by one, gauging their attitudes.

Judge Corsned was slowly pacing the room, while Faubourg leaned on the mantelpiece of the fireplace lighting a clay pipe. Mistress Farouche stood near her son, wringing her hands with worried vehemence. Wanhope was seated at the desk facing Pere, riffling amongst documents and occasionally casting a glance at the boy. Charlatan Fugle was attentively stationed at the elbow of the senior ranking pontiff.

He was very nervous, and with good reason. Despite his callowness, he knew what he divulged this morning could get Amoret burnt at the cross. So he was desperately trying to clear his mind of all the petty niggles and personal disappointments he'd experienced when the scales had fallen from his eyes, revealing his former favourite for what she truly was: a liar, a cheat and a fornicator. There was no place here for grudges nor was it an opportunity to settle scores.

Her life was at stake and only he could save it.

If he was lucky.

"Master Peregrine," Corsned addressed him, exuding a civility he did not associate with her manner, "do not be alarmed that you are in any trouble here yourself. We are fully aware that you were taken against your will."

"I wasn't," he jumped in.

"Peregrine. Consider what you say, and show respect to Her Worship," his mother soberly advised, keen to steer him from upsetting the Judge at this delicate stage.

"I'm sorry, Your Worship. Please forgive me," Pere apologized. "But I wasn't abducted. I went of my own free will."

"Indeed? Well, we can understand that Artemis led you astray with empty promises."

He couldn't contest that because he believed she had.

"The point is, you are absolved of any blame in these matters," Corsned reprieved. "Our concern is Artemis's asocial behaviour and heretical conduct. To establish these facts we require your testimony."

Pere nodded.

They wanted him to swear lies, but he was determined not to because his integrity was unswerving. Above all, though, he still could not find it within his kind, loving heart to depose his impassioned attachment to Amoret in spite of the pain she had caused him.

"Excellent. Let us begin with the incident involving Mistress Alecost," Corsned broached. "Tell us in your own account what happened there."

Hesitantly, he looked at his moccasins and shuffled his feet.

"Peregrine," Mistress Farouche cajoled.

"In his own time, Warden," Corsned said.

"Mistress Alecost came to call for me on that day," Pere eventually began. "She took me riding on her dray. We stopped at a copse on the edge of the Thirlborh Road to go for a stroll, and she proposed to me."

He touched the ring still adorning his finger.

"This is the ring she gave me," he declared, surrendering it to the Judge. "I think it should go to her family."

His mother confiscated it instead.

"What happened next, Master Peregrine?"

"I refused her," he said. "She didn't take too kindly to my reply and insisted I accept her, forcing that ring onto my hand. Then she assaulted me, sexually."

A murmur ran through the other women.

"I see," said Corsned, "then what?"

"I tried to fend her off, naturally, but she was too strong. As luck would have it, Amoret was riding by and came to my rescue."

"She killed Mistress Alecost," Faubourg put words into his mouth.

"No, my Lady. I did."

Another bout of murmuring ensued, more pronounced and protracted.

"*You* did?" queried Corsned. "Or you *think* you did? She may have been merely stunned and Artemis finished her off, couldn't that be the case?"

"No!" he stuck to his story. "I killed her. She was dead after I hit her with a branch. She was going to stab Amy in the head."

"Are you familiar with therapeutics, Peregrine?" Faubourg asked ingenuously, puffing on her pipe. "Are you an apothecary or a soothsayer?"

"No, m' Lady."

"Then how did you know Mistress Alecost was dead?" Corsned took up the line of interrogation like a starving dog snaffling a bone from a butcher's shop.

"Amoret said –"

"Ah! *Amoret* said!" the Judge gleefully interrupted. "And is *she* acquainted with the therapeutate?"

"No."

"So you only had *her* word for it, is that not so?"

"Yeah, I suppose, but – "

"Precisely how did Artemis determine Mistress Alecost was deceased?"

Pere thought about his answer a moment.

"By doing something to her neck, I think."

"So, in fact, Artemis could've done *anything* to Mistress Alecost once she had convinced you that she was dead from your blow."

"I don't …"

"You've already admitted, young Master, that you know little if anything of the therapeutic arts. Can you say without any doubt that Artemis did *not* do anything additional to Mistress Alecost's body while she was 'doing something to her neck'?"

"No," Pere honestly stated.

The first nail in the coffin had just got hammered home.

"Go on with your account," Corsned encouraged.

"Well, we were frightened and didn't know what to do …"

"On the contrary, young sir, Artemis knew exactly what to do, didn't she? She *robbed* the corpse. We searched the Selcouth folly and discovered Mistress Alecost's belongings hidden there in saddlebags."

Pere gloomily recollected.

Another nail in.

"Pray, continue."

Swallowing hard, he went on. "Attercop and Skaines …"

"The Deputy Wardens, Your Grace," Faubourg informed Wanhope.

"They came along the Thirlborh Road and spotted Mistress Alecost's dray abandoned, so Amy and I rode back to Selcouth."

"And there you were talked into going on the run with Artemis, yeah?" prodded Corsned.

"We were eloping."

"That's a new name for becoming a fugitive from the law."

A chuckle rippled through their number.

Only Pere did not laugh.

"Continue, young Master."

"Attercop and Skaines turned up at Selcouth."

"Whereupon they were immediately engaged in both unarmed and armed combat with Artemis, I believe."

"Of sorts," Pere vaguely confessed.

"Come come, young sir! Deputies Attercop and Skaines sustained severe bruising and abrasions, plus Artemis discharged a firearm at Deputy Attercop!"

"She wasn't aiming *at* her!" he claimed. "She hit the building!"

"So she's a bad shot! That doesn't mean she wasn't *trying* to shoot Deputy Attercop."

Third nail.

Something occurred to Pere suddenly. "They were out of their jurisdiction."

"They were officers of the law pursuing a line of enquiry into a *murder*. I think those could be deemed mitigating circumstances, don't you?" Corsned parried. "Continue."

"We escaped further into Mandrake County and they gave chase, firing upon us and endangering our lives greatly. They shot our horse." He glanced at the Judge, but saw this moving tragedy failed to soften her steely resolve. His sympathy ploy washed up, he went on. "We met a kindly farmer who gave us a ride on her cart. The Deputies shot her as well."

"Did you inform this farmer of your situation?" Faubourg dipped in.

"Yeah."

"And she freely aided and abetted your cause?"

"Yeah."

"Accomplice to a fugitive murderer," Corsned condemned. "Deserved what she got. Had she been a true, upstanding citizen she would have surrendered you to the Deputies." She motioned for Pere to carry on.

"We used the farmer's cart to escape, but at the junction with the Excelsior Road we crashed into a caravan of coaches."

"And to whom did these coaches belong?"

"They were Royal carriages, Your Worship."

"Be specific."

"Her Royal Highness the Atheling Princess Anheires."

"Did she have companions travelling with her?" Corsned delved.

"The Chancellor of the Treasury, the Governor of the Sceptral Cabal, one of the Goshen Primitials and four Douzeper Knights."

"I understand these very important ladies and gentleman were on their way to Mandragora Demesne, yeah?"

Pere nodded confirmation.

"I also understand the Douzeper Knights there present chased Deputies Attercop and Skaines away, believing them to be assassins of some description. Tell me, did Artemis lead the Atheling Princess and her delegation to believe the Deputies to be a regicidal threat?"

He couldn't lie. "Yeah. But they'd already assumed it themselves."

"Nevertheless," Corsned said, "Artemis did not dispel this misconstrued theory."

"No. Neither did I, though."

"You are not under suspicion here, young Master, as I made

clear at the beginning. The fact is, Artemis seized upon this error and wove her own web of deceit in order to vanquish her pursuers, ingratiate herself into company no one would dare contend with and secure herself a comfortable hideaway at Mandragora Demesne. Is that not so?"

"I suppose," he answered, non-committal.

Fourth nail.

"And when you arrived at Lady Mandrake's abode?"

"Lady Mandrake kindly took us in …"

"Labouring under the same delusion as the delegation that Artemis was a heroine who had saved the Atheling from an assassination attempt," Corsned threw in.

"We were given hot baths, a change of clothes and were invited to sit with the rest of the party at dinner."

"Did you meet anyone new? Foreigners, perhaps?"

"There was a Countess there. She was from Paladin."

"I see," said Corsned. "Was she there for any particular reason?"

"To meet the Princess, I think."

"And did this Countess represent any group or faction?"

"I don't know."

"A confederacy, maybe?" Corsned relentlessly wheedled. "Does *Antichthon* ring a bell?"

"Yeah, it does."

"Do you know what the Antichthon Credo is, My Child?" Wanhope spoke for the first time, icily observing the boy.

"No, Your Grace," Pere humbly pleaded ignorance.

"It is a fundamentalist sect of the Icarusians. Not only do they support the blasphemy that all humankind were created by *gods* that came out of the eye of the sun, but they also sacrilegiously claim those gods came from a world parallel to our blessed Gaea that lies beyond the sun."

Dark mutterings and cursing condemnation hissed around the room.

"That's impossible," Pere insisted, relying on the validity of his scriptural studies. "Nothing is akin to Our Provident Mother."

"Quite so," Corsned agreed, "but the Antichthon Confederacy strives to root this preposterous claptrap in Paladin through brain-wash indoctrination and other radically manipulative methods. And if they succeed there, where do you think they will turn next?"

Pere chewed his lower lip thoughtfully and suggested "Charlemagne?"

"Zoe forbid it, but yeah," said Wanhope. "So you can perhaps now grasp the importance of your testimony here today, My Child. What you divulge could help repel the heathens from the gates of Holy Goshen City itself and deny them their iconoclastic desire to sack the Aten Delubrum therein and so rend the very fabric of our most sacred creed."

The Adiaphoron gazed at the ceiling and crossed herself with the sign of the saltire.

"I suppose they talked a lot of politics at Mandragora Demesne," Corsned resumed. "Very tedious to a young berd's mind, I'll wager."

"The Countess and Lady Mandrake did," Pere said.

"Indeed? Don't happen to remember anything in particular, do you?"

"No, Your Worship. But they discussed the Queen's plans for the crusade."

"Really?"

"Did you have anything to drink at this soirée, My Child?" Wanhope asked. "Reflect upon your zeal to the reverence of Zoe Almighty, My Child, and answer truthfully."

Pere hung his head in shame and said, "I did, Your Grace."

"Can you be more candid, My Child?"

"Wine, Your Grace."

"I am partial to a fine drop of the grape myself, My Child. All things in moderation," the Adiaphoron submitted. "Was there anything else offered to you, My Child?"

"Gin, Your Grace."

"An excess?"

"Very much, Your Grace."

"Constant prayer will serve you better than shame, My Child," Wanhope prescribed. "Was there anything you drank which may have *looked* like wine, particularly *red* wine, My Child?"

Pere bit his bottom lip.

But he couldn't lie, certainly not to the cloth.

"There was, Your Grace," he confessed, starting to snivel.

"Come, My Child, purge your seity with us. You have no enemies here."

"I ... I believe ..." he cleared the phlegm clogging his throat, "... I was told it was a wine, but it was also referred to as ... *Ichor* ..."

Sharp intakes of breath abounded and someone mumbled something like "Abomination!"

Fifth nail.

He burst out crying and buried his face in his hands, blubbing, "I am *so sorry*, Your Grace!"

"Hush, My Child," Wanhope calmly sympathized. "I trust you recited the Purgatory Prayer when you uncovered this Heresy?"

"Yeah, Your Grace."

"Then you have nothing to fuel contrition. You have renounced the darkness of Malison's consorts. Be not ill at ease with your naivety."

Although they were only words they made him feel better to enough of an extent as to stem his tears.

Corsned waded back in. "So after you were tricked into imbibing allegiance with pagans, what happened?"

"The ... the delegation left."

"Why?"

"The Primitial drank the Ichor and – "

"*The Primitial?*" Wanhope indignantly echoed, flabbergasted, all soothing reconciliation gone from her tone. "Do you know what you say, boy?"

"She was tricked, Your Grace. She didn't know what it really was, as I didn't myself. I didn't mean to suggest anything otherwise," Pere excused. "After that the Princess refused to stay in the house any longer."

"And?" Corsned pressed.

"I played cards with Lord Hilding while the ladies withdrew to the study for brandy and cigars, then I went to bed at around four seventy-five."

"Then myself, the Sheriff and your mother turned up, yeah?"

"Yeah."

"To catch Artemis in the act of raping Hilding Lord Mandrake!"

"No!" Pere ruefully refuted. "I don't believe that!"

"That *is* debatable, Your Worship," Faubourg verified.

They'd have to settle for five nails instead of six.

"Well, thank you, Master Peregrine, you have been most helpful to our enquiries," Judge Corsned enthused, pleased with the results. "But if we may impose on you a tad more, I am sure there are some points the Adiaphoron will want to clarify."

Pere gulped dryly and turned to the Adiaphoron.

"My Child," Wanhope said, taking up the whip, "I can vouch for the steadiness of your fidelity myself from the reverent humility you have demonstrated and the honesty in your confessions. Charlatan Fugle has additionally expressed her contentment that you are indeed a good and pious Zoetic and a joy to teach."

He smiled at the local priestess, for like the majority of her parishioners he was fond of her. She was a young, trendy reformer in the stuffy, stolid system of worship she was ordained to minister and permeated its dusty carcass with fresh ideas.

Fugle regarded him coolly, her amiable disposition tempered by the presence of her Adiaphoron.

"But are you sure in your own heart, My Child?"

"In the sacred names of Australopithecus, Habilis, Erectus and Sapien," he canted, crossing himself with the shape of the saltire and reciting one title per point.

"It is easy to say the words, but it takes faith to believe them," Wanhope remarked, ignoring the standard show of orthodoxy as irrelevant to the assurances she sought. "Whom is the dark twin of Zoe Almighty?"

"Malison," Pere quickly replied. "The Purveyor of Deliquium."

"Whom is the birth child of Zoe?"

"Gaea, Our Provident Mother."

"How was this conception achieved?" Wanhope persisted.

"The Benign Creator Zoe shaped her daughter Gaea from her own divine matter and nurtured her into life," he loosely quoted from the Primordial Precepts.

"Whom did Gaea give birth to?"

"Hominidae."

"Whence did Hominidae spring forth from?"

"The Primordial Oceans of Our Provident Mother."

"Name the progeny."

"Australopithecus, Habilis, Erectus, Sapien."

Wanhope adjusted her bifocals. "And the first recorded Sapiens."

"Our exalted forebears Xanthe and Yeven."

"How many children did they beget?"

"Two, Your Grace."

"And they were?"

"The twins Charis and Mares."

"What aspects of these twins were peculiar?"

"Charis was the epitome of goodness and Mares was her exact opposite and equal."

"What did Mares do?" Wanhope further tested his scriptural knowledge.

Pere hesitated, pre-empting where this line of inquiry was going. "He raped his twin sister."

"And what came from this incestuous union?"

"A girl child."

"Name?"

"Chimera."

"And she became?"

He didn't answer.

"Come, My Child," Wanhope coaxed. "Your learning has been exemplary thus far. What did Chimera aspire to?"

"She became the Primogenitor of the ... the Giaours."

"With whom did she mate?"

Pere refrained from answering again, concentrating on fractiously interlacing his fingers in his lap instead.

"With *whom* did she mate?" the Adiaphoron insistently prevailed.

"Peregrine!" his mother hissed behind him. "Answer Her Grace!"

Finally, he uttered, "With her father, Mares."

"While her mother Charis did what?"

"She traversed The Pangaea to mate with the Six Seas and became the Primogenitor of the Littoral tribes."

"And from which tribe is our blessed regal House of Gerent descended?"

"Charlemagne, through Mulciber and Monte Creston."

Wanhope paused, reclining in her seat and steepling her fingers while the boy remonstrated on what she had elicited from him under the duress of her inquisition.

"Artemis is a Giaour, is she not?" she eventually broke the silence with.

"Yeah, Your Grace," Pere admitted.

"Did you know this before you threw yourself into her power?"

"Yeah, she told me."

Disapproving castigation was grumbled by some of the assemblage.

"So you put aside your piety and gave yourself to her, of your own free choice?"

"Yeah, Your Grace."

"You cast away all your sacred instruction and guidance for *a sordid, heretical issue of a bastardized race born out of foul incest?*"

Pere started crying.

"Spare us your tears, My Child," Wanhope implored. "We can understand you may have been unduly influenced considering the tenderness of your youth. However, this does not vindicate you wholly from your failure to effectively exercise self-discipline in this instance, which is precisely the reason why I question your otherwise fastidious fidelity. Darkness resides in the hearts of all humankind, My Child, and we must be vigilant of its iniquitous temptations and endeavour to resist these demoralizing lures. Therefore, in view of your deplorable lapse in credence, I am to recommend that you be confined to a seclusion cloister until such a time as when you have re-attained true faith."

"No!" Pere squawked.

"Is that necessary, Your Grace?" Mistress Farouche timidly tackled. "Surely Charlatan Fugle would be more than capable of giving the boy the extra tuition he needs."

"You underestimate the ramifications of your son's straying, Warden," Fugle said, "and overestimate my abilities."

"Indeed," her Adiaphoron ratified. "Too much temptation remains in his path if he were to stay here. He requires solitude and constant tutelage. The Eunuchs will be better able to offer him those benefits."

"Where, exactly?" Farouche asked, her fighting done.

Pere stared at his parent, distraught by the apparent ease with which she was abandoning him to this fate.

"Farren Eyrie."

"That's over five hundred kilometres away!"

"Would you prefer him burnt as a heretic?" Judge Corsned fielded. "If he were anyone else but the Watch Warden's son he would be. You are indebted to professional courtesy, madam."

Farouche looked around at the band of officials, feeling like a mouse in the middle of a viper nest.

"I am grateful for that," she said, "but I was hoping he would marry."

"So he shall, I'm sure," Wanhope predicted. "When he returns from his restorative absence absolved of his misgivings, he will be more eligible than he is now as a tainted sinner. What decent, eco-fearing woman would want to connect herself with the consort of an idolatrous desecrator?"

The Warden bowed to the priestess's superior astuteness.

"May I suggest that the Charlatan does take charge of the boy until proper arrangements can be made, Your Grace," Corsned said to Wanhope, who simply gave the nod to the notion. She turned to Fugle to ask, "Do you have room in your private quarters, Charlatan?"

"Yeah, no problem, Your Worship," Fugle complied.

Slumping back in his chair, Pere felt utterly gutted.

He had hoped to save Amoret, yet he wasn't even able to save himself.

Though he'd never visited an eyrie he had a pretty shrewd idea what to expect. He was aware the cloisters were stone buildings with no heating, no beds, no nothing; and he'd heard tell that the Eunuchs slept on the floor, ate on the floor, prayed on the floor and that was *all* they did.

He'd also come by a rumour that they flogged each other with flagella; but whether this was part of their religious practices or some sort of gratification done in secret, or even if it was true, he didn't know.

What was clear was that his foreseeable future looked very bleak.

Corsned clapped her hands together and rubbed them. "Then I believe our business here is concluded for now, ladies. All that remains is for Master Peregrine and myself to commit his testimony to writing."

There were ten of them already, and the blood purge had only just come to Rampick.

She knew some of them by sight. Not their names since she was an outcast who only frequented their community occasionally as it suited her, but she had seen their faces on the streets when in town. Some she remembered had looked down their noses at her then or made prejudicial comments behind their hands. Now, though, they were on the receiving end of social rejection for some contrived reason or another, and they didn't like the taste of their own medicine one bit.

The odd one out was old Gaby Cailleach: a virtual fixture at

The Creaking Meat Tree and a perpetual overnight resident here in the gaol-house once her drinking was done. She was lying curled up on the floor of Amoret's cell and had been there for the past two days, apparently forgotten in the fray of arrests being warranted on Judge Corsned's authority. It was a very strong possibility that she might get inadvertently burnt as a heretic rather than thrown back out as a vagrant drunk who had served her stir.

The lot of them were crammed into three cells measuring approximately four by two metres apiece, each designed to detain two captives at a stretch. In the rare event of a big brawl breaking out in the tavern across the road, the Watch Warden utilized the coal cellar as an overflow, which was marginally warmer and more comfortable than the regular dungeons.

Amoret sat in the corner of her stinking prison as far away from the slop trough as she could possibly get, leaning her back against the bricks and closely observing her three fellow inmates.

One woman with a wild mop of ginger hair was sitting on the rough, splintery wooden bed inconsolably weeping into her hands and wailing despairingly. Her clothes were dishevelled and grubby; largely from having lived in them without taking them off for a few days, but it did look as if she was often in that kind of state anyway. Amoret vaguely identified her as the old spinster who pedalled curiosities around the coffee houses and taverns in these parts, and she had obviously had the misfortune to appear in Rampick at the wrong time. She was undoubtedly a typical candidate for the paranoid inquisition's fervent purification mandate. And if she didn't stop crying soon she would also become a candidate for being repeatedly punched till she did, for Amoret didn't know how much more she could take of her pathetic lamentations.

The third woman in her cell stood at the tiny aperture in the wall barred by steel grating, her fingers hooked through the holes and her eyes gazing dolefully out at the pastel blue sky visible. She wore the trappings of a manual worker, perhaps being a farmhand or apprentice to a town artisan. She was one Amoret didn't recognize and so could only guess as to why she might be under suspicion (probably for yawning in church or something similarly ludicrous).

Just then the red draped figure of Charlatan Fugle glided into the cellblock.

And it was as if the Matronit herself had walked in bearing a pardon for every poor wretch imprisoned therein. The place erupted into a discordant vocal competition to beg her audience, each and all eager to put his or her case forward whether confessing, appealing or protesting. Banging and rattling the bars on their cages like deranged monkeys, their desperate faces pressed into the gaps to vie for precedence. Only Amoret stayed where she was, ardently refusing to grovel to one who represented her persecutors.

Fugle ignored their howling pleas best she could, for her mission there was not to redeem any of the damned. She was bringing someone new in.

At first Amoret thought it was yet another victim.

"More fodder for your inferno, Juju!" she bitterly scolded above the other racket.

Then she saw it was Pere.

Her heart leapt with joy at the sight of him and she scrambled up to push her way past the other two appellants clinging to the cell bars. But her excitement sank like a stone again when she considered why he would be coming in here.

"Pere! They haven't convicted you, have they?" she anxiously wanted to know.

"No. I came to see you," he thankfully said. He held out a hand and she took it and squeezed it tightly. "I bought you some nourishing food," he added, kindly offering a thick cut beef sandwich through the bars to her.

"What's this? A last meal?" she callously joked.

"I know how inferior the gaol food is. I used to cook it, remember," he tried making merry, only to have the refrain dry up in his throat. "You deserve better than that." Pere mournfully glanced round the cell. "And this."

"For what I did to you I deserve to be in this Erebus!" she cursed herself.

"Hush!" he soothed, stroking her face. "I forgive you, if you'll forgive me."

"You have nothing to be reproached for, darling."

"I will have tomorrow."

Amoret frowned at him. "Why?"

"I'm to be called as a witness at your trial."

"As a defence witness?" she vainly hoped.

"Prosecution," Pere whimpered, close to tears. "I'm so sorry!"

Amoret blinked as if just waking from a dream. "I meet my death tomorrow, then."

"There was nothing I could *do!*"

"You were my only hope, Pere," she numbly uttered, releasing her grasp on him. "I felt they might ... just *might* listen to me with you on my side. What a *fool!*"

"Oh, Amy! They twisted my words! I told them the truth and they made it what they wanted to hear! I couldn't save you! I couldn't save myself!"

"What do you mean?"

"I'm to be sent to Farren Eyrie for meditative realignment."

"*Indoctrination?* Those damned narrow-minded *bitches!*"

"It is nothing to what you face," Pere dismissed his own penalty. "If only I could've done *something!*"

"Don't upset yourself," she consoled. "There was nothing you could do. Their minds are already made up. The trials are just a farcical show! Examples to the rest, reminding them to toe the line or else!"

"Your trial will be as fair as can be, My Child. You have my word," Fugle optimistically projected. She wasn't completely convinced herself that the proceedings would serve any true moral justice, since political expediency featured too prominently for righteousness to play a significant part. But her religious convictions bound her to the Zoetic Church, so she would be in allegiance with it the whole distance. She believed this was no time for procrastination; this was a time to pick sides or get caught up in the middle like the unfortunate wretches languishing in this prison.

"Who asked you, Juju?" Amoret rudely snarled. "What's your affair here, anyway? Come to gloat at the condemned? To congratulate yourself for being on the winning side? Sanctimonious *bitch!*"

She spat at her.

Pere gasped in shock. As did the rest of the inmates, for they were certain this insult would drive the paragon of redemption from their desperate pleading and abandon them to their impending doom.

"Amy!" Pere cried. "It was Charlatan Fugle who brought me here and persuaded Corsned's guards to let me see you! I owe her a lot of gratitude! And so will you!"

"It's all right, Peregrine," Fugle said, producing a handkerchief from her cuff to wipe the spittle from her brow. "I would be angry and afraid if I were in Mistress Artemis's position."

"I make no apology!" Amoret asserted. "You'll have the pleasure of seeing me burn tomorrow, after all!"

"Perhaps not," Fugle said. "My business here is to talk with you, because I am to be your defence spokeswoman."

Amoret laughed, surprised to say the least. "A *Charlatan?* Speaking for a *Giaour?* Is Corsned looking for some inside information so she can trump up more charges?"

"I volunteered," Fugle conveyed. "No matter what you are labelled as amongst society, you are still fundamentally one of Gaea's children and you deserve a fair hearing the same as anybody else."

"And you think you'll make a difference, do you?"

"I can try."

"No thanks," Amoret declined. "There'll be enough trying going on tomorrow without you as well."

"Amy?" Pere questioned her decision.

"You're rejecting my help?" Fugle asked, confused.

"I'll manage alone."

"How?"

"I don't know, but I sure as Erebus won't be using the line of defence you were banking on," Amoret revealed. "Conversion."

"It's an option that will be offered you," the minister assured her. "And I recommend you consider it."

"I'd rather *BURN!*"

"Amy!" Pere entreated. "You can't *do this!*"

"You have sealed your own fate, My Child," Fugle melancholically lamented. "May Zoe have mercy upon your seity."

She went to bless her with the sign of the saltire, but Amoret furiously slapped her hand away, snarling, "Don't you *dare* put your damned hex on me! *Juju!*"

Pere just stood there and stared disbelievingly at Amoret.

"Come, Peregrine," the Charlatan induced him. "There is nothing more we can do here."

The boy turned and started to go with her.

Amoret grabbed his arm. "I love you, Pere. Always remember that."

"Do you?" he doubted.

"Of course!"

"Not enough to spare yourself so we may be together for the rest of our lives," he interpreted. "You'd rather throw your life away as a *martyr!* Your Uncle Semeion was right. You are a stubborn fool, Amy!"

"It's too much to ask!" she pleaded. "I would be changing a part of my very nature, not just the way I pray! I would be betraying my *people!* My *ancestors!* I would be betraying *myself!* Would you rather have me a feckless, spineless *convert?*"

"I'd rather have you alive in my arms," Pere earnestly declared, tears tracking down his cheeks. "But it's clear that you don't value me or what I feel as highly as you value your principles, and prefer to be sacrificed to them than betrothed to me."

He shrugged off her grip.

"Pere!" Amoret mewled, reaching for him again.

"When I weep inconsolably tomorrow it will be as much for myself as for you."

And with that he left.

"*Pere!*" she almost bayed.

But he was gone.

Leaning against the bars, she sobbed.

Suddenly, someone audaciously stole the sandwich from her grasp.

"*Hey!*" Amoret yelled, looking round angrily to see the culprit was Gaby Cailleach, obviously roused from her drunken slumber by the hullabaloo. She went after the thieving old hag, who had shuffled away into a corner to ravenously consume the stolen tasty snack. "Gimme that back!"

"*Arrgh!*" Gaby cried in pain, regurgitating what she'd torn off.

Something metal clinked on the cell floor and Amoret stooped down to sift it from amongst the half-chewed bread and meat. She held it in the palm of her hand to study it, oblivious to Gaby wolfing down the rest of the sandwich while her attention was distracted.

She immediately guessed what it signified.

A way out.

VIIII

It was Tertiday, Rupelian 17th, AD 4004.

And it was today she died.

They came for her at around 1:80 in the morning before breakfast had been served up. Two of Corsned's soldiers stormed in accompanied by Warden Farouche officiously rattling the gaoler's keys, and they threw open the door to Amoret's cell.

"Now we don't want any trouble," Farouche warned, presenting a set of shackles.

Brandishing batons, the soldiers lunged at Amoret, who was still huddled in the corner where she had retreated yesterday to sob her heart out. They roughly grappled her to her feet and shunted her to the Warden for the restraints to be painfully applied. She didn't attempt resistance because she had long since resigned herself to the inevitable demise awaiting her. She felt she had very few reasons left to live anyway.

Her solitary chance of escaping the infernal pyre meant recanting her inherent beliefs to swear servitude to a church that had persecuted her people; a prospect that revolted her to the pit of her stomach and offered no kind of existence worth the abhorrent shame.

The only berd she had ever truly loved had rejected her for her adherence to this very principle. And if that wasn't bad enough, he was himself due to be confined to an eyrie, where he was likely to spend the rest of his youth being indoctrinated into dogmatic altruism and maybe even end up sanctified as a Eunuch.

Without Pere and her faith there was no future.

Better to die a martyr.

They bundled her out into the corridor, shoving her and calling her derogatory names that somehow didn't carry the sting they once did. Fettered at the wrists and ankles, she shambled along, all the fight in her having dissipated into mindless, unquestioning compliance to their overbearing attitude. She just didn't care any more.

Amoret was pushed and prodded up the wooden stairs and likewise driven into the front office of the gaol-house. There she was forced to respectfully stand to attention before the Warden's desk, currently occupied by Judge Corsned, Adiaphoron Wanhope and a little weasel of a woman with wire-rimmed spectacles and greased-back hair who looked like some sort of clerk.

The authoritarians regarded her closely without speaking.

Corsned kicked off. "Amoret Artemis. You are hereby charged with murder, kidnap, assault and theft."

"Is this the trial?" Amoret asked, looking around the room, which just contained those mentioned and the Deputy Wardens, who were poised by the street door.

A soldier thumped her in the belly, causing her to cry aloud and double over.

Gauntleted hands intolerantly hauled her up straight again.

"You will be taken from here to the town hall and there you will be publicly tried for those crimes lodged against you," Corsned went on. "Prior to that event, I am bound by legislation to offer you the opportunity to make a full and frank confession to said crimes."

The Judge unfurled a ready drawn up, copperplate-scripted document and extended a reservoir pen for Amoret to sign it with. Amoret gawped at it dumbly. All charges being brought were neatly listed but written in so much switchback legal jargon that it was impossible for anyone other than a lawyer to decipher it. Since she neither had one nor was one she didn't bother reading it in detail.

"What happens if I sign that?"

"You hang instead of burn."

"Oh, great!" she sardonically cheered. "For a minute there I thought I'd be in the same damn boat!"

Another punch in the belly folded her up.

"If I had the time, Artemis, I'd torture a confession out of you," Corsned let her know.

"You'd be wasting the time you haven't got," Amoret cockily remarked.

She hawked up mucus and spat it onto the dotted line.

The soldiers waded in with their batons.

"I'll take that as a definite 'No'," Corsned said, carefully folding the paper and binning it.

Resurrected from the floor by her minders, Amoret wiped away blood streaming out of her nose with a shaky hand. "You can take it and shove it up your *FUD!*"

Down she went again.

"Then these crimes will be deliberated upon along with those aspects being considered by Adiaphoron Wanhope and Mistress Gombeen." Judge Corsned turned to her ecclesiastical associate. "Your Grace."

"My Child," Wanhope began, adjusting her bifocals and gazing steadily at Amoret, "as a practising Icarusian you are in breach of the Anti Thaumaturgy Laws passed by the Arval Counsel and are therefore deemed by the Zoetic Church as a Heretic. This reprehensible occultism is further compounded by the fact that you are a Giaour of Chimeran descent."

"What do you want? An apology?" Amoret flippantly countered, earning herself another crippling body blow from one of the soldiers.

"Of sorts," Wanhope admitted. "We prefer the term 'conversion', though. This will spare your miserable skin, but it is not a get-out clause. There are strict conditions to be observed."

158

Amoret got her wind then asked, "And what delights do they entail?"

"To begin with, absolute recantation of the arcane arts under the duress of corporal ordeal, followed by the purification of your seity via solitary confinement and the deprivation of all secular materialism and social interaction; so that we may have a clean slate to work with, as it were. Then you will take priestly tutelage and scholastically study the Incunabula scriptures for a period of ten years. Of course, all your worldly possessions and interests will be automatically forfeited to the Church."

"Physical *and* mental torture," Amoret mused. "There's a price for everything. Even salvation."

"Pray, what did you expect? A warm embrace and a wet kiss?" Wanhope asked. The other two chortled. "The Church is a bastion of moral and ethical enlightenment, and it does not take lightly the application of any gentile for orthodoxy."

"Yeah. I've often said the Zoetic Church is a real *bastion*."

Amoret reflexively cringed, anticipating another beating, which failed to come since the soldiers didn't understand her veiled allusion.

"I presume your answer is in the negative," Wanhope guessed.

"I'd rather freeze in Erebus," Amoret stated.

The Adiaphoron scowled at the mere mention of Icarusian iconography. "May Zoe have mercy upon your seity, pagan!"

"Mistress Gombeen," Corsned addressed the weasel-woman at the end.

"According to municipal records you have not made any contributions to the Frithgild surtax, Mistress Artemis," Gombeen imparted, consulting her papers. "In fact, you have not made contributions to *any* taxation levied by the Crown. Have you a personal exemption from the Queen herself, madam?"

Her familiars chuckled.

"I don't live in Brecham County," Amoret flatly informed her.

"The Frithgild is an individual taxation, madam, payable by every citizen in the land regardless of where they live. Our information comes directly from the Mandrake County municipal accounts, held by the Duchess of Brecham in the absence of Lady Mandrake's co-operation with Excelsior Montis."

"My home is on Mandrake's estate," she weakly excused herself instead. "She's exempt."

"No, no, madam," Gombeen irritatingly corrected. "Lady Mandrake only *thinks* she is exempt, when in fact she is just as liable as yourself. Many of her tenants willingly pay their dues as required. Whereas, I'm sorry to say, many others have been lulled into the same false sense of security as yourself, no doubt perpetuated by Lady Mandrake in her persistent 'rebellion' against the Crown. You should have covered your own back, madam, and not relied on her apparent benefice."

"So what's your deal?"

"No deal, madam," Gombeen said. "You can pay the total sum of your arrears including all other levies defaulted on, and both the Sceptral Judiciary and the Crown *may* favour you with leniency when your penalty is deliberated."

"How much?"

The tax inspector referred to her figures, "Forty three thousand five hundred and ninety one signats, forty seven ducats."

Amoret patted her clothes, shrugged and said, "Heck! Left my purse in my other britches."

This time the soldiers gave her a thrashing.

"All right! All right!" Corsned curtailed their enthusiastic discipline. "We want something left to burn for the crowd. Take her to the town hall."

The two soldiers unceremoniously hauled the punch-drunk prisoner onto her feet and dragged her towards the street door, which Attercop obligingly opened for them.

"Give my regards to thy uncle, Giaour," Attercop taunted Amoret as she was swept beyond the threshold.

Amoret looked back over her shoulder to challenge Attercop, but it was too late to concern herself with petty rivalry.

Her audience was waiting.

Outside, a mob of eager hecklers rose into full derisive,

scorning, abusive vociferation at her very appearance and instantly launched a hail of rotten fruit and mouldy vegetables, indiscriminately pelting her and her escorts. The soldiers tried warding off the missiles homing in on them personally, cursing the howling throng for their misjudged aim. Amoret had no such luxury, with her forelimbs restrained by the shackles. Incapable of self-defence, she had to endure the unbridled brunt of the attack, letting spoilt produce splatter her face and go into her eyes while less decayed rootstock bashed against her like small boulders.

She glanced around the sea of faces lining the main street, estimating that perhaps the entire populace of Rampick had turned out for the spectacle of her being frog-marched along the parade to certain death. Merchants had deserted their stores; artisans had abandoned their workshops; journeywomen had neglected their crafts; househusbands with babes in arms forsook their chores; farmers had left the land; shepherds had left their flocks in the crofts; even children had wagged the morning off school to hurl torrents of profanity at her.

Never before had she been so popular, nor so afraid.

They'd come to gloat, relieved that it wasn't them or their kin. They'd come to see the Giaour burn as a scapegoat to absolve them of their sins.

As she gauged the screaming horde she saw none of them possessed separate identities any more. They all wore the same face; one fraught with fear and demonized by ignorant hatred. A face she was well familiar with yet hadn't seen in such vast multitude.

It frightened her more than her fate.

In spite of this, Amoret bravely walked the gauntlet with head held high (when she wasn't flinching and ducking at incoming projectiles), unashamed and unrepentant before these persecutory bigots and their blind loathing.

The humiliating procession passed the parish church, where a gathering of the most loyal of its regular congregation lorded it over her as she went by; singing homage to the omnipotent prowess of their deity and showering her with handfuls of salt.

161

Accompanying their sanctimonious hymns was the resonating drone of the church's pipe organs emanating from the venting at the summit of the towering obelisk.

Eventually they entered the market square, which was literally packed with impatient onlookers vying for the best spot to view the execution that everybody seemed to have accepted as a foregone conclusion, delayed by the inconvenience of the trial. Peddlers of varying trades plied the milling mass with assorted wares, sating and amusing them temporarily while they discontentedly awaited the main attraction.

Amoret's gaze was irresistibly drawn to the centre area of the square, where an enormous wooden saltire mounted high on a stake rough-hewn from a tree trunk dominated the attention like an awful harbinger of doom.

Under the gesticulating direction of Widdy Loon-Slatt, soldiers and lumberjills darted back and forth between several parked carts and the cremation site, unloading kindling wood to stack up against the cross's support post. High above this hurly burly, carpenters were cobbling together a makeshift platform to access the edifice itself.

She watched with a morbid fascination, knowing she would be on there before the day was out.

The thought made her feel sick.

Her nerve wavered for a moment and suddenly conversion became a very appealing alternative to martyrdom. Not through any weakness within her character, but solely as a natural part of the instinctive will to live.

Steeling herself, though, she rediscovered her courage and put the disgusting worm of capitulation right out of her mind. She would not bend to these oppressive tyrants and give them the satisfaction of witnessing her do so. That would be worse than death; it would be life with no soul.

She was taken into the town hall then, a squat building situated at the rear of the square, its dressed stone façade marking it out as a structure of some communal significance amongst the plethora of half-timbered affairs surrounding it. This was to where the local dignitaries gravitated every so often to pool innovative ideas and useful input for the greater good of the town, but usually ended up drinking themselves stupid on fine wines and talking balderdash.

The courtroom was immediately discernible from the amount of people crammed into its limits. Normally it was a meeting chamber for the aforementioned personages of renown. For now, however, it had been shoddily converted, via pushing tables together and borrowing chairs from elsewhere, to accommodate the capacity crowd (the likes of which it seldom enjoyed in its other purpose, if ever).

Silence fell when the prisoner was brought in, save for the odd whispered slight.

She was led down the aisle between the public gallery seats, glares of enmity searing into her, and the soldiers forced her onto a bench at the far end of the room. They then sat either side of her, closely sandwiching her.

Some woman neatly attired in her best suit and collar, who looked like a quill-pusher of one description or another, stood up from her seat at the double bank of tables heading the proceedings. Officiously, she ordered, "Court in session. All rise!"

Everyone dutifully did except Amoret, until her guards made her observe the courtesy.

"Presiding, Her Worship Judge Thesmothete Corsned of Brecham County Sceptral Judiciary Bar; Her Grace Adiaphoron Golem Wanhope of the Brecham County Diocese; Chief Inspector of Municipal Revenue for Brecham County, Mistress Chalan Gombeen."

A door opened at the back of the room and the three introduced came to assume their positions at the top table, obviously having slipped out of the gaol-house and travelled to the town hall along the back streets whilst Amoret entertained the hoi polloi on her walkabout.

"Thank you, Madam Clerk," Corsned said, settling in.

"Be seated!" the Clerk told all present.

"The Accused will rise," Corsned demanded.

Begrudgingly, Amoret got up a second time.

"You are Amoret Artemis, lately resident at Selcouth folly on the Mandragora Estate in Mandrake County in the Realm of Montaigne, are you not?" the Judge formally affirmed.

"I am."

"Born Fourteenth of Aquitanian in the Year of Our Word Three Thousand Nine Hundred and Eighty One in an unknown location in Cadmia, were you not?"

"I was."

"Madam Clerk, would you please read the charges laid against the Accused," Corsned delegated.

"Your Worship," the Clerk said, bowing before continuing. "Amoret Artemis. You are hereby charged with the following crimes: Murder, two counts ..."

"What do you – "Amoret started to question.

"Silence!" Corsned curtly asserted, banging a gavel to stress her point. "Carry on, Madam Clerk."

"Heresy, four counts. Abduction, one count. Assault, six counts. Firearms offences, two counts. Theft, five counts. Tax evasion, seventy five counts," the Clerk finished.

Murmurs spreading through the assembly disrupted the quiet.

Corsned banged the gavel to subdue it before resuming. "How do you plead, Artemis?"

"Not guilty to all charges," Amoret sternly refuted the allegations.

"Let the records show the Accused's plea. You have refused representation offered to you by the parish Charlatan, have you not?"

"I have. I will defend myself."

"Let the records also reflect that, Madam Clerk."

"Your Worship," the Clerk acknowledged, speedily noting the details in shorthand.

"We shall begin with the tax evasion charges. Mistress Gombeen, if you please ..."

The inspector riffled her papers importantly, cleared her

throat and then said, "Mistress Amoret Artemis. The accounts of the Duchess of Brecham's tax collectors, to whom the task of recovering revenue in Mandrake County has fallen, show clearly that you are in debt to the Crown for unpaid levies over the last sixteen years, inclusive of Poll Tax, Wool Tax, Window Tax, Roof Tax, Chattel Tax, Income Tax and Excise Tax. At the varying rates of those dues over said period, the total amount calculated as owing equals forty two thousand five hundred and sixty nine signats, thirty four ducats."

A shocked gasp gripped the spectators.

It was a small fortune.

"In addition, there is non-payment of the Frithgild surtax newly introduced last year; the sum of which, plus forfeiture penalties, totals one thousand and twenty two signats and thirteen ducats. Adding this to the other defaulted payments brings the debt to a grand total of: forty three thousand five hundred and ninety one signats, forty seven ducats." Gombeen squinted at Amoret through her wire-rimmed spectacles. "You were offered the chance to discharge this debt earlier this morning, were you not?"

"I was," Amoret truthfully confirmed.

"And you refused."

"If I could've paid them I would've. Except the Frithgild. That's blood money."

Disgruntled jingoism erupted in the gallery.

Corsned banged the gavel, silencing it.

"You could have paid, Mistress Artemis, of your own free will. There was nothing stopping you contacting the Mandrake County Municipal Revenue office and registering yourself at any time during those sixteen years."

"When I was younger, I was led to believe Lady Mandrake was exempt from the taxation laws," Amoret feebly excused. "And my uncle and I were very poor when we first came to Montaigne."

"Why did you think Lady Mandrake was exempt from taxation, pray?" Gombeen persevered.

"We had heard she was a bit of a renegade noble, constantly

at odds with the monarchy, and we were also led to believe she'd declared Mandrake County as autonomous. We didn't want to upset her since she was about the only person who had shown us kindness by allowing us to stay on her estate rent free."

"I see ... and you believed these qualities afforded her special dispensation?"

"Yeah, madam."

"Unfounded though they were."

Amoret nodded her answer.

"Speak for the Clerk's records, Artemis," Corsned requested.

"Yeah," Amoret said aloud to Gombeen.

"I would like to call the witness Mistress Mag Jougs, revenue assessor for the Duchess of Brecham's estate," the inspector announced.

"You may be seated, Artemis," Corsned granted her. "Madam Bailiff."

The Brecham County Sheriff, who had been standing to one side, stepped forward and hollered, "Call Mistress Mag Jougs!"

At the front of the room near the double doors, Warden Farouche repeated the Sheriff's command. The sound of echoing footsteps prevailed in the corridor outside until Attercop and Skaines brought in a buxom woman in knee breeches and tailed coat. She trotted up the aisle alone and dutifully stood on the opposite side to Amoret, facing her. Jougs removed her hard felt hat and bowed to the presiding judges.

And Amoret vaguely recognized her.

"You are Mistress Mag Jougs, revenue assessor for the Brecham estate and County?" Gombeen asked her.

"I am, madam."

"Did you or did you not present yourself to Mistress Amoret Artemis here and her uncle Master Semeion Ducdame on the Eighteenth of Zanclean in Anno Dictum Three Thousand Nine Hundred and Eighty Eight?"

"I did, madam."

"Was this not for the required registration of taxable influx?"

"It was, madam," Jougs unhesitatingly claimed, though exactly how she was able to remember the events without referring to any form of notary was beyond Amoret because she couldn't herself; although, she had only been a little girl at the time.

"And did Mistress Artemis and Master Ducdame express any intention or obligation to register in their new homeland?" Gombeen pressed.

"They did not, madam."

"You mean they had been allowed into the Realm of Montaigne by the authorities as refugees and they *refused* to make any worthy contribution to the state's welfare, even after the liberal graciousness they'd had bestowed upon them?"

"'Twas so, madam. Master Ducdame fended me off with a rapier blade, threatening to run me through if I darkened their door again."

Dim recollection dawned on Amoret and she smirked at the memory of Jougs dancing through the door of Selcouth, her uncle close behind pranging the assessor's fat bottom with the tip of his foil.

"Did he, indeed? Not the sort of gesture you would expect a grateful immigrant to make, now is it?"

"No, madam," Jougs agreed.

"But of course, Mistress Artemis and her uncle were not strictly 'immigrants', were they, Mistress Jougs? As you later discovered."

"They were not, madam. I took the liberty of checking with the Immigration Office of Foreign Affairs at Excelsior Montis, and there was no record of an application made under the names of either Artemis or Ducdame."

"So, in fact, they were *illegal aliens*, were they not?" Gombeen concluded, slyly regarding the Accused.

"It appeared so, madam."

"I object!" Amoret blurted, bolting to her feet. "We were brought into this country under the guardianship of Lady Mandrake!"

"Yeah, but *illegally* all the same, madam!" Corsned shouted her down.

"*I was only SEVEN YEARS OLD!*" she yelled, rattling her shackles. "You can't hold *me* responsible for the actions of others!"

"Subdue that prisoner!" Corsned barked at the soldiers.

They did.

"Sadly for you, Artemis, we can," the Judge disappointed her. "Continue, Mistress Gombeen."

"Did you report this to your superiors and the Sceptral Judiciary, Mistress Jougs?" Gombeen resumed examining her witness.

"I did, madam."

"And was it acted upon?"

"'Twas not, madam. I was told there were a lot of 'political factors' at stake, owing to Lady Mandrake's influence abroad at that time."

"This was during the Cadmian Revolt, was it not?" Gombeen clarified.

"Indeed, madam," Jougs answered.

Amoret remembered this because the plunder of gold deposits in Cadmia by marauding Arimaspi was how she and her uncle first came into contact with Mandrake. Ever the opportunist, the rogue noble was involved in the murky and dangerous trade of double-dealing, simultaneously smuggling supplies for both the Arimaspi and the Cadmians along the Ruelle Canal, which she purposely built to facilitate her mineral mining enterprises in both those warring states. As a lucrative sideline she was also smuggling out any refugees who could afford to pay a princely sum.

Fleeing the persecution of Giaour communities at the hands of the conflicting partisans and invaders, Amoret and Semeion stowed away on one of the ore barges bound for the Arimaspian Gulf. Inevitably, they were discovered at port, but Mandrake herself was there to kindly stay the ship's captain from throwing them into the harbour. Taking pity on them, she put them aboard her personal vessel and sailed them to a new life in Montaigne.

"So, any action was shelved," the inspector assumed.

"Indeed, madam. Until it was forgotten."

"Thank you, Mistress Jougs."

"Artemis?" Judge Corsned said. "Would you care to cross-examine?"

"No, Your Worship," Amoret declined, seeing little point.

"You may step down, Mistress Jougs."

"That concludes my case for the Municipal Revenue Service," Gombeen wrapped up, tamping her documents into an ordered stack as Jougs left the chamber.

"Thank you, Mistress Gombeen. Due deliberation will be given to the evidence in concurrence with the other matters still outstanding," Corsned informed the court. "We will now move on to the charges of Heresy, for which Adiaphoron Wanhope will open the questioning. Rise for Her Grace, Artemis."

"My Child," Wanhope addressed the upstanding Amoret. "You are a practising Icarusian, are you not?"

"I am," Amoret firmly asserted.

Murmurs complaining of her brazen heathenism beset the gallery.

"You have imbibed of the blood of your icon, have you not?"

"Freely."

Shockwaves rippled through the onlookers.

"Even though knowing this was flouting the specific laws implemented by the Arval Counsel of the Zoetic Church?"

"Because of them," Amoret flagrantly antagonized.

Some of the spectators got very agitated at this remark, shouting and threatening to kill Amoret before she got anywhere near the bonfire outside. Corsned banged the gavel several times but was unable to quell the disturbance.

"Remove those people!" she demanded instead.

Warden Farouche and her Deputies obeyed, wrestling the troublemakers out of the courtroom.

"And anyone else who causes affray within this court will be held in contempt!" the Judge sternly reprimanded the public present. She turned to the Adiaphoron, saying, "Pray, continue, Your Grace."

"Earlier this morn you were offered the opportunity to convert to the divine enlightenment of the Zoetic faith," Wanhope went on. "Which you refused."

"I did," Amoret said proudly.

"Your precise words being 'I would rather freeze in Erebus'."

"I would."

"Well, I am sorry to disappoint you, Artemis, for it very much sounds to me as if you will burn in the sky by the weight of this unashamed blasphemy. You are quite clearly an unrepentant pagan and Giaour of Chimeran descent." Muted agreement issued forth from the gallery. "I call the witness Master Peregrine Farouche," the Adiaphoron invoked.

Amoret's heart leapt at the mention of his name and she hastily scoured the courtroom with her eyes to see where Pere was, for she hadn't spotted him when she was initially brought in.

"Be seated, Artemis," Corsned required.

The soldiers dragged her down onto the bench.

"Madam Bailiff."

"Call Master Peregrine Farouche!" the Sheriff reiterated.

Pere materialized out of the room where the three judges had come from, Charlatan Fugle escorting him to the correct position. He was plainly dressed in the usual russet tunic he wore when skivvying in the gaol-house kitchen. His fresh, youthful complexion was unadulterated by cosmetic enhancement and his golden hair flowed over his shoulders.

Head bowed, he threw Amoret a fleeting sideways glance and killed her with that single look.

So sweet and innocent was he.

She ached for him.

"Master Farouche, My Child," Wanhope began. "You are a good and faithful acolyte of the Zoetic doctrine, are you not?"

Pere didn't reply; he just nervously eyed the gathering.

"Pray, speak, My Child. You have nothing to fear," the Adiaphoron gently coerced.

Charlatan Fugle tentatively placed a hand on the boy's arm, reassuring him.

"I … I am, Your Grace," he shyly uttered.

"Adherent to the letter of the Incunabula like all devout Zoetics?"

"Yeah, Your Grace."

"You purge your seity from the rigours of the day by reciting the Purgatory Prayer every night before you go to bed, do you not, My Child?"

"I do, Your Grace."

"And you accept no false gods or icons into your heart?"

"No, Your Grace."

"How then do you explain your recent transgression, when you were inveigled by Artemis here into an intimate relationship?" Wanhope relentlessly probed.

"I thought … I thought I loved her, Your Grace," Pere frankly answered. "I thought she could help me escape to adventure and new horizons."

"Ah … yeah. Such desires are within us all at your age, My Child. And did Artemis live up to these expectations?"

"No, Your Grace."

"What did she turn out to be instead?"

"A liar."

"*Pere!*" Amoret cried, leaping up.

The attendant soldiers slammed her onto the bench again.

"Hold your tongue!" Corsned admonished, banging the gavel. "You will have your chance soon enough, Artemis!"

Order restored, the Adiaphoron pursued her line of questioning. "Did she tell you she was a Giaour before you began the relationship with her, My Child?"

"Yeah."

"Pretty damn honest for a *liar!*" Amoret interjected.

Corsned hammered the table again.

"I won't warn you again, Artemis! Any further interruptions and we'll be adding contempt to your list of charges!"

"Is that going to make a difference?" she angrily countered.

Ignoring her, Wanhope asked Pere, "And did this worry you, as a pious and righteous Zoetic?"

"A little at first, but I saw illicit excitement in it too," the boy confessed.

"A factor no doubt played upon by Artemis," Wanhope surmised.

"I think she found it somewhat thrilling to be corrupting a devout."

"*Pere!* That's not *true* and you *know it!*" Amoret abrasively contested, causing him to shrink back in fright.

"Damn you, Artemis!" Corsned ranted. "Another word and these proceedings will take place in your *absence!* Do I make myself clear?"

"Yeah," Amoret said, relinquishing the point. "Your Worship."

They'd done a real job on Pere. The thought that perhaps he was bargaining her in exchange for getting off the hook himself flitted through her mind, then she privately cursed herself for thinking him capable of such spite.

"In that case, I presume she did all she could to bring your faith into degradation," Wanhope said. "For example, plying you with the foul communion the Icarusians call Ichor."

Gasps resounded amongst the spectators.

"She never forced me to drink it," Pere defended.

Wanhope glanced at Corsned and vice versa.

"But she *did* influence you, did she not?" the Adiaphoron rephrased.

"Yeah, she did."

"Tell the court of a particular incident that occurred at Mandragora Demesne, My Child."

He looked to Fugle for support and she smiled at him.

"Amy ... that is, Mistress Artemis and I were at Mandragora Demesne enjoying the hospitality of Lady Mandrake after a series of events that had led us to seek refuge under her roof. There we met a Countess Ahithophel from Paladin, who was a member of the Antichthon Confederacy ..."

Murmurs ensued.

The boy carried on. "She, like Mistress Artemis, was an Icarusian, and while we were dining they encouraged me to imbibe Ichor."

Gasps.

"Madam Bailiff," Wanhope said to Faubourg. "Show the court Exhibits A and B."

Faubourg rummaged among a quantity of carefully labelled items arranged on the Clerk's table. Selecting two, she held them aloft. The first was an old, battered pewter goblet engraved with elaborate designs. The second was a loop-headed cross.

"Exhibit A in the Bailiff's left hand is an Ichor Grail, used during the communion ritual of the Icarusians to *drink* the *blood* of their god. Exhibit B is an Ankh, the symbol of the Icarusian creed, also utilized in the ritual," Wanhope educated those unfamiliar with the articles, which was virtually everybody other than herself and Amoret. "They were found at Selcouth folly, the home of Artemis and her uncle."

Many spectators seemed disgusted at the very sight of the objects.

"What other blasphemy did they try to instil in you, My Child?" the Adiaphoron enquired, returning to the matter in hand.

"They likened their communion to the Primordial Renascence."

A lot of those present crossed themselves with the saltire and muttered terrible oaths towards the perpetrator of this abominable slander.

"Well, I think that covers the four counts of Heresy cited. The fact Artemis is an unrepentant Giaour and pagan, admitted to before this court by her own blasphemous tongue. The fact she wilfully corrupted a young berd and led him astray from his otherwise unfaltering pursuit of the Zoetic faith. The fact she wilfully flouted the express forbiddance of Icarusian practices by the Arval Counsel's Anti Thaumaturgy Laws, admitting to 'freely' imbibing in the abhorrent filth known as Ichor. And the fact she did blaspheme against the Zoetic Church still further, implanting the evil seed into this young berd's mind that her diabolical idolatry can be *assimilated* to the *divine sacramental rites* of the *orthodox creed!*" Wanhope glared down her nose at Amoret. "May you burn in the sky, Giaour!"

"Do you rest your case, Adiaphoron?" Corsned troubled her.

"I do, Judge."

"Your witness, Artemis," she invited the Accused.

Amoret stood, her eyes fixed on Pere, who cast his gaze to the floor to avoid hers.

"Master Farouche," she casually commenced, shuffling towards him.

"Do not approach the witness, prisoner!" Corsned churlishly disallowed.

The guardswomen pulled her back to the bench.

Unruffled, Amoret started once more. "Master Farouche ... during the course of our intimate relations, did I ever bully or harry you into doing anything you didn't want to do?"

He glanced at her then said, "No. Except ..."

"Yeah?"

"Except stay here in Rampick. You made me do that."

"You wanted desperately to leave this town, didn't you, Pere?" she pressed him. "To escape the tyranny of your mother."

"*THAT'S A LIE!*" Warden Farouche bellowed from the front of the room.

"Warden!" Corsned chastised her, banging the gavel. "Kindly keep your own counsel! Or I will have you *removed!*"

"Begging your pardon, Your Worship," the Warden humbly apologized.

"My mother is not a tyrant," Pere contradicted. "What she wants for me is not the same as what I wish for myself."

"And what was she planning for your future?"

"Marriage."

"In other words, the protraction of the drudgery you are currently trapped in and so much despise," Amoret expanded. "Isn't that how you see the prospect of marriage?"

"Yeah," he said, bowing his head in shame.

"When you met me, what led you to believe that I could break this cycle of hopeless yearning to throw off the chains burdening you?"

"It was because you were a Giaour."

174

The spectators mulled this over, disconcerted.

"You came to me *because* I was a pagan to your religion? Your faith couldn't offer you any way out of your strife, so you sought salvation in a heathen?"

"I knew Giaours were nomadic," Pere rectified. "I thought … I thought you and your uncle would be moving on to the continent … especially with the blood purge coming."

Judge Corsned huffed at his use of that term, but let it pass in favour of getting this trial over and done with as soon as possible.

"So you *used* me?" Amoret cuttingly summarized.

"No! It wasn't like that!"

"That's the way it's coming across!"

"*Pah!* And *you* didn't use *me*, I suppose? Don't say you weren't flattered by a young berd looking twice at *you!*"

"Yeah? I could do better than *you* in a *bordello*, boy!"

"*Desist! Desist!*" Judge Corsned demanded, pummelling the table with the gavel. "This is a *courtroom!* No place for *lovers' tiffs!* Kindly stick to your questions, Artemis!"

Inhaling a deep breath, Amoret calmed herself before continuing. "Let's recap. You wooed me as a lover because my nomadic heritage attracted you and you thought it could be a means to an end, right?"

"*You* did all the wooing as I recall," Pere corrected, not wanting himself portrayed to the court as a trollop.

"Okay, okay. But you don't deny you had a motive for accepting my advances."

"No."

"But I refused to take you away from all this, didn't I, Pere?"

"Yeah."

"And what were my reasons?"

"You were *afraid* … for both of us," he answered. "Because of the blood purge and the coming crusade. Because you're a Giaour."

"Not because I'm a liar, right?"

"You lied to me by fobbing me off with empty promises," Pere laboured the point. "But I understand your reasons for doing that now, and I agree that they were justified fears. In all other respects you've been true to me, though I can't condone some of the actions you have taken to get your own way."

They stared at each other.

She would never have believed it of him, to be so set against her.

"Are you done, Artemis?" Corsned asked.

"No further questions."

"You may step down, Master Farouche."

Pere gladly did, but only moved to the foremost row of the gallery seats. Amoret did not take this as a promising sign, for it suggested to her that he would be called to testify on the other charges levelled at her.

"We have thus far heard the case for the charges of tax evasion and Heresy," Corsned briefly reviewed. "Now I will personally present the evidence for the remaining felonious charges. The first of which will be the two counts of murder cited. The Accused will rise." She diverted her attention away from her documentation and settled it on Amoret. "Artemis, you are hereby charged with the premeditated murders of both Mistress Avoirdupois Alecost, former landlady of The Creaking Meat Tree public house, and your own kin Master Semeion Ducdame."

Amoret gasped, genuinely shocked.

Pere clapped a hand to his mouth, equally devastated by this news, and cried, "*No!*"

"This second charge has been brought relatively recently owing to the discovery of fresh evidence just yesterday," Corsned informed the court. "Master Ducdame's body was found dumped in a pond not more than a few metres distant from Selcouth folly. And as my first witness I would like to call the officer of the law who made the discovery, Deputy Warden Caitiff Attercop. If you please, Madam Bailiff."

The guards reminded Amoret to sit.

"Call Deputy Warden Caitiff Attercop!" Faubourg summoned.

Snapping her head round, Amoret watched Attercop come strutting self-importantly up the gallery aisle, clutching the lapels of her coat as if she were posing for a portrait.

She remembered the Deputy's parting remark when she had left the gaol-house that morning: *'Give my regards to thy uncle, Giaour.'*

"Deputy Warden Attercop," Judge Corsned addressed once her witness was in place. "Can you tell the court precisely how you came upon the body of Master Semeion Ducdame?"

"I can, Y'r Warship," Attercop obliged. "My self, Deputy Warden Skaines, Watch Warden Farouche and the County Sheriff had perceeded to Selcouth folly in order that we might search it for everdince. I found the corpse of Master Ducdame dumped in a pond some thirty odd metres away from the building."

"And how did you come to be that far away from the site?"

"Call of nature, Y'r Warship."

"I see. And how long had Master Ducdame been lying there?"

"The apoceth'ry, Mistress Wiccan Mountebank ..."

"Whom I will be calling later for confirmation purposes," the Judge notified the court.

"She examined his remains and estermated he had been in the water for nigh on three day or more."

"What conclusion, if any, would you draw from this, Deputy, in view of your experience as an officer of the law?"

"Only one, Y'r Warship."

"Which is?" Corsned was intrigued to learn.

"That he were brutally slain by his niece Amoret Artemis and gotten rid of."

"*LIAR!*" Amoret suddenly and raucously roared, leaping to her feet. "*YOU KILLED HIM!*"

"*Subdue that prisoner!*" Corsned yelled, beating the hammer.

The soldiers grabbed Amoret. But the bondage restraining her wrists unexpectedly came adrift at this crucial moment, partially liberating her. She violently swiped one of the guards in the face with the manacles and chains, knocking her out cold, and then she grappled the opposite into a headlock. Like greased lightning, she unsheathed her captive's holstered pistol and slammed the soldier onto the floorboards.

Attercop and the Sheriff were just reaching for their shooters.

Unfortunately for them, Amoret got the drop on them.

"*Payback time, Attercop!*" she raged, cocking two of the flintlock's four hammers.

"*AMY!*" Pere squealed, launching himself from his chair, only to be pulled back by Charlatan Fugle.

"*Fico!*" Attercop whimpered, stumbling backwards.

The gun went off.

And everybody in the room hit the deck.

Including Attercop, narrowly eluding the 10mm twins that almost evacuated the contents of her skull onto the wall behind her.

"*Amy!*" Pere beseeched, Fugle still preventing him rushing to her side.

"*Let go of him, Juju!*" Amoret shouted, training the pistol on the minister. She shuffled over to them, the leg irons restricting her gait.

Fugle did as bid and Pere ran to embrace his lover.

Warden Farouche and Skaines, scrambling down the aisle on all fours, drew their weapons ready to do battle with the emancipated recidivist. The Sheriff and Attercop too were quickly recovering and preparing to dispense justice.

Amoret had no other choice.

She spun Pere round, hooked her arm about his neck and jammed the pistol's barrels to the side of his head.

"Amy?" he worriedly queried.

"Stay back!" she cautioned the courtroom occupants in general, wild eyes trying to keep everyone with a firearm under surveillance. "*I'll kill him!*"

"You're not making things any better for yourself, Artemis!" Corsned placated from under her table.

"Shuddup!"

"You're *DEAD*, Giaour!" Warden Farouche guaranteed. "Whether you harm my boy or not, I will *KILL* you!"

"Lose the boom tubes!" Amoret commanded, having no truck with bravado. "Or he dies!"

"She be bluffing, Warden!" Attercop professed. "She b'ain't got the guts!"

Proving the validity of her threat, Amoret cocked the other two hammers of the pistol.

"*Amy!*" Pere cried.

"*Lose 'em! All of you!*"

"Do as she says!" Faubourg instructed her subordinates, surrendering her sidearm first.

Begrudgingly, the rest followed suit.

"In the name of Zoe Almighty!" Warden Farouche swore, tears welling up in her eyes. "I will hunt you down and *kill you*, Giaour!"

"C'mon, kid!" Amoret inveigled Pere, dragging him back towards the room from where he had been called. "Move it!"

"Amy! You're *hurting me!*"

"I'll do more than that in a minute, you whining brat! I'll put your brains on your *mother's shirt!*"

"Damn you to the sky, Giaour!" Mistress Farouche sobbed.

They disappeared into the room and slammed the door.

"Here," Amoret said, passing the pistol to Pere while she wrenched the key round full circle in the lock then grabbed a chair, which she rammed under the doorknob at an angle. "That'll hold 'em for a minute."

"Oh, Amy!" Pere sighed. "For a moment I didn't think you were going to use the key I gave you in the gaol-house. Skaines was oiling the shackles and I guessed they were meant for you, so I stole the spare key while she wasn't looking and hid it in the sandwich."

"Thievery, eh? Whoever taught you that?" she sarcastically wondered, busy divesting herself of the leg irons with the aid of said key.

"I was on tenterhooks all the time, praying you'd get free."

"For a moment I wasn't going to use it," she revealed. "I'd

179

almost resigned myself to martyrdom. Until that about Uncle Semeion came up ..."

She stifled a tear.

"Oh, Amy," he tenderly sympathized. "That was a real blow. Do you think it was Attercop who ... "

"Killed him? Yeah. Either her or her idiot sidekick Skaines."

"Bandits, maybe."

"Nah. I reckon they happened across Semeion when he left us that day, and knowing Semeion he probably gave 'em what for, so they killed him."

Scraping and thudding at the door alerted them to the urgency of their situation again. Amoret hastily hurtled to the single sash window in the antechamber and heaved it open. It baulked and groaned in its runners, delaying them even more than they'd already delayed themselves. All the while, the noises and voices behind the door were getting louder as efforts increased to break through.

Exerting her strength, Amoret managed to finally shove the window upwards, facilitating their emergency exit. She leaned out into the back street, glancing this way and that to check for any soldiers hovering around.

The coast was clear.

"C'mon," she beckoned Pere on, relieving him of the pistol.

She lifted him through the window.

Then she discharged the gun's last loads into the wall near the door, causing much panic in the adjacent chamber and dissuading pursuit a little more, but she knew it wouldn't be long before they realized she'd expended her quota of shot. Tossing the depleted weapon onto the floor, she clambered out into the street where Pere was anxiously waiting for her.

"This way," she said, snatching his hand and trailing him southwards.

"We're heading round to the market square?" he doubted her choice.

"Excellent cover," she explained. "We can lose ourselves in the crowd."

Just then a window in the town hall fled open.

"*There they are!*" a voice hollered after them.

"Fico!" Amoret cursed, glimpsing Faubourg raising her pistol. A shot rang out and Amoret collapsed, screaming in pain.

"*AMY!*" Pere screamed with her, freaked out at the sight of arterial scarlet pouring from her thigh.

"Holy Icarus! She got me!"

"I winged her!" Faubourg triumphantly proclaimed.

"No!" Pere helplessly denied, crouching over her wound and attempting to stem the flow with his hands. He only succeeded in smearing it over himself. "*NO! Please, Zoe! NOT NOW!*"

"It's a graze!" Amoret bravely played it down, grabbing his wrists and firmly pressing his hands onto the injury.

"*A graze?*" Pere fractiously twittered.

"Don't worry about it," she said, quickly ripping a strip off her begrimed shirt and improvising a dressing.

"*Don't worry?*"

"Stay right where you are, Giaour!" the Sheriff was advising as she climbed into the street. "If you know what's good for you!"

"C'mon, Amy!" Pere cajoled, pulling her up. "*C'mon!*"

Shambling to her feet, Amoret lurched on at his behest.

Another shot buzzed past as they cornered into the alley flanking the town hall. Then a third sprayed shards of brick onto them. They floundered along fast as they could, the pattering footsteps of their pursuers gaining at an alarming rate.

Coming out into the square, they forged straight into the mob, desperately trying to mingle.

"*STOP THAT GIAOUR!*" Warden Farouche could be heard bellowing in their wake.

People began taking notice.

"*STOP HER! SHE'S A CONVICTED HERETIC!*"

"'Oi!" one burly woman challenged them, realizing they were the quarry.

Amoret lunged at her and smacked her on the nose. She put the opponent out but also fell over herself from the sheer momentum of her swing.

That was it then.

The mob closed ranks, and hands fell upon Pere to yank him clear as fists and feet trounced Amoret.

"*NO!*" Pere screamed hysterically, wriggling to get loose but failing miserably. "*NO! NO!*"

He could only watch, blubbering, as both physical and verbal abuse rained down onto his beloved. Empathically feeling in his heart every blow landed. "*NOOooooo!*"

At last his mother, Faubourg, Attercop and Skaines broke up the party, warding off the assailants and reclaiming Amoret for themselves.

Judge Corsned arrived soon after, her entire retinue of soldiers at her heel.

"Well done, ladies," she commended. "Take her to the apothecary, get her cleaned up and patched up, then we can reconvene. Though, I fear consideration for re-trial may be necessary."

Discontented tumult swelled through the crowd.

"Get back!" Attercop and Skaines harried the masses.

"No, Your Worship," Warden Farouche disobeyed.

"What was that, Warden?" asked the Sheriff, surprised.

"Do I hear insurrection, madam?" Corsned indignantly enquired.

"This Giaour has proved her guilt enough," Farouche reckoned. "She burns today, and she burns *now!*"

"No, Mama!" Pere importuned her favour. "No!"

"A court of law decides her guilt, not *you*, Farouche!" the Judge spelt out. "Now take her to the apothecary, damn you! And I will endeavour to forget this incident."

The immediate circle disputed her authority and started jostling her.

"Hold, you scoundrels!" Faubourg chided, drawing her truncheon and striking at those within reach. "Hold, I say!"

Farouche pointed her pistol at Corsned.

In hesitant response, the chaperone soldiers went for their artillery. But before they could clear holster, the crowd restlessly swelled forwards again, swamping them and sucking them into its turgid underbelly where they couldn't jeopardize the will of the people.

"Mama!" Pere gasped.

"*I'm* the law in this town, Judge."

"Farouche!" Faubourg chewed her out. "What on Gaea do you think you're *doing?* Put that thing away this *instant!*"

"Too late now, Sheriff."

Attercop jabbed her Thunderbus into the Viscountess's midriff and disarmed her.

"This is lynch mob justice, Farouche!" Corsned reminded these rogues as Skaines similarly held her to ransom. "And I'll see *you* lynched for it!"

"Take them away!" the Warden directed her minions.

"Oh, Mama!" Pere lamented, distressed at the magnitude of what his mother had done.

"Don't worry," she consoled. "I've got the backing of the whole town. I'm their elected peacekeeper, and I'm doing exactly what they want me to do."

She pulled Amoret up off the ground.

"C'mon, Giaour! You've an appointment … with *death!*"

X

The drum thudded, sombre and monotonous, heralding the coming capital punishment.

Widdy Loon-Slatt fumbled in her britches pocket, removed her watch and checked the time. The hands read it as 2:37. She frowned, shook it, and then held it to her ear to make sure it was still ticking. It was working perfectly well, so she assumed it was correct since she had set it by the parish church clock whilst on her way to the market square that very morning.

She hadn't reckoned on the Judge finishing the trial at least until well into the afternoon, but the drummer-girl was now beating out her cue to get the bonfire prepared for the official lighting up. In response, Loon-Slatt frantically hurried her helpers to get stacking the wood on a bit sharpish while she scrambled up the ladder onto the platform to get a better view of the death march.

When she'd gained this advantageous height she surveyed the scene in its entirety, marvelling at the number of self-righteous citizens who'd turned out specially to witness this event. Most of them were probably too scared not to attend in case it counted against them as reasonable doubt in respect of their character.

Some of the residents and business establishments with property girding the market arena had rented their upper storeys to avid enthusiasts keen to get a really superb view. There was even somebody in a cape cavorting about on one of the house roofs directly opposite, lugging something cumbersomely lengthy, which Widdy guessed might be a telescope. Now that was dedication.

Shifting her gaze to the town hall, she saw the tipstaffs Farouche, Attercop and Skaines strutting along behind the drummer. They were keeping a close guard on their prisoner to protect her from the jeering mob's malicious intent toward the scapegoat; but despite the animosity expressed, the vast throng respectfully parted at their approach to let the entourage pass through.

Oddly, there was no sign of the Judge or the Adiaphoron, both of whom always accompanied the condemned to the cross as a matter of course; the former to oversee the legal procedure of the sentence and the latter to administer the Saving Grace. There weren't any soldiers with them either; only Charlatan Fugle and Farouche's boy brought up the rear of the party. This was very irregular to the usual practice, but as long as the warrant was in good order it was no concern of hers how the condemned was delivered to her.

Loon-Slatt cackled and rubbed her hands together.

She fleetly descended the ladder and went to monitor the progress on the laying of the fire bed below. On the whole it was nearly complete. A few more cords of lumber remained to be built in but that could be done during the formalities. Provided the actual pyre itself was ready for torching at the specified moment then things would go smoothly, and she'd have another faultless execution under her belt.

Snatching a coiled rope off one of the lumber carts, she scurried over to receive the procession.

"Warden," Widdy greeted Farouche when they reached centre stage. "Where be the Judge and the Adiaphoron?"

"Mistress Loon-Slatt," Farouche said. "They were … unavoidably detained … we are to proceed in their absence. This Giaour is to be executed forthwith."

"Have you got yon warrant?"

Farouche showed her the business end of her pistol. "This is all the warrant I need."

"Right," Loon-Slatt caught on quickly. "What happens now?"

"Well, you can either do your duty or you can step aside and let us do it for you."

"Will I still be paid my gratuity?" she asked, stroking her bristled chin as she considered her options.

"Yeah. The town will pay you," the Warden promised.

"Then I says that be all the warrant *I* needs." She rubbed her hands again then paused. "Who'll be giving the Saving Grace if the Adiaphoron b'ain't doing it?"

"Charlatan Fugle," Farouche nominated.

"I'm afraid I can't, Warden," Fugle protested, her conscience pricked by this anarchic insurgence. "This is an illegal execution you are contemplating. Tantamount to *murder!* I cannot be a party to this!"

"In case you've forgotten, Charlatan, this gy brutally slew a member of this community!" Farouche said, motioning to Amoret, who hung limply between Attercop and Skaines, bruised and bleeding. "Not to mention her own *kin!*"

"Sinking to that level ourselves doesn't make us better!" Fugle argued. "If anything it makes us *worse!* I'm merely here for the guardianship of your son's fidelity, and I prefer to remain in that capacity alone."

"Then *I* will do the honours, Warden!" a pompous voice volunteered.

Wanhope floated forth from the crowd.

"Your Grace," Farouche said, aghast. "Are you sure?"

"I am an ordained priestess," Wanhope sniffily stated the obvious, as if conversing with simpletons. "Besides which, I cannot send even an unholy Giaour to the sky without satisfying myself that I have done everything in my power to redeem."

"We would be most grateful, Your Grace," Farouche ingratiated.

"Right, that's that sorted," Loon-Slatt impatiently concluded. "Let's get her up yon ladder and get a nice blaze going."

"I don't think she can climb," Skaines said, hefting her share of Amoret's listless weight.

"Tell you what. I'll go up first then I'll toss this here rope down and you tie her on this end," Widdy proposed, selecting Attercop for that particular task. She gesticulated to Skaines, suggesting, "You can come with me and give me a hand with the pulling, big, strong lass like you."

Her plan was generally accepted as sound.

Enthused, she grinned and vanished up the ladder like a rat up a drainpipe. Skaines heaped Amoret onto her partner and followed after the masked woman, though at a comparatively slower pace.

Within the minute the rope came dangling from above and Attercop wound it round Amoret's waist, tying it off securely with a bowline knot. When she'd done this she signalled to Loon-Slatt that the load was prepared for hoisting.

Once Skaines had squirmed her obesity onto the platform and regained her breath, she joined Loon-Slatt, taking up the slack behind her. They started systematically heaving their prize catch aboard, operating so slickly in unison that Amoret practically flew upwards to meet them.

Pere watched the rapid, jerky elevation of his beloved, much as he could through the incessant tears blurring his vision. Part of him prayed the rope wouldn't break and let her plunge to certain destruction whilst another part prayed it would to spare her this public disgrace.

"Be strong, Peregrine," Charlatan Fugle bolstered him, wrapping him in a soothing embrace. "Survival of the fittest is Zoe's will."

"This isn't anything to do with any god!" he furiously shunned her. "This is *blind hatred!*"

He went to appeal to his mother for a reprieve. Although he knew it would probably be of little use, he felt he could not rest until he had tried every avenue, as the Adiaphoron had said about doing everything in her power to placate even the most implacable.

"Mama! You can't *do* this!" he pleaded with her, tugging at her sleeve to distract her from the ensuing spectacle. "It's a *travesty!*"

"It's the will of the people, boy," she emptily dismissed his entreaty. "It's the will of Zoe."

"No it's *NOT!*" Pere exclaimed so fiercely his mother looked at him dazed. "It's *your* will!"

"I am the appointed preserver of law and order in Rampick!" she enunciated. "I have my duty to this parish, which includes dealing with thieves and murderers!"

"Your *duty?* You neglected that the minute your own narrow-minded vengeance made you threaten a *Judge* with a pistol! And this …" He ripped the badge from her doublet and brandished it like an unholy object. "This means *nothing* any more!"

He threw it in the dirt.

She swiped him a flat handed smack across the face.

It was the first time she had *ever* really hit him with malevolence.

Pere clutched his cheek, shocked, and stared into her eyes. A bemused, painful realization at what she'd just done shone brightly there.

"Charlatan!" Mistress Farouche shouted, avoiding her son's plaintive gaze. "I thought you were taking charge of this boy?"

"Yeah, Warden," Fugle said, stepping forwards, her eyes inflamed with indignant detestation of what she'd seen happen.

"Then keep your word, madam, and keep him in hand!"

The Charlatan led the lad away, making no riposte. In her mind, however, she was saying plenty.

On the platform, Loon-Slatt and Skaines were busy slicing their hauling rope into lengths with a knife and lashing Amoret to the giant saltire, affixing a limb of hers to each shaft of the X-shaped pillory.

Meanwhile, Adiaphoron Wanhope was ascending the ladder as best she could in her flowing robes. Behind her, Attercop was lending supportive accompaniment and simultaneously hoping the portly priestess didn't fall, else she'd be fetched off too and more than likely squashed. After much panting and labouring on the Adiaphoron's part, they finally gained the plinth where Loon-Slatt helpfully hiked Her Grace on by hooking an arm between her legs and bunking her up as if she were a sack of potatoes.

"My Child," Wanhope said breathlessly, adjusting her garbs and strolling dignifiedly as possible to the trussed convict. "You are an unholy abomination of Chimeran descent. A *Giaour*. Born of despicable lust and incest. A *mistake* of Mother Nature. A living *abortion!* Yet I humbly come to you to grant you the rite of the Saving Grace."

She took the jewel laden silver saltire hanging around her neck, kissed it then hesitated.

"Could you ... erm ..." she said to Loon-Slatt, flapping her hand indicatively towards Amoret's lolling head.

"Ooar, Y'r Grace," obliged Loon-Slatt, moving to grasp Amoret's blood matted hair and yank her head upright so the priestess could apply the saltire to the brow.

"Sacred Zoe Almighty, immarcescible provost of divine luminescence and radiance, we beg your indulgence in this mortal's termination. May this mortal's life have amounted to enriching and evolving the great scheme all humankind endeavours to serve and improve upon with each transient generation. May your incandescent benefaction smile upon this mortal's termination and find purpose still for the corporeal husk. May more bounteous produce issue henceforth from this mortal's termination now your will be served. Aten."

"Aten," Loon-Slatt, Skaines and Attercop repeated in harmony, miming the saltire on their torsos with their index fingers.

"Nazar!" Amoret croaked in retaliation.

"Unworthy heathen!" Wanhope chided.

She flounced off.

Widdy leaned in towards Amoret's face and said, "How'd you like your stake, Giaour? Well done? 'Cos that's how you be gonna get it!"

"Fico!" Amoret cursed her.

Cackling, Loon-Slatt dropped the prisoner's head.

And cleared the deck.

When everybody but the condemned was back on terra firma, Loon-Slatt removed the ladder and assumed her role as mistress of ceremonies. She called for the woodpile to be doused in flammable oil and her assistants unquestioningly did as she bid them; immediately muscling large barrels off a cart, uncorking them and generously anointing the neatly laid fire bed with viscous liquid.

Still cackling and enjoying her vocation, Loon-Slatt fetched herself a stick of wood, dipped it in one of the barrels and struck a match to light the oil on the end of it. She then toured the whole circumference of the pyre's base, setting it to burn in the bottoms of the stacks.

The crowd gasped at how greedily the flames devoured the accelerant fluid.

Pere couldn't bear to watch, preferring instead to nuzzle his face into the Charlatan's cassock.

Amoret was left stranded on the cross, the flames wreathing themselves around the stake beneath her, licking higher and higher towards her. So close she could feel their blistering heat.

All delusions about the glory of martyrdom had vaporized.

She didn't want to die.

There was no glory in it whatsoever, only … *finality.*

Desperately, she looked up to the sky and cried, "*Empyre above! Help me!*"

But the sun just gleamed at her, offering her about as much salvation as a beacon would to a drowning sailor whose ship had already splintered on the rocks.

Cloying smoke engulfed her in a billowing black pall, stinging her eyes and wracking her lungs, forcing her to hopelessly quit her earnest plight for mercy and turn her face away from the celestial idyll she had worshipped all her life, which had failed to bestow its divine intervention in her greatest moment of need.

Here she was, dying to defend the honour of the Icarusian faith, only to discover at this crucial juncture that it was a fanciful deceit. Myths and fables contrived to explain the machinations of a world beyond the scope of humankind's comprehension. Attempting to alleviate the compunction of relentless struggles by filling the void of ignorance with rational, tangible sense. Attributing the wild, random nature of this ungoverned ecosphere to an insubstantial entity that was responsible but not answerable. Giving everyone something to blame everything on, whether it is named Icarus or Zoe or whatever.

Deep in her heart, as probably in everyone else's, she'd known it to be so for a long time, yet had never revoked her reverence. To cast the spells of prayer and go through the motions of inefficacious ritual was far better than to confront the emptiness of the prevailing truth.

The very emptiness she now confronted.

Leaping flames stretched for her, warping and charring the boardwalk at her feet.

Faith had gotten her into this mess, but it didn't look as if it were going to get her out of it.

Just then, as if sent from the eye of Empyre itself, a long steel bolt suddenly arrowed through the smoke and embedded itself deeply into the cross's stout angle beam, millimetres shy of her left hand.

She stared at it, breathing hard from fright. She'd seen its type before many years ago whilst still roaming the continent with her uncle. It was a miniature ballista bolt, its point barbed and acting as a grappling hook on its target. Its shaft was coiled with a length of rope, the loose end of which was taut and trailed off back to wherever it came from.

The tight rope juddered a few times as though someone at the other end of it was testing the firmness of purchase, then it bowed downwards as it took weight, causing the bolt's head to creak ominously in the beam.

Below, shrouded by the smokescreen, the crowd gasped in amazement.

Dramatically, a figure completely cloaked in a waxed leather cape came sliding down the tensile rope on a crudely modified horse harness, wafting through the intensifying blaze as if it were nothing more than a harmless curtain.

Amoret could only gawp in astonished awe as the figure landed feet first on the platform, drew a curved sword and expertly chopped away her bindings so as she could gratefully fall into its rescuing arms.

"Who … who *are* you?" she wanted to know, curiosity burning as fervently as the planking under them. "To who do I owe my life?"

Pulling aside the protective scarf hiding its identity, the figure revealed a familiar, friendly visage she was overjoyed to behold.

"Come!" Countess Ahithophel hurried. "There is no time to lose!"

To emphasize this, shots fired blindly from the ground broached the smoke.

Ahithophel hastily cut the rope she'd come flying in on and unwound the coils off the bolt shaft.

"How're we going to get off here?" Amoret troubled her saviour, avoiding the avaricious flames consuming the wooden platform and the bullets buzzing by at all trajectories.

"Don't fret!" Ahithophel reassured her, scouting the crowded town agora. "I have an accomplice!"

At that very moment a cart overloaded with loose straw and furiously powered by a team of frenzied horses came clattering into the square, scattering the crowd in all directions. The driver spared the animals none, callously flogging their hindquarters and bellowing goads at them while her passenger fired rounds from the revolving magazine of an eight-barrel Octobus rifle above the heads of the people to urge them into speedy departure.

Both team and cart deliberately swerved towards the Warden and her Deputies, who'd been taking indiscriminate pot shots at the invisible antics happening aloft, disrupting the shooting party and causing the custodians to dodge clear for fear of being trounced beneath hooves and wheels.

"Here's our ride!" Ahithophel said, shoving the sword into its scabbard and swaddling Amoret in her cape. "Hold onto the rope!"

Amoret and the Countess grasped the dangling rope, which had caught fire but was only slowly smouldering as it had been treated. They ran backwards together as the cart came swooping round to their left, then with an encouraging cry they rushed forwards and swung out.

The platform collapsed into the inferno almost as soon as their toes abandoned it.

They let go of the rope and flew without wings for a moment before hitting the bull's-eye, their plummet broken in the encompassing pillow of thickly wadded, thoroughly soaked straw.

The driver instantly thrashed the lathering horses into action again, turning the cart about and cantering towards Farouche and her henchwomen; the three of whom were thanking their lucky stars for a chance at a rematch with these daring rescuers.

Hastily, they began repriming their spent weapons.

The passenger on the cart called "Hold!" and let two rounds go over their heads, dissuading retribution. This frightened Attercop so much she dropped all her balls and spilt her morsing-horn's supply of black powder before she could reload.

Skittering the steeds to a halt, the driver brought the cart broadside against the only people remaining in the market square. Dropping the reins, she reached to her waist and extracted a quad-barrel sidearm as the masked shooter climbed down from the forward bench of the vehicle and approached the dumbfounded women and boy.

Farouche's finger twitched on the trigger of her pistol, as did Skaines'. Attercop hovered at the back, edging herself behind everybody else.

Widdy Loon-Slatt, completely unarmed, shrieked and hightailed it.

Pere, encircled in the Charlatan's shielding hug, gawped at the mysterious figure as it sashayed into their vicinity.

Removing the concealing mask, the passenger exposed their true self.

"Mandrake!" Farouche snarled.

"The very same," Mandragora said coolly. "I want your son, Warden. No buts."

"*Never!*" Farouche denied, raising her gun.

It was the last thing she did.

Mandragora adeptly flipped the Octobus stock round and chinned the Warden, sending her sprawling onto the ground in cold unconsciousness.

"Okay, so there was a butt," she joked.

Skaines inaccurately discharged her first shot at Mandragora, skimming her and making her fall backwards. The cart driver rapidly responded to this attempt on her Lady's life, giving Skaines an equally close shave, only to have Skaines defensively blow her from her perch and send her spinning like a top. Ahithophel reflexively joined the fray, putting in Skaines' right eye with a shot from her pocket pistol.

Taking evasive measures, being as she was totally without firepower, Attercop grabbed Pere and tried wrestling him from the Charlatan's maternal mollycoddling.

"Leave him be!" the minister resisted her, clutching the boy closer to her bosom. But despite her earnest efforts, the Deputy simply pistol-whipped her until she let go and crumpled into the dirt dazed, leaving Pere to fight his hated enemy tooth and nail.

"Let that boy go, bitch!" Ahithophel demanded, training her aim onto the desperado Deputy.

Winning the tussle, Attercop pressed Pere to her and set the Thunderbus to his temple, yelling, "*I'll kill him! Afore thine very eyes, I'll kill him stone dead!*"

Mandragora brought the Octobus's sights onto Attercop.

"Let him go! I'll blow your stupid block off, Deputy!"

"*I'll kill him!*" Attercop squeaked, cocking all four hammers and privately praying her bluff would be enough to get her out of this situation alive.

It wasn't, for Pere rumbled her.

"Shoot her!" he cried. "She didn't reload! *Shoot her!*"

Nobody desired to take the chance and Attercop hissed her

sibilant snigger, reckoning she had it made.

So Pere clasped her gun hand in both his and forced her to squeeze the triggers.

"*PERE! NO!*" Amoret shrilly screamed at him.

The hammers snapped onto the flints, sparking nothing.

"*Damn thee!*" Attercop cursed, thumping him at the nape of the neck with the pistol before dropping it and going instead for her blade. Before she could unsheathe it Mandragora and Ahithophel both scored hits on her, taking her down.

Groggily, Pere slumped into a lethargic heap.

"*Pere!*" Amoret anxiously yelped, vaulting over the side of the cart and rushing to his aid. "Pere! Are you okay?"

"Yeah," he groaned, rubbing his neck. "I think so."

"Oh, my darling!" she mewled, embracing him to her chest. She glanced at Mandragora, "Can we get him to a therapeutic?"

"He'll have to wait till we get back to the Demesne," Mandragora regretted. "We'll need to refresh the horses there before heading on to Havenstrand to catch the morning boat to Monte Creston. I'll get my quack Merryandrew in from Slackton then, but we've gotta split right now, kid, so look lively."

"C'mon!" Ahithophel corroborated the urgency, climbing into the cart's driving seat and taking the reins.

"You intend us to go with you?" Amoret asked.

"Yeah. Do you think we do this sort of thing for fun?" Mandragora said.

"Maugre! C'mon!" Ahithophel rudely interrupted.

Amoret scooped Pere up in her arms and carried him to their transport, where, with the help of Mandragora, she carefully laid him in the straw.

It was then she noticed something out the corner of her eye.

Attercop was crawling along on her belly, still alive and affecting a surreptitious exit.

"She's *mine!*" Amoret claimed through gritted teeth.

"Forget it, sister!" Mandragora said, clapping a staying hand on her shoulder. "We're behind schedule as it is. If you go after her we won't be waiting when you're finished. You catching my drift?"

"That bitch killed my horse!"

"Hey, I'll buy you a new one! Just get on!"

Amoret looked at her and said, "Are you gonna buy me a new uncle too?"

"Fico!" Mandragora muttered, lifting the Octobus and priming it.

She aimed.

Fired.

Attercop flopped down and lay very still.

"Satisfied?"

"No," grumbled Amoret. "I swore I'd do it with my bare hands!"

"You'll just have to make do with that," Mandragora told her. "Now get on! Or the next person I shoot will be *you!*"

Believing she wasn't jesting, Amoret clambered aboard.

Gadding the team, Ahithophel swung the cart around and cracked the straps against the horses' backs to gee them into a gallop.

The cart bounced and rattled out of the square.

Leaving the saltire to burn to ash.

Unnoticed.

EPILOGUE

Havenstrand, Rundale County, Montaigne North West Coast.
Quartoday, Rupelian 18th, AD 4004

Amoret awoke.

And life felt really grand for the first time in a long time.

Outside, the wailing shriek of wheeling gulls and the more distant clamour of the dockyards reminded her she was in Havenstrand. But not much longer would she be there, for she knew she was bound that very same morning for Monte Creston on the clipper *Oggin Parbreak*, which was due to set sail at 2:15 sharp.

Stretching and yawning, she threw aside the bedcovers and groped for the new clothes she'd strewn on the floor the previous night when she came reeling back to the boarding house after an extremely enjoyable evening of revelry with Ahithophel and Mandragora. Finding them, she lazily slipped into their comfortable fittings, taking care not to disturb the dressing wrapping the gunshot wound to her leg. She then hobbled to the latticed window of her room to look out on the harbour.

A tranquil sea lay before her, hazy sunlight glistening off the gently fluctuating surface that disappeared into the sky at the edge of the horizon. Fishing launches playfully bobbed along on it, venturing onto the calm waters to reap the advantage of the fair weather's favour.

She smiled contentedly.

A new life beckoned, and the best of it was she would be

spending it with Pere. Nothing could blemish the euphoria she felt about that fact. Not any of her aching injuries or even the hangover throbbing in her head.

After they'd left Rampick in a cloud of dust yesterday, they called at Mandragora Demesne. There they changed their clothes, gathered some provisions for the long journey ahead of them, got Amoret examined by Mandragora's personal apothecary and fixed themselves up with a fresh team of horses and a more suitable, swifter carriage. Then they hit the road again, stopping only once at Almsham post house to renew the team before the final stint.

When they arrived in Havenstrand at about 4:00 that evening, Ahithophel took Amoret to another therapeutic to get a stock of the medicaments she needed, including a large majolica pot of arquebusade. Mandragora and Pere, meanwhile, went on a shopping spree, buying yet another change of clothes for all four of them to vary their styles from the descriptions of them that probably would've already been put out on the judicial grapevine.

The boarding house where they were lodged was a discreet, low-key affair away from the main port and any prying eyes that may be taking an interest in its comings and goings. Mandragora had booked them rooms two days prior to the fracas so suspicion would not be aroused locally or otherwise. She'd used the place before, apparently, when she'd felt the need to play her dubious business dealings close to her chest, and swore by the integrity of the landlady.

Later on that night, Mandragora and Ahithophel took Amoret for a celebratory drink around the town taverns while Pere rested. They plied her with copious quantities of wine and song and showed her one heck of a good time; to so much of an extent that Amoret thought she'd be pretty crippled with the after effects of the booze come morning. Yet here she was, bright-eyed and raring to go.

Mindfully, she checked the time on the new pocket watch Pere had bought her (on Mandragora's money, of course). Its integrated numerical dial told her it was 1:78, which meant there was plenty of time for her to take Pere somewhere special for breakfast as a celebration just between the two of them. It was the least she could do after partying with their hostesses till about 5:20 that morning.

Turning the watch over lovingly, she read the inscription Pere had had engraved on the rear. *My Beloved Amy You Will Forever Have My Heart* the curling copperplate calligraphy affectionately declared.

A smile creased her lips again and a lump rose in her throat.

Re-pocketing the timepiece, she exited the room with a definite spring in her step, and it wasn't just down to the fact she couldn't walk properly. Humming cheerfully, she went to the chamber adjacent to hers and knocked at its door to waken her sweetheart.

She waited a few moments, but he didn't come to answer.

"Pere?" she said, tapping a second time. "Pere? Are you awake?"

No reply.

Trying the handle she found the door unlocked and so peeked inside. "Pere?"

His bed was empty. Neatly turned down and looking very unused for some considerable time.

Well, he did go to bed a lot earlier than she did. Perhaps he was out on the quay taking a breath of sea air. Why he would want to do that was beyond her since they'd be getting quite enough of that once they were onboard the *Oggin Parbreak* and riding the swell. Still, she knew how he loved the beauty of nature, so she sidled off to test this theory.

Pausing outside Ahithophel's room, she rapped on the door.

Again no response.

Either she'd gone to breakfast or was still recovering from last night's frolics.

Whistling as she went, Amoret continued along the corridor and began descending the stairs, where she met a chamber-bachelor on the ascent with an armful of clean linen.

"Morning," Amoret greeted him.

"Good morning, ma'am," he courteously reciprocated, curtseying briefly.

"Say, you haven't seen the guest from Room 9 have you?" she asked. "Blonde berd about your height …"

"Yeah, ma'am. He went to the docks with Mistress Mandragora and the other lady."

"Right. They must've gone for a stroll before breakfast."

"Oh, no, ma'am. This was a long time ago."

Amoret stared at him. "What d'you mean? When did they leave?"

He stifled a yawn. "About five-ninety this morning."

"*What?*"

"They woke me when they passed the servants' quarters on their way out the back entrance," the young man divulged. "I looked into the hallway and Mistress Mandragora paid me a ducat to stay quiet about their going."

Amoret jostled past him, causing him to spill the linen. Frenetic, she dashed down the rest of the flights, bounding several steps at a time to hasten her progress, her wounded leg all but forgotten.

Mistress Byre the landlady was just coming in through the front door, propping her walking cane in a rack nearby reserved for such articles. Amoret ran straight up to her, aggressively grabbed her by the lapels and slammed her against the passage wall.

"Where are they?"

"Who?" Mistress Byre nervously gasped, shocked by the unprovoked attack.

"Where've Mandragora and Ahithophel gone?" Amoret expanded. "Where've they taken Pere?"

"I thought you knew," the robust woman said, genuinely bemused by her violent interrogation.

"Knew *what?*"

"Mistress Mandragora asked me to commission old Oakum's schooner to ferry them across to The Pangaea last night. She said you'd be joining them when you can get passage on the *Oggin Parbreak* clipper next week and paid your room up for another five-night."

"The clipper sets sail this morning!" Amoret corrected.

"No it don't," the landlady asserted. "My niece is a cabin-girl on the *Oggin*, and it don't dock here again till next Quartoday."

"*Damn them!*"

Amoret rushed outside into the street, futilely scanning the horizon.

She glanced round and saw a girl coming along the cobblestone road leading a fallow mare on a halter.

"Hi there, girl!" she curtly beckoned. "Loan me your mount! I have to get to the docks! *Quickly, you oaf!*"

"It b'ain't my mount, ma'am," the youngster said timidly. "She belongs to a Mistress Artemis who's staying at this house."

"*I'm* her!" Amoret revealed, astonished. "*I'm* Artemis!"

"Her name be Yaud," the girl introduced, trustfully surrendering the halter. She fumbled in her jacket pocket for a few moments then produced a crumpled scrap of paper. "There was this note to be given to you 'n' all, ma'am."

Amoret impatiently snatched it from her.

It was the purchase receipt, but scribbled on the back in Pere's open, rounded script was the message:

Amy, I hope you will love Yaud as much as you loved Favel. I picked her out specially because she reminded me of him. Please don't be angry for our abandoning you in this horrid way. Lady Mandrake and Fran said they could not let you die on the cross, but it is too dangerous for us to take you with us at present. I said I wouldn't go without you, but they insisted, if only as repayment for them saving your life. How could I refuse them after their brave kindness to you, darling? Lady Mandrake says she will send you passage when things are settled where we're going. Please take care, and always believe that you are the only one I will ever love. Pere.

She stared out at the wide, vast sea.

"Pere!" she whispered, a tear splashing down her cheek.

Her hand screwed the note up and threw it away.

Hoisting herself onto Yaud's bare back, she tugged the mare's mane and enforced a turnabout, stupendously impressing the callow stable girl with her horsewomanship. Digging her knees into the steed's ribs and smacking her haunch, Amoret drove her into a canter towards the docks.

Woman and beast instantaneously melded like a well-engineered machine, almost as if they'd been together forever. She could've nearly fooled herself that it was Favel she had back between her legs.

They hurtled through the narrow streets like demented steeplechasers, Yaud's hooves clattering noisily on the cobbles. Along the way they frightened doddering old berds, sent dogs into fits of crazed barking, scattered hens and pigs left to wander the neighbourhood, burst through streamers of laundry strung across the passageways, jumped market barrows laden with fresh seafood fare and generally upset unassuming residents quietly going about their daily chores.

Their unchecked behaviour improved none when they reached the docks. They cut and swerved recklessly around the hustling, bustling stevedores and the multitude of cargoes being painstakingly heaved off the wharf and into the holds of the moored ships via windlasses. Quite rightly, they received much colourful castigation for their irresponsible invasion of what was a heavily industrialized area.

Amoret's plan was to find a Jill Tar willing to have her working passage onboard her vessel, for she had no money to pay her way since all the coin she'd spent at Havenstrand had come from Mandragora's purse. Failing that, she intended to stowaway in freight bound for Monte Creston.

She spotted a likely looking old salt sitting on a barrel and smoking her clay pipe while she watched the world pass her by. Her complexion was tanned and weather beaten, her beard thick and white, her garments shabby and she looked just like a sailor down on her luck. There was no telling if she actually owned or commanded a boat, but even if she didn't there was a strong possibility she might be able to point her in the right direction.

Bringing Yaud to a stop in front of this woman, Amoret said, "I'm looking to work passage to the continent."

"Ooar?" the old salt remarked.

"Do you know of any ships bound for Monte Creston?"

"Ar, but there b'ain't none taking on crew, gy. I should knows 'cos I been asking myself, with being a deckhand for nigh on forty year. It be all this blood purge lark. The captains daren't take on casual crew for fear of yon customs 'n' immigration."

"Do you know of any ships, anyway?" Amoret pressed, dwelling on the stowaway idea.

"Are you looking for passage to The Pangaea, did you say?" somebody else asked from behind her.

Amoret turned to square up with two frock-coated women who looked distinctly out of place here. They were too clean-shaven and groomed to be swabs but not resplendently attired enough to be officers in the Sceptral Navy.

"Yeah," she cautiously replied. "Have you a boat?"

"Ar," one said. "Whole fleet of 'em."

The other sauntered around Amoret, studying her. "We could use a strong gy like you."

"We'll even pay you in advance," her associate promised Amoret, removing something from her coat pocket. "Hold out yer hand."

Amoret did, and a huge coin was dropped into her palm.

She gawped at it stupidly.

It was a Real Signat. Effectively worthless as currency owing to the high base metal content, they were specifically minted to look and feel like a fortune in order to bribe gullible subjects into the combatant services of Her Majesty Queen Pherenike #9 in preparation for the impending crusade.

"Press gang!" Amoret had chance to utter, realization dawning on her.

Then a club struck her.

Recruiting her for duty.

Printed in the United Kingdom
by Lightning Source UK Ltd.
125205UK00001B/68/A